LAURA GALLIER

THE
DELUSION

Provide feedback on the book and submit communication through
the online form at www.TheDelusionBook.com

Housetop Publishers
Cypress, Texas

First Paperback Edition: October 2012

The characters and events portrayed in this book are fictitious. Any
similarity to real persons, living or dead, is coincidental and not
intended by the author.

The Delusion: a novel / by Laura Gallier - 1st ed.
p. cm.

Summary: Owen Edmunds' frantic search to find a cure for his
terrifying hallucinations turns into a desperate mission to protect
others when he becomes convinced that he's actually the *one* person
who sees the truth.

ISBN 978-0-9883658-0-3
Library of Congress Control Number: 2012950481

[1. Fiction—Fantasy/Paranormal. 2. Fiction—Christian/Suspense.
3. Fiction—Ghost.]

Printed in the United States of America

For my mother, Linda McClendon,
who has put up with plenty of my story telling!
Thank you for believing in this book and in me.

CONTENTS

It doesn't matter whether you want to be in a spiritual battle or not —you are in one. The battle is between good and evil, and you are the prize.

Dr. Charles F. Stanley

1. Critical Day

By March of my senior year, eleven students at my high school had committed suicide. What a sickening realization it was to discover their deaths had been provoked. I could see what was tormenting and inciting them, but it didn't matter. I was hard pressed to get anyone to believe me.

I realize you likely won't believe me either. Admittedly, my story is twisted and bizarre and nearly impossible to accept. Still, I'm holding out hope that, in the end, you'll turn out to be one of the rare ones—one of a small minority willing to venture beyond the five senses to see what is almost always completely and intentionally unseen.

It all began on what I assumed would be a typical Monday.

The deafening thunder woke me before my alarm had a chance. I fumbled through my twisted flannel sheets until I found my phone.

5:53 a.m.

I dropped my Droid and grabbed my pillow, but I was too late. A burst of lightning lit up my room and jarred my eyes open before I could cover my face.

Another day of rain. I was so not surprised. It was like a gang of storm clouds and depression stalked our Texas town and refused to relent, bringing a random chill with it. I'd lived in Cypress, a Houston suburb, as long as I could remember and never needed to wear a fleece hoodie the week after spring break—until now.

The press loved it. The ominous drizzle was the perfect backdrop for their continuous news coverage. Each time a suicide occurred, reporters converged on our campus in a mad race to be the first to broadcast the story.

Out of the eleven students at my school who had taken their own lives since August, I was friends with five of them—really good friends with one of them, Bobby Kellogg. It sucked.

Thanks to the media, the nation was now captivated by the so-called Cypress Suicide Saga and obsessed with our climate-confused city. Lincoln Forest High School had become the eighth wonder of the world, the ultimate reality freak show. It felt like all of humanity stayed perched on the edge of their seats wondering who would off themselves next, and how.

This was not the way I'd envisioned my senior year.

There was a new theory every day about why it was happening. The last suicide was a month earlier. A popular guy named Steve Hopkins crammed a few too many pills down his throat. He used to sit two rows from me in my calculus class. Now his empty chair was a constant reminder that few things in life are as permanent as death.

People said Steve's decision to quit the baseball team two weeks before taking his life was a sure sign he was spiraling out of control, and parents blamed the school for overlooking such an obvious indicator. So now even the faintest hint of laziness would get you yanked out of class for an intervention in the counselor's office.

"Owen?"

I swear, the only time my mom called my name was when she wanted something.

"I'm on it, Mom."

My dog Valentine remained draped over the foot of my bed like a wet mop. We'd found her a few years earlier on Valentine's Day, hence the name, although Psycho would have been more fitting. She growled at the most random times and refused to eat dog food. Unless we served her table scraps, she'd just as soon go hungry.

"Owen?" She was getting closer. I didn't like when my mom came into my room. She usually ended up knocking something over.

"Mom, go lay down. I'll make breakfast in a minute."

I stretched, then peered into the hallway. Valentine took a peek, too.

Most people hang pictures on the walls, but that would never fly in my house. My mother leaned on the walls most days just to keep from toppling over. I watched her put one boney foot in front of the other the best she could. Her silky robe looked three sizes too big and made her pale bird legs look even thinner. Her hair was still wrapped in a towel from after her bath, which, to my knowledge, was more than ten hours ago. Go figure.

Even though she faced away from me, I could tell she was crying. But I'd quit trying to console her about a decade ago. Instead, my attention was on Valentine, who growled as ferociously as a fat, golden-haired house pet can.

"Oh, stop it," I said. "You're not scaring anyone."

I headed downstairs to the kitchen and made the usual, scrambled eggs and toast. Some days I really resented having to make my mom breakfast. Today was one of those days. For the most part, I'd learned to accept her for the drunk she was, even though she insisted she was just a hip single mom with an uncommon appreciation for alcoholic beverages. Fortunately, with the exception of incessantly correcting my grammar and requiring that I learn a new scholarly word every day—including its root word language of origin—she pretty much left me to myself.

I showered and threw on a black T-shirt, jeans, and my gray Abercrombie pullover. It was cool outside, which meant it would be even colder in my school.

I headed out the door, dodging the deluge of water pouring down from the porch and making a beeline for my Rally Yellow Camaro. There wasn't much elbow room with all six-foot-two of me in the driver's seat, but I couldn't complain. It was a hot ride. It was my birthday present when I turned sixteen. Okay, my mom was a near failure as a parent, but she managed to do a few things right.

Driving to Jess's house, my thoughts digressed to the usual: second guessing my decision to go premed at UCLA in the fall.

I'd wanted to be a doctor ever since I put a bandage on Tommy what's-his-name's knuckles during a game of street basketball. I was only nine at the time, but something stirred in me when I was able to calm him and stop the bleeding. I wondered, though, if I actually had the makings of a good doctor. Maybe babysitting my mom my entire life had created a pathetic need to take care of others. Yuck. I hoped that wasn't the case.

And there I was, 602 Delano Lane. I used to think I had a big house until the first time Jess invited me over. She lived in a modern-day mansion. Although I never understood how my mom banked six-figures working a few hours a day as an online English professor, with Jess's dad there was no mystery. He was a prominent real estate agent and investor, and according to Jess, a brilliant man except when it came to being a husband and father. I'd met Mr. Thompson once, and he seemed nice enough, but you never know about people.

I managed to pull into the driveway despite the torrential downpour. I sent Jess a text, then headed up the slippery steps and held out an umbrella as she opened the massive front door. She zipped her jacket, and we ran to the car.

Jess and I had seen each other around school since our freshman year, but we'd never hung out until lately. She wasn't a preppy girl—the kind I usually went for—but she was fun and was hailed as one of the hottest girls in the school. She was also quick to speak her mind, and a little on the wild side. I liked that.

I wondered how long we would go on like this before she'd want to assign an official label to our relationship. So far she hadn't brought it up.

I turned the air to hot, then cold, then warm, but nothing blasted the haze off the windshield. Jess finally got the temperature just right, and by the time we neared the intersection two blocks from our school, we could see fine.

There they were, the sign people, as we called them. Weirdos came out to our school in droves and shouted and held up signs, protesting as if our suicidal student body was defiling their holy planet. Their posters said all kinds of crazy things. My personal favorite: *The devil lives at Lincoln Forest High.*

It always annoyed me the way religious people ascribed power to a fictitious satanic being.

"I'm so sick of this," Jess said.

I used to find it all amusing, but even I had to admit, the hostile scene was becoming unsettling.

A lanky guy with stringy red hair shook a fist. "It's the end of the world," he said. Wouldn't you know it; traffic stopped, putting him right outside Jess's window for a good ninety seconds.

A short lady rocked back and forth just inches away from the crazed redhead. She held a candle stick that couldn't sustain a flame during the downpour. She, too, peered through Jess's window. Let's just say that if looks really could kill, Jess would have had no pulse.

"Why do they hate us, Owen?"

"They think we're evil and cursed. But who cares what they think? They're all lunatics."

Jess dug through her purse as an excuse to look away.

And that's when I saw them: the television network vans. That could only mean one thing. I felt the familiar sense of dread and began making mental predictions about who, among the people I knew, was most likely to have killed themselves.

We finally turned on the side street by our school. What a frenzy. A dozen news crews stood in the rain.

As we turned into the parking lot, a disgruntled woman stood a few feet away clutching a young child in one hand and waving a smeared handwritten sign in the other.

Jess glared at her with disgust. "Who would bring her kid to this war zone?"

I parked the car and tried not to make eye contact with the deranged lady as I ran around to open the car door for Jess, but I got distracted. The woman whirled around as an out-of-breath police officer grabbed her arm, knocking her waterlogged sign to the ground.

"You're not allowed to be on school property." The officer was annoyed, but who could blame him? The sign people had been there since November. The hostile woman flailed her arms and yelled something about the First Amendment. The boy by her side looked terrified.

Jess opened the passenger door and ran under my umbrella.

"Sorry, I was going to get that for you," I said above the commotion. Lately I felt like the rain had seeped through to my brain and washed away my ability to focus.

A girl named Samantha and a guy I didn't know dashed up to us, splashing my pant leg in the process. "Jamie Longmire killed herself at six o'clock this morning," the guy said, matter-of-factly. "She took her dad's gun and pulled the trigger. I heard she did it in the bathroom."

"What?" Jess's lips quivered. "She's in my third period class."

Samantha's eyes narrowed, and she leaned in even closer. "She *was* in your third period class. Not anymore."

7

A blonde reporter shoved her microphone between Jess and Samantha. The invasive light from the TV camera made us all squint.

"Tell me, did you know Jamie? Did you know she was having suicidal thoughts?"

Jess struggled to find words that matched her emotions. "I did know her but . . . I mean . . . I didn't . . ."

"I knew her very well," Samantha said with an inordinate amount of zeal. "She seemed, like, a little down the last few weeks, but we're all kind of down, ya know?" Samantha's face radiated. There was no disguising her excitement at the notion of appearing on television. Disgusting.

While grabbing my hand, Jess turned away from the reporter and strode toward the school. "I can't take this, Owen. I can't do this anymore."

"Jess Thompson, what do you mean by that?" Uh-oh. Principal Maxwell appeared out of nowhere. Her swollen eyes, soggy hair, and tattered rain boots looked pitiful.

"I'm going to arrange for you to meet with a counselor today."

"But I don't need to—"

"It's not up for debate." Mrs. Maxwell pulled a pink slip from her coat pocket to schedule the appointment.

"Can Owen come with me?"

She sneered. "This is a counseling appointment, not an opportunity to play footsies under the table with your boyfriend."

"But—"

"Just go, Jess," I said. I spoke calmly in hopes of offsetting the pandemonium closing in on us. "Talk to the counselor. It'll be fine."

Truth be told, I liked the idea of Jess going to speak with someone. She'd seemed depressed the last couple of weeks, and I was worried about her.

I squeezed Jess's hand to offer some reassurance, and I could tell she liked that.

We walked through the double doors by the library where a few students were hugging. Most of them looked like zombies. Apparently earphones were the escape of choice.

My former chemistry teacher Mrs. Barnett—my favorite teacher of all time—stood in the hallway smiling at students as they passed by, apparently attempting to bring some warmth into an otherwise dismal environment.

I walked Jess to her first period class, and when we stopped at the door, I took a good look at her for the first time that day. The rain made her hair wavy. Of course she insisted it was frizzy, but I thought it was pretty.

"I like your hair," I said.

"Thanks." She tried to crack a smile, but a second later, she looked away. Tears pooled in her eyes.

"It's gonna be okay." I cupped her chin with both hands and drew her eyes to mine. "I promise."

While I did hold out hope that she and I would be okay, the promise was a bit much. I couldn't promise anything.

I stopped at my locker and tried not to think about the fact that Jamie Longmire's locker was right down the row from mine, or that she was still alive just a couple of hours ago. Two stern-looking men in gloves rummaged through all of her belongings. I caught a glimpse of one of them thumbing through what looked like a journal.

Should I have been nicer to her? Gone out of my way to say hi? Those dreadful familiar thoughts stomped across my mind. This was the twelfth suicide this year, and the twelfth time I'd wondered if there was anything I could have done to make a difference.

My best friend Lance came up next to me.

"Hey dude," he said. "Did you hear about number twelve?"

"Yeah. It's crazy, right?"

Lance had had my back ever since he jumped between Roy and me in the fifth grade. Roy threatened to kick my butt, but Lance—a shorter, smaller kid than me—stood between us and told Roy he would wake up in the "ISU" if he dared to throw a fist. He was referring to the ICU but got confused and said the wrong thing. We still laughed about that.

Lance and I agreed to talk later and both went to class. I sat in the second seat from the window in English Lit and shook my head in disbelief that yet another student was dead. The two guys to my right struck up their usual conversation, exchanging what had to be exaggerated stories of fooling around with one girl after another. The only thing more annoying than hearing about their sexual experiences every day was their insistence on bumming answers off me every time we took a test.

"So Owen, you've hooked up with Jess, right?"

I had nothing to say to those losers. Fortunately, the teacher's timing was excellent.

"Okay, get your laptops open, and bring up your homework."

That was the last complete sentence she formed all period. The rest of my classes went about the same. The suicides were hard on the students but even more draining on the teachers.

A new sense of helplessness breathed down my neck. Whereas the suicides used to feel like isolated incidents, they now seemed more like a plague. I just wanted to get through the day, so I could go to basketball practice and work out some of my frustration.

Practice went by fast. We did some intense drills in preparation for Thursday's game, then Coach dismissed us right on time, and Lance and I went back to his house to lift weights. I was glad it was just the two of us. He and Meagan had been going out for over a year, and it got old having her around all the time. She was a nice girl and all, but—at the risk of sounding eight years old—he was my best friend first.

I headed back to the school to pick up Jess from dance practice. Although most of the sign people were gone by five o'clock, a few odd balls at the main intersection still shouted nonsense. One man rang a tarnished bell and wore a sign that said, "Do you hear the death?"

What in the world?

I pulled up outside the auditorium and took in the repulsive view. A couple of months earlier, a few shabby tents had popped up in the grassy acreage behind the baseball fields on the west end of the campus. Now there were at least a hundred. The property was owned by some old guy who was supposedly making bank off the thrill-seekers and freaks who paid him to camp out there. It was absurd. I'd never cared enough to come by at night, but rumor had it they did chants and worship rituals or something.

As if that wasn't bad enough, there was a constant parade of minivans, SUVs, and luxury sedans. All of suburbia came to take photos of the bogus scene. One guy, who looked like he'd quit his job with a traveling carnival, sold T-shirts: "I survived a day at Lincoln Forest High." I watched a soccer mom look both ways, then cross the street to go buy one. "You've got to be kidding me."

The rain finally slacked off to a mere drizzle. No sun in sight, but at least I could stand outside my car and look up at the drab sky. I couldn't get used to the chilly wind blowing around me this time of year.

Jess came out and sank into the passenger seat, and we drove out of view of the chanters, campers, and cameras.

"So, have you picked out a prom dress yet?" My attempt at girl talk. "No," she whispered.

It was clear I wasn't going to get much out of her, but I asked another question anyway. "Did you meet with the counselor today?"

"Yeah."

She sipped her bottled water and stared aimlessly out the window. I tried not to show how worried I was about her.

"I know what you're thinking, Owen."

So much for my poker face. "Did the counselor teach you how to read minds?" My stab at comic relief fell flat.

"You think I'm gonna get depressed and—"

"Shut up, Jess!" I'd never used that tone with her, and she glared at me. I was taken aback by the intensity of my own response.

We said very little until I drove past the grand entrance to her neighborhood and pulled over by the woods that stretched behind all the mega-houses. Finally, a smile graced her face. We'd done this before, on days like today when the world was closing in on us and suffocating our free spirits.

She flew out of the car before I did and darted down the slippery hillside toward the trees. I let out a belly laugh and ran after her, determined to catch up. I've never liked losing to a girl, and I imagine I never will.

Mud flung from her Nikes and hit me in the face. I resisted the urge to pass her and instead let her lead the way to what was becoming "our spot" in the woods—a patch of rocks peeking out from the brush under a tight cluster of towering pine trees.

I love that feeling of being out of breath but unable to wipe the grin off my face. We collapsed on the rocks, knowing any second the cold would seep through our clothes. Jess crossed her arms over her bent knees and sucked in air. I did the same.

Other than the occasional car horn and bird chirp, the sound of our breathing dominated the open air.

Jess lifted her chin and asked, "Owen, do you ever feel, like, really depressed sometimes? It's hard to explain." She turned to face me. "There's this heavy feeling that weighs down on me, almost like it's pressing on my chest or something. Like this strange misery of sorts that creeps up all of a sudden. Do you know what I mean?"

I felt like I was swinging at a curve ball I never saw coming. "Is it like . . . a sad feeling?" I could tell she was disappointed that I couldn't identify with her depth of emotion.

"It's more than feeling down. It's like this awful emptiness drops over you for no reason at all. It happens during random times at school or when you're alone in your room. Do you ever feel that?"

I tried not to pause too long. "Well, I guess I sometimes . . ." I trailed off, reluctant to admit that I didn't understand at all.

"It's this eerie unhappiness that follows me around, and even though I try super hard to ignore it, it finds me. Especially when I lay down to sleep. It's like turning the light off calls on this miserable feeling to seek me out. And I wonder if that's what happened to Bobby Kellogg and Jamie Longmire and the others. Were they so smothered by this feeling that they decided to end it all?"

I wanted to say something profound. "I . . . don't know." So much for that.

I pride myself on having a logical answer for everything in life, but in that moment, I was at a loss.

Jess glanced straight ahead, "I think—" She froze mid sentence. "Do you hear that?"

Not this again. Last time we were in the woods together, she said she heard the sound of rushing water and insisted I needed to figure out where it was coming from. We looked around a while but didn't see anything. I was no more interested in tracking down the source of the liquid mystery today than I was then.

"Jess, let's not worry about what that sound is, okay?"

There was no point in telling her to ignore it. Once something piqued her interest, she was hooked.

"I think it's right underneath us," she said.

"There's probably a drainage ditch nearby or something."

"Seriously, Owen. It sounds more like a river than a drainage pipe. Listen."

I felt zero compulsion to comply, but out of respect for her, I closed my eyes and silenced my breathing.

And there it was—only I didn't just hear it. I felt it. It seemed to stir right under us.

"It has to be some sort of underground drainage system." I straightened my legs and folded my hands behind my head, as if that would convince her that our work was done here.

She wasn't buying it.

"Alright, fine. Hand me that." I pointed to a jagged rock.

"You think you can break ground with that?"

I peeled back the top layer of sludge and drove the rock straight down into the damp dirt. Truth is, part of me was afraid that if I didn't start digging, Jess would resurrect the discussion about her feelings, and I would have nothing but lame advice.

For half an hour, I slammed, ground, and dug into the dirt with both hands and the rock. By then, I couldn't feel my fingers, and blowing on them had stopped helping. I might have given up except that the sound grew louder the deeper I dug. It sounded like an ocean—not so much the crashing of waves but the swift movement of tides peaking and collapsing.

About the time I noticed my favorite pullover was completely drenched with mud, I felt myself plunge forward. I gasped—a knee-jerk reaction to the sensation of falling as my arms sank into the earth, stopping just short of my shoulders. I dropped the rock and clenched my fists as an army of needles punctured my hands. It took me a second to process that my hands were actually immersed in warmth, not needles.

I pulled my arms out and in one continuous motion, bolted straight onto my knees and spread my fingers in front of me, examining both sides of my hands. They were fine—becoming bone-chillingly-cold by the second, but fine.

"Owen, are you okay?"

Jess peered down at the hole, her jaw gaping open. We both lunged forward onto all fours, placing our heads ear to ear to get a closer look at the confounding sight.

About a foot below a hallow expanse, a body of water—I assumed it was water—raced by. It was impossible to see how wide it was, though it wasn't entirely dark. The water itself had what I can only describe as an iridescent glow.

"Have you ever seen anything like this?" Jess said.

I didn't know which was more mystifying—the glow, the torrential sound, or the odd gap of space between the dirt and water.

I shook my head.

I laid down flat on my stomach and placed one arm in the hole to feel around. I thought maybe I'd touch a concrete slab or some structure bracing the ground, but there was nothing.

I pulled my arm out and Jess planted her face as far into the opening as she could. Her words echoed. "This is awesome!"

She sat back, wiped the mud off her face, and pulled her small water bottle from the pocket of her hoodie.

"Here." She took the lid off and handed me the empty bottle. "See if you can scoop some of it out."

I pressed my cheek to the ground and stretched out my arm. I felt the warm water flood the bottle and pulled out our "official sample."

Sitting on the rocks, Jess hovered right beside me with her eyes glued on our discovery. I held it up and turned it back and forth, inspecting it intensely in the sparse sunlight.

"It looks like normal water," Jess said, clearly disappointed.

"Maybe there's some kind of rock under the water that's making it appear to glow," I said.

"Give me that!" She playfully jerked the bottle from my hands, spilling some of it. "I'm gonna drink it."

"Oh, no you're not." I snatched the bottle back. "We don't know what it is."

"Owen, it's pretty obvious it's just water. Don't you ever do anything daring?"

"Of course, but . . ." How could I politely explain that drinking from an unidentified source is dumb, not daring?

Jess took the bottle from me and pressed it to her lips. I took it right back and held it in the air beyond her reach. "You're not drinking that," I said.

"Seriously? You're gonna tell me I'm not allowed?"

Great. I came across like an overbearing parent. Now she'd definitely want to drink it.

"Give me the bottle." She waved an open hand in my face and left it there. "I can have it if I want."

Most of the time, her persistence was endearing. Right now, it was leaning toward obnoxious.

Her hand was a millimeter from my chin. "I understand if you're scared, Owen, but I'm not. Give . . . me . . . the bottle."

I couldn't believe she went there. "I'm not scared! I'm just looking out for you."

"I can look out for myself, thank you."

I considered pouring the bottle out and insisting that we leave, but I wasn't trying to force my will on her. I wanted to protect her.

Surely what I was about to do next would prove that.

I closed my eyes and emptied the bottle into my mouth. The heated liquid slid down my throat and pooled in my stomach.

"Owen! You idiot!"

"Huh?"

"I wasn't really gonna drink it. I can't believe you did that."

I launched the water bottle into the woods and tried to come to grips with what I was feeling. My heart pounded inside my chest. I was furious. I was hurt. I was humiliated. And I wanted to laugh, all at the same time.

"I was just trying to see if you would give in to me or not," she said. She faced me and leaned in so that her cheek was inches from mine. "Owen, I didn't mean to—"

"Lie to me?"

Her eyes opened wider than I'd ever seen while her mouth hung in an open silence. She abruptly buried her head in my neck and threw her arms around my shoulders. I hugged her back. We held each other without so much as a twitch.

Apparently my stupid stunt accomplished what I'd intended. She realized that I cared about her. I only hoped I would survive another day to see how things progressed between us.

Jess eased back and clutched my frostbitten fingers. She appeared genuinely remorseful. She might actually have apologized—something she seldom did—but thuds of swollen rain drops interrupted the moment.

"We'd better get back," I said, looking far off into the woods.

"Yeah, okay." She wiped her smeared eye makeup with her damp sleeve and extended an arm to help me up. I chose to forego her assistance. I don't think I'm the only guy who detests being called an idiot, and while I genuinely forgave her during our hug, I felt the need to prove I could stand on my own.

That's when it hit me. My stomach was hijacked by a disturbing sensation. Somehow the liquid that had warmed my insides upon entry now turned to ice in my belly. I figured I'd vomit.

"Are you okay?"

"I'll be fine. My stomach just feels a little weird." I knew if I elaborated on how awful I suddenly felt, it would seem like a serious guilt trip. Besides, my head started pounding, and the last thing I wanted to do was keep talking.

We found our way to the car despite the blinding rain. The sun wasn't supposed to set for another hour, but the storm ushered in a premature dusk. The chill radiating from inside me created a desperate desire to feel sunlight, but that wasn't going to happen.

As I made the quick drive to Jess' house, I had two goals: get her home safely, and don't barf in the car. I suppose she could sense that I was about to hurl. There was no lingering goodbye. She flung the door shut and disappeared in the rain. I saw the front door of her museum-like house open

19

and close, and that was my cue to speed home to my toilet bowl and flannel sheets.

I clung to the steering wheel with every turn and contemplated the possible diagnoses. The most probable: I had just ingested some ravenous parasite that was feasting mercilessly on the lining of my stomach and giving birth to ice-cold larva at an astounding rate. *Don't panic.*

I careened into the driveway and came to a halt behind my mom's BMW. I came close to demolishing our brick-encased mailbox, but it stood unharmed.

I had to use my shoulder to push my car door open. Once out, I thought I gave the door a good shove, but it swung in slow motion and stopped short of closing. "Am I really that weak?" I used both hands to push it closed and, in the process, dropped my keys onto the rain-soaked pavement. By the time I grabbed them, I had a full-blown migraine, the shakes, and what felt like ice cubes festering in my abdomen. I tried to throw up, but nothing came out.

I reached the front door, and anxiety grabbed hold of me. The porch was spinning. How was I supposed to get my key into the keyhole? Finally, something went my way. I gave the knob a twist, and the door opened right up.

I normally wouldn't ask my mom for help, but the feeling that death was breathing down my neck compelled me to call out to her. And I needed to know where she put the bottle of ibuprofen and that pink stomach relief stuff.

"Mom?" My keys crashed onto the hardwood floor. I stumbled toward the couch.

"Mom!"

I buckled and landed flat on my back just short of the sofa.

"Are you here?" For all my effort, I couldn't project my voice beyond a whisper. I rubbed my eyes with one hand and covered my mouth with the other. *Calm down, Owen. It will be o—*

A blast of thunder interrupted my pathetic attempt to soothe myself.

With the exception of the hallway, there was not a single light on. I suddenly realized my mom wasn't home—no doubt in such a hurry to visit her boyfriend that she forgot to lock the door.

I recognized the patter of Valentine's nails tapping along the surface of the floor, but I was too disoriented now to see where she was.

"Help me, girl."

I laid there in fetal position and dug my fingers into my sides. My forehead radiated heat, but my gut remained ice cold.

It occurred to me to call someone, but I couldn't imagine where my cell was.

I surrendered to the pain and let my eyes drift shut. I allowed myself to consider the real possibility that I might not survive my stupid act of chivalry. At least Jess would know it wasn't a suicide. Surely she would tell the truth about what happened.

As fear gave way to exhaustion, one final coherent thought passed through my mind.

If I die, Jess will blame herself.

I didn't want that.

2. Abnormal World

Flickers of light penetrated my eyelids, confirming what I already knew. I was dead.

A slobbery tongue slurped the side of my face. *My dog is dead, too? How puzzling.*

My eyes parted and revealed a solid block of light piercing through the sunroof above my head. I was still on the living room floor. My headache was gone, thank God, but my back was killing me—an obvious consequence of having spent the night sprawled out on a hardwood surface.

About the time it registered that I had cheated death and would live to see another day, I felt that awful sensation in my stomach. A bag of ice lay burrowed in my midsection.

I sat up like an arthritic grandfather. My mouth was parched. From the looks of things, my mom still wasn't home.

The clock on the coffee table read 7:43 a.m. Clearly I wasn't going to first period.

I bent my knees and tried to get a feel for whether I could stand. I elected to lean on the couch and then put my feet under me. That worked.

"Oh crap. Jess." I normally picked her up by seven. I looked around for my phone, but didn't see it anywhere. I figured it was in my car, which was great because I relished the idea of getting outside to feel the sun.

I stood in the driveway, looked up, and inhaled. The air was humid and cool, but it was incredible to feel sunshine on my face.

Sure enough, my phone was in my car. Jess hadn't called. Weird. I sent her a text: **Sorry I didn't come get you today. R u at school?**

I came inside and tossed my phone on the kitchen counter. I liked the fact that I could fix whatever I wanted for breakfast without worrying about my mom's appetite for a change. I was famished and dying of thirst. Maybe if I ate something hot, like oatmeal, it would melt that freeze in my belly. I microwaved my meal and ate it, but the ice remained.

Perhaps a steamy shower will do the trick, I thought.

It didn't.

I opened my closet door to grab something to wear and noticed my room was darker than before I showered. The sun was fading. How typical. I contemplated staying home—I had a stomach ache, after all—but if I wanted to exempt out of finals, I had to go.

I was dressed and ready to head out by 8:33 a.m. Jess responded to my text: **Drove my car to school. Wasn't sure if u r sick or maybe mad at me.**

I responded: **I'm not mad. Promise. Just slept in. On my way.**

The sun had officially checked out. The wind blew harder than usual.

It dawned on me that I hadn't done my calculus homework, but I figured I could finish it before fourth period.

I had only taken a few steps down my driveway when an unfamiliar noise caught my attention. I looked in the direction of the racket, but saw nothing. It sounded like nails on a chalkboard—no, more like hundreds of claws in a frenzy scouring a jagged rock.

I reached for my car handle but turned again, sensing the dreadful clamor was closing in on me.

A jogger entered my line of sight, and my mind reeled.

"What . . . is . . . that?" I said aloud.

My body went numb as I tried to make sense of the ghastly scene—a slender, attractive brunette out for a morning jog with what looked to be cumbersome, eight-foot chains dragging behind her. The four bulky metal tails grated against the cement, drowning out the rhythmic cadence of her tennis shoes pounding the street. I watched in disbelief as the chain links snaked, staggered, and slapped the pavement.

The woman tilted her head from side to side, seemingly on beat with whatever song played through her earphones.

Is this some sort of joke?

As she ran past me, my eyes traced the chains up her tan legs and muscular back, all the way to a chunky, tarnished shackle fastened snug around her neck. The metal links were bound to the collar just under her ponytail at the top of her spine and draped down like clanking tentacles. They drug on the ground behind her like a hideous train flowing from a bridal gown.

As if that wasn't troubling enough, from the back of her head spewed several thin braided cords. They jutted straight out several inches, then hung down to the small of her back, swaying from side to side and smacking the chains.

"She's jacked up." I don't know if I said that out loud or not.

It was more than a bizarre spectacle.

It was somehow *wicked*.

She finally ran out of sight. I could have gone to the edge of my driveway to take a longer look, but that was the last thing I wanted. I needed her and her freakish metal trappings to get lost. The revolting sound lingered, and once again I desperately wanted to vomit but couldn't.

I needed a second to get my wits about me so I decided to go back inside. I don't know when I dropped them, but my backpack and keys were at my ankles. I normally wouldn't have left my backpack on the driveway—I kept my laptop in there—but I was so rattled by what I'd just seen that I only grabbed my keys.

I flopped down on the sofa. The ticking of the wall clock was the only sound in the room, and that was far too quiet. My mind kept replaying the unsettling soundtrack of those grotesque chains dragging behind that otherwise unassuming woman. I had to get up.

I went to the kitchen to splash cold water on my face, and then returned to the sofa and began mulling over possible explanations for having seen Freddy Kruger's girlfriend jog by my house.

Maybe she's training for some triathlon and the weight of the chains and cords are helping her bulk up, I reasoned.

Perhaps she's a clown by vocation—not a happy one that goes to birthday parties but a creepy, fright-filled clown that leads haunted hotel tours—and she's about to go to work.

Maybe she was on lockdown in a prison and somehow broke free.

While wearing athletic gear.

And earphones.

None of my theories added up, but I felt more relaxed after switching on the TV for a bit. No one appeared to have metal appendages slinging behind them, not even on the Shopping Channel.

I glanced at my watch: 9:06 a.m. I concluded I had overreacted and needed to release the throw pillow from my death grip and move on with my day. The icy feeling in my abdomen was making me paranoid, that's all.

I locked the door, and as I walked to my car, I felt my lighthearted outlook on life returning. Unfortunately the sight of my jostled backpack plopped right where I'd dropped it made me feel uneasy all over again. I couldn't get the awful image of the jogger out of my mind.

What was so scary about her? I asked myself. It was hard to explain, but I guess it was the way she looked enslaved, as if, without her knowledge, something sinister had claimed her as its own.

"That's ridiculous," I said as I put my car in reverse. "This isn't Star Wars. Get over it. Owen, get it together."

I backed out of my driveway and prayed one of my traditional atheistic prayers. "God, I don't believe you exist, but nonetheless, could you please keep that scary, Bloody Mary looking jogger lady from crossing my path again? And get the ice out of my stomach while you're at it."

I noticed that someone—no doubt some deviant kids— had spray-painted the word "rage" in large lowercase letters on the fence across the street. What losers.

I made it to the stoplight at the end of my neighborhood without seeing any joggers, or cars for that matter. I waited for the light to turn green and thought about Jess. I questioned whether I would tell her—or anyone—what I saw this morning. Maybe in a few days, after the disturbing mental image and eerie sound stopped stalking me.

The light turned green, and I drove forward, casually glancing at the grocery store parking lot on my right.

"Oh my God!"

I jerked the wheel left without turning my head. My eyes were locked on a well-dressed man at the gas pump. Were those really chains draping behind him and cords protruding from his head?

"Please, no."

My attention jumped to the young lady two pumps down. She had them, too.

I slammed into the curb on the grassy center median. Someone laid on his horn. I came to a complete stop, but my mind was reeling.

"Get out of the road!" a guy said. The seemingly concerned woman in the passenger seat beside him opened her door and mouthed something in my direction.

They, too, had fat shackles around their necks.

My car was sprawled across both lanes, but I couldn't move my arms. A young mechanic walked out of the auto repair shop across the street and peered through my window from the curb. He turned sharply back toward the shop, and I heard the unmistakable sound of chains clattering against the cement. I closed my eyes.

"Not again. This is not happening!"

My eyes opened just in time. The man who had honked at me was now rapidly approaching my car. I managed to rouse my hands into gripping the steering wheel, fully convinced that if I didn't drive away, he'd kill me.

I threw the car in reverse with no concern for whether I hit the mutated guy or not, then sped in the direction of my house. I don't know if the light was red or green, but I went right through the intersection into my neighborhood and straight home.

Like a bad case of déjà vu, I flung my car into park and rushed to the door. I raced to the bathroom and locked myself in, refusing to look toward the mirror hanging above my sink. I dropped to my knees and clutched the sides of the toilet.

After several minutes, it was clear I wasn't going to barf, but I dreaded getting up. What if I looked in the mirror and saw a steel collar around my neck with grisly chains and revolting cords protruding from my head? I was terrified to look, but I had to know.

I stood and swallowed without any saliva in my mouth, then inched my way around toward the mirror. I kept my eyes closed for fear of beholding my monstrous reflection. I hadn't noticed anything different about my appearance when I showered this morning, but everything had changed since then. I was now officially psychotic.

I flashed my eyes open and let out a sigh of relief. No demon dog collar. I turned to check the back of my head, and didn't see any of those freaky dreadlocks either.

I still couldn't stand the sight of myself. I hurried to my room and crammed my face into my bed pillow. I was beyond delusional. I needed to be locked up, or at the very least, sedated. My mind started replaying the events.

Did I run over that guy? Did someone follow me?

I peered out the blinds like a paranoid schizophrenic, then yanked them shut.

Did I lock the front door?

I shot downstairs to double-check, then ran back to my room and pushed my desk in front of my door. Then I climbed under my covers and hid for the next six hours.

I drifted in and out of sleep, wrestling over what I did or didn't see. It's a hard thing to accept that you're a crazy person—that your formerly sound mind is now overrun by hallucinations just because you did something rash the night before.

My phone was in my car and would stay there forever as far as I was concerned because leaving the house was no longer an option.

My mom never came home. How typical.

Eventually I pulled the covers down and looked for the clock that normally sat on my bedside table. In all my frantic flailing, I had knocked it to the floor.

3:28 p.m.

I sat up and took a panoramic look around my room. My stuff was the same, but I felt far removed from my surroundings, like I was homesick even though I was at home. I tried convincing myself I'd been sleeping all day, and this morning's horrifying events were merely lingering images from a fever-induced nightmare. But I knew better. My desk was in front of my door—irrefutable proof.

It dawned on me that I was missing basketball practice. Then it occurred to me that I might have a life-sucking brain tumor. What if, while I sat barricaded in my room, I needed to be rushing to the nearest emergency room?

I was desperate to talk to someone—Jess, Lance, my mom—anyone who knew me before I became delusional. My cell was my only link to the outside world. I wondered if I could grab it and get back inside without being mauled by steel-trapped humanity.

I dared to pull one slat of my wooden blinds up a half inch. I didn't see anyone outside my house.

I put on a sweatshirt and pulled the hood over my head, then dug in my junk drawer until I found sunglasses. I grabbed my Louisville Slugger baseball bat and took slow, calculated steps down the stairs. Valentine sat poised by the front door wagging her straggly tail.

"No walk today, girl. No way."

I clutched my bat in one hand and slowly turned the lock on the door with my other. Visions of this morning's jogger overwhelmed my mind. I imagined her leading a charge against me the instant I cracked open the door— the disgruntled guy who honked at me earlier right on her heels.

I peered through the sheer curtain panel. The coast was clear, but I still feared for my life.

My hand hung lifeless on the door knob. I could hear my heart stampeding. My stomach was subzero. But I had to act.

I swung the door open and leapt to my car. In seconds, I had my phone and was back inside. I slammed and locked the door, then pressed all my weight against it. I struggled to calm my heavy breathing.

Jess had texted me: **Where r u?**

I lost the urge to call her. How do you tell your prom date you're seeing metal things hanging from people?

I retreated to the couch and called Lance. His voicemail picked up.

"Hey, Lance. It's me. Listen, I know you're at practice right now, but can you call me right away, like, as soon as you get this message? Something . . . really terrible happened to me today. I mean, I'm okay, but I'm not okay, I guess. Just call me. Thanks."

I sent him a text: **Call me!!**

I had mixed emotions about contacting my mom. I couldn't remember the last time I sought her comfort. I only recall coddling her a million times. Oh well. I called her anyway.

"Hello?" She sounded unusually happy. I instantly felt a tad better.

"Hey, Mom. Where are you?"

"I stayed across town at Teresa's house last night, but I brought my laptop with me so I've been getting some work done while we visited today. You remember my friend Teresa, don't you?"

Yeah, right. She was at John's house. Or Frank's. I couldn't remember the latest guy's name, nor did I care.

"I'm sorry. I should have let you know I wasn't coming home," she said. As usual, our parent-child roles felt reversed.

"I've had a really, really bad day, Mom."

"You have?" She sounded genuinely concerned. "What happened?"

"I don't feel good. I'm kinda . . . seeing things or something. Scary things."

"Oh." She was taken aback, as evidenced by the long pause. "What do you mean, scary things?"

"People don't look right. It's hard to explain. When are you coming home?"

"I'm leaving in half an hour. How about I pick us up some chicken on my way home?"

"No, Mom—please just come straight home."

"Um, okay. I can do that."

My mom was so different when she wasn't drinking. She was actually responsive. It was nice.

I counted down the minutes until she came home. What would I tell her? If I spilled my guts she'd head straight for her liquor stash. If I couldn't handle something, I knew she couldn't, and drinking was her one and only crutch. Well, that and pathetic men. Besides, my story would probably drive a Baptist preacher to drink, much less an alcoholic.

I clung to the sofa and took comfort in seeing normal humans on TV. Why didn't the people outside my house look normal? I can't stand when things don't add up or make sense. I sat there drowning in my own cognitive confusion. I turned the TV volume way up and hoped the dialogue would overshadow my anxiety.

Even with *Wheel of Fortune* blaring, I heard the door to the garage shut. I muted the TV and turned toward the kitchen, anticipating seeing my mom turn the corner.

"I'm in the living room, Mom."

I heard her fumbling through the mail. I resented that she went traipsing down to the mailbox at the end of the driveway when she got home instead of coming straight in to check on me.

"You got a letter from UCLA."

"Great, Mom—can you please come here?"

I heard her opening another envelope while I wasted away on the sofa. Finally, I heard the sound of junk mail hitting the recycle bin.

"Oh God, no," I said. I tried to deny the noise reverberating in my ears: metal dragging the tile floors, then the hardwoods. I couldn't bring myself to look. I stared at the floor.

"How are you feeling?" Her voice was kind. I could see her silhouette in my peripheral vision, but I dared not turn my head.

My phone dinged at me. Jess sent me a text: **U ok? Im worried. Call me!**

My mother lowered into the lounge chair directly across from me. A nauseating quiver slivered all the way up my spine.

"What happened to you today?"

"I told you. I've been seeing some really terrifying things."

"Are you high on something?"

Her words infuriated me, slapping me out of my stupor. I glared straight at her and was pleasantly surprised to see that nothing about her appearance was out of the ordinary.

I was still angry, but that made me more relaxed than I had felt all day.

"Mom, you know I don't do drugs. I would never do that."

"Well, you sounded strange on the phone today. You wouldn't be the first teenager to get high."

She wore a flowing skirt with a loose-fitting silky blouse. A scarf shrouded her neck. I sank back into the couch, relieved to see my normal mother. On any other day, that would be somewhat of a disappointment, but today, it was a life saver.

Why did I think I had heard the dreaded clamor of chains scraping across the floor? Maybe it had come from outside. Or maybe I was a certifiable basket case.

My mom shifted her weight, removing her shoes and folding her legs into the side of her chair. I heard a clanking sound. *What the—*

"So are you ill?"

She reached across her chest up to her shoulder and unwound her scarf a layer at a time. I contemplated how much I wanted to disclose. It was foolish to tell her everything. I decided I would explain that something wasn't right without delving into specific details.

"I just don't feel like—"

The air depleted from my lungs. My mother's scarf cascaded to the rug, and in its place, a hulking, gray-tinted shackle squeezed her throat. There was no hiding my terror. I must have looked like I'd seen death.

"What, Owen? You don't feel like what?" She paused a moment, then leaned in toward me. "You're scaring me," she said.

The irony was almost as thick as the contraption encircling her neck.

I felt myself inhale. "I just . . . don't know . . . what else to tell you." I tried to be nonchalant but over did it and sounded robotic instead.

My mom put one foot on the floor, then leaned in and extended her hand. I shuddered backwards into the depths of the couch cushions. She pressed her eyebrows together in dismay.

"Hand me the remote, Owen!" She was agitated. I should have known she wouldn't press me for more information. She was an expert at changing the subject.

The remote was at the end of the coffee table, beyond the grasp of us both.

"I'll get it."

Too late. She was already on her feet. My mouth gaped open as a wall of chains draped over the back of the chair and formed a metallic canopy. There were too many to count. She bent to grab the remote and a dozen or so gnarly cords slid and dangled down her left shoulder. As the chains jerked from behind the chair and onto the floor, it was like a crate loaded with pots and pans hurled down from the second story of our house and shattered at her feet.

I sprang up and cupped my hands over my ears, astounded at the noise. She didn't notice—the noise or my adverse reaction.

"Owen, bring me a Diet Coke out of the fridge. And take some Tylenol. That'll make your headache go away."

In the midst of my catastrophic mental breakdown, I had two oddly ordinary thoughts. One, I didn't have a headache and never said I did. And two, as far as I knew, there weren't any more Diet Cokes in the fridge.

"Mom?"

"What?" She flipped through the channels totally unaware that I was dying inside.

As badly as I wanted to choke her, I loathed the site of that shackle gripping her throat. Where did it come from? Was it really even there?

Feelings of despair overwhelmed me. Either I needed serious help, or she did.

"What, Owen?" Her tone was insensitive and demanding, of course.

"Never mind." I should have known better than to look to my mother for consolation. She didn't have it in her.

I walked to the kitchen and fought the tears pooling in my eyes. I opened the fridge. Just like I thought, no Diet Cokes. I slammed it shut.

"Why is this happening to me?"

I grabbed the bills and envelopes stacked by the fridge and launched them at the floor. My anguish had turned to full-blown rage, but my reasoning mind wouldn't let me lose all control.

What are you gonna do? Start tearing up the place? That won't make the chains go away.

I collapsed into a chair at the breakfast table and rocked back and forth like a lunatic. As if on cue, Jess's silver Mercedes pulled up in front of my house.

"Thank God."

I darted out the door at the back of the kitchen and sprinted through the garage toward the driveway. I didn't care if some scary figure lurched at me. If I could just get to Jess, my world would flip right side up, if even for a moment.

Her driver's side door opened. I don't know if I smelled her perfume or just wanted to so badly that I imagined it, but a sweet scent beckoned me to move even faster in her direction.

Sensing I was headed right for her embrace, she reached out to me.

But I stopped just short.

I couldn't hug her.

I couldn't hug anyone wearing a shackle and chains.

3. Neurological Despair

I couldn't sleep. The fact that it was two o'clock in the morning didn't matter. Nothing mattered. All of mankind, including the people closest to me, had turned on me—morphed into metal-clad freaks overnight. I didn't know if they were out to harm me, but I feared them either way.

Jess must have been hurt by the way I treated her earlier. I stopped just short of her reach, then turned my back and ran away without offering the slightest explanation.

I couldn't bring myself to respond to her flood of text messages. I was too frightened to try to reconcile with her.

I laid there next to Valentine in my king-sized bed, and for the first time ever, contemplated suicide. I figured that was more evidence that I wasn't in my right mind and tried to focus instead on reaching a levelheaded conclusion. I kept getting hung up, though, on one distressing thought: I felt cursed, but it was everyone else who looked cursed.

I detest confusion.

I powered up my laptop. Everything that exists in the universe and beyond is described in great detail on the Internet, right? I searched "people wearing chains," but all that came up was stuff about fashion trends, jewelry, and some blog about a supposedly hilarious picture someone took of a Walmart shopper.

I looked at countless websites about alien invasions, but none of them described anything like what I was experiencing.

I decided to search "seeing things that aren't there." Unfortunately, that didn't help my anxiety level any. Within minutes, I determined I was most likely suffering from Schizoid Personality Disorder—a diagnosis that scared me so bad I slammed my laptop shut and buried every inch of my body under the covers.

It's a strange thing to hope you have a brain tumor, but I started wishing for that over some incurable mental disorder. At least brain tumors are sometimes operable.

I concluded I needed to have my mother drive me to the hospital first thing in the morning, even if it meant undergoing some major surgery, or worse, a one-way ticket to the nearest insane asylum.

By 5:30 a.m., I was so hungry I was nauseous. That freeze in my stomach didn't help matters.

I left the perceived protection of my room for the kitchen and chased down a peanut butter and jelly sandwich with an enormous glass of milk. Sitting at the breakfast table, the silence was driving me nuts—or more nuts, I suppose.

Misery was far too pleasant a word to explain my mood, and I had never experienced anything close to this degree of loneliness.

I rinsed my dishes and started back toward my room. My bed was the only safe place on the planet to me, but that wasn't saying much, because even there I felt threatened.

As I passed my mother's bedroom, I noticed she was sprawled across her mattress in a drunken coma. I took a closer look hoping not to see them, but the harness still groped her neck and a mass of chains and cords flung in every direction.

What if I take a closer look while she lies there passed out? I thought.

My steps were swift and deliberate. I flipped on the fan light above her and stepped up to the foot of her bed. She was lying on her back but angled onto her right side, her hair disheveled and her mouth hanging open.

The jumbled mass of chains eerily framed her petite body, and at that distance, the cords now appeared to be braided strands of dark leather-like material embedded with tiny peculiar specks of something sharp. They were slightly thicker than a pencil and appeared pliable, like cable wires.

I had to take a closer look.

Do I dare touch it?

I braced myself against the mattress and leaned in to examine the chain dangling nearest to me. It was an out-of-body experience of sorts watching my hand glide in slow motion toward the metal. The links were more massive than I realized—each at least four inches long and half an inch thick. As the tips of my fingers reached just short of a link, I sensed it would be uncomfortably cold to the touch.

41

"Here goes," I whispered.

Finally, I made contact. It was bone-chillingly cold. I jerked away for a moment, then leaned in again, only this time I used the entire palm of my hand to clutch the gigantic chain. I couldn't wrap my fingers all the way around, and I couldn't hang on for long, cold as it was.

I put my palm to my mouth and blew. I hadn't realized I was trembling until then. My fingers thawed a bit, and I determined to touch the chain again, only this time I'd use both hands and give it a vigorous tug.

It occurred to me that the unpleasant racket of colliding chains might wake my mother, but then I recalled a disturbing reality—it seemed I was the only one who could hear them.

I grabbed the icy chain links and pulled as hard as I could, but I was no match for them—they were physically impossible to lift, even slightly.

I let go and blew warmth on my hands again, then zeroed in on the bizarre apparatus hanging from the bottom link of the chain. It was a half cylinder with a hinge in the middle, some sort of open cuff. It had dents and dings, no doubt from being dragged all over creation behind my mother, and it appeared scorched on the inside.

Ignoring the cold, I ran my finger around the curves of the cuff. I thought I felt an engraving of some kind, but my finger was going numb. I leaned in to take a closer look and observed that there really was something chiseled in the cuff. They were crooked, sloppy letters, as if hand-carved by a childish craftsman.

david allen barrett

A name? Who is that?

42

No doubt, my delusions were getting even more farfetched.

I counted fifteen cuffs in all, each suspended from the ends of individual chains. I took a step to my right to examine another one, but my attention shifted to two straggly cords intertwined among the chaos. As I clutched one, I imagined the bony pinky of a haggardly witch. It was encrusted with sharp fragments of what appeared to be bone and glass, and I felt as though I was handling a thorny rose stem. It sliced my finger.

Just as I released it, I thought I saw something—something written.

I blinked hoping the vision would miraculously go away. Surely the word "bitterness" was not etched into the black pigment on that cord. Yet another brain-bruising observation.

My determination to take a closer look at the freaky objects only served to intensify my psychotic state of mind.

As I dashed toward the hallway, my mother jostled in her bed, prompting me to look over my shoulder. She remained asleep, but before I turned back around, something unfamiliar lured my eyes to the wall above her headboard. I beheld the word "victim" displayed in black lowercase letters. I turned off the light and kept charging toward my bed.

I laid there for who knows how long until my mother called my name.

"Owen, you gonna make breakfast?"

I didn't answer.

Was it the depression, the ice in my stomach, my psychotic episodes, or my body physically shutting down that pinned me to my mattress?

I had to come clean with someone about my hallucinations, but who? Some psychiatrist looking to land more grant money while I sat rotting in a maximum security facility?

I heard my mother's chains coming down the hallway. She burst into my room without the slightest inkling of motherly affection.

"Owen, get up."

I didn't say a word or move a muscle. She got louder.

"Get outta that bed."

I took my time sitting up, then glared at her with the most "I don't care" expression I could muster and asked, "Mom, who—"

"Owen, are you okay? You look awful!" Her tone now carried a rare hint of concern. She stepped closer, pulling her chains along.

"No, I'm not okay. Who is David Allen Barrett?"

She flinched.

"Mom, do you know him? Is he a real person?"

I'd always known my mother had secrets from her past that she kept hidden from me. I could only hope she would be honest with me about this.

She turned toward the window, then snapped her head back at me with furious intensity. "Where did you hear that name? Have you been snooping around?"

"So you know him?" I said.

I don't need you conjuring up the past. That's none of your business!"

My mother's rebuke didn't faze me. "That name means something to you?"

She turned to storm out of my room, but I grabbed her arm and turned her around to face me. Her chains gathered at my ankles.

"Mom, I don't care about your past. I'm not trying to dig up dirt on you or anything—I swear." I pulled her in close and peered down at her.

"Please, just tell me, is David Allen Barrett someone you know?"

Sadness poured over her face, then she clinched her fists. "Yes."

She pulled away from me, and I let her go. She didn't care to ask any questions. She left my room in a hurry and clanked down the hallway.

I tried to come up with some justification—a formula of sorts—that would explain how I saw that man's name etched on a cuff dangling from one of my mother's chains. My emotions see-sawed up and down from relief—*maybe I'm not a schizoid*—to rage—*why is this happening to me?*

I heard the front door slam. I glanced at my phone and saw that Lance had called three times. Jess sent me a text: **What's the matter with u? Have u lost your mind?**

Interesting.

I kept my ring tone silenced and retreated to my bed where I concentrated so hard that I finally grew weary enough to get some sleep. I woke up at 1:15 p.m. with a headache and the same awful cold feeling brewing in my belly. I made another peanut butter jelly and sat at the breakfast table with my back to the window for fear I'd see another screwed up human.

I needed a plan. Surely I could come up with a rational next step despite the utter confusion of my circumstances. I grabbed a notepad and pen. I had to go back to the source of when and where this madness began. It started just after I made the asinine decision to drink whatever substance Jess and I found in the woods. I needed to know what it was, what was in it.

Mrs. Barnett came to mind. She was my chemistry teacher in the tenth grade and adored me—I was one of her best students. Maybe she could help me figure out what I'd ingested. What excuse would I give her for having the liquid tested? I drew a blank, but for now, I knew what I needed to do. And I dreaded it.

I threw on some jeans, a T-shirt, and my American Eagle baseball cap. I snatched a bottle of water from the fridge and poured the contents down the sink. I considered looking for some gloves but decided that was an unnecessary precaution. It was a little late for prudence.

Now all I had to do was get in the car and drive to the woods behind Jess's neighborhood. But that was easier said than done—my new agoraphobia threw a major kink in my plan.

Keys in hand, I stood at the front door and waited for my fear to subside. It never did. I took a deep breath and prepared to dart out the door when I saw my cell light up. It was Jess.

"Hello?" I wondered if it was a mistake to answer the call.

"Hey, it's me. What's going on with you?"

"I, ah, don't feel well."

"Well I'm sorry about that, and I'd like to be there for you, but you're making it very difficult. Why did you leave me standing by myself in your driveway yesterday? And why have you ignored all of my texts?"

"I'm just going through something really . . . scary. After I drank that stuff in the woods, I got deathly sick and things went haywire."

I paused, knowing I was about to expose my insanity.

"Jess, I've been seeing things. I thought it was all in my mind, but then something happened with my mom this morning, and now I'm just not sure. Does that make sense?"

"Um, not really. Have you gone to the doctor?"

"Yeah," I lied. "I'm waiting on the results of the lab work." I didn't want to admit I was too scared to go to the doctor—or anywhere, for that matter.

"Are you sure this isn't about prom?"

"What?"

"I've heard from several people that you said you'd rather go with Cindy Rutherford. Are you avoiding me now because you don't want to tell me that?"

Seriously? Jess was still in high school world, and I couldn't identify. I wanted to tell her how ridiculous she was being, but all I could come up with was, "I barely know Cindy."

"Well, like, five people today told me that you'd rather go with her. Prom is only a month away. I can't believe you would pull this."

Although nothing about the prom scene was even remotely appealing at this point, I assured her repeatedly that I wanted to go with her, but she insisted the rumors were true. I finally got tired of going back and forth with her.

"You know what, Jess, you're right. This is all just a big scheme to get you to break up with me."

She paused for a moment. "Are you serious?"

"No!" The anger in my voice now mirrored hers. "I'm feeling sick Jess. Can you just please try to understand?"

"Oh, I understand just fine."

She hung up on me. Wonderful. Was I wrong to expect a little more compassion from her?

I went back to finding the nerve to leave my house. I actually liked that it was drizzling. Surely that would discourage metal-bound joggers from taking to the streets.

I counted to three, then opened the door just wide enough to squeeze out. What a relief to get in my car and lock myself inside. I backed out of my driveway and took a second look at the graffiti on my neighbor's fence with the word "rage" on display for all to see. But could everyone see it, or just me? Another drop in the sea of confusion.

I kept my eyes on the road, dreading what I would see if I allowed my gaze to drift. Vehicles drove by, but the rain helped obstruct my view.

As I neared Jess's neighborhood, I realized how much I missed her, even though she was seriously self-absorbed today. Guess I was too, but given my circumstances, I felt slightly justified.

I pulled over in the same place I always did and headed straight into the woods. I was nervous, of course, but I arrived at Jess's and my spot unscathed. The hole I'd dug had filled in a bit, but was still easy to find. It served as another tangible reminder that I wasn't dreaming up the events of the past forty-eight hours.

Having done this once before, I grabbed a rock and dug through to the mystery fluid with relative ease. The feel and sound of rampaging waters was just as intriguing as the first time I'd sought it out. Finally, I saw the glowing substance through an opening in the dirt. I laid on my stomach and got the sample.

While driving home, I noticed two little boys running up a driveway, having a blast in the afternoon rain. It made me smile—then slam on my brakes. I stared at their backs, seeing nothing out of the ordinary—not a single chain or cord. Had the poison finally passed through my system?

A kind-looking lady walked onto the porch holding towels for the waterlogged boys.

"Ugh!" I punched my steering wheel. She was shackled.

Frustration bombarded my mind. The kids had no metal on them. Why? And why did that lady have two chains while my mother had more than a dozen? What were those weird cuff things hanging off the ends?

As if I wasn't aggravated enough, I pulled up to a stop sign that had "die" written on it, in black lowercase letters, of course.

I drove the final mile toward my house agonizing over how much I wished I had a father to run to. Not a coach. Not Lance's dad. My own dad. I'd never met him and, according to my mother, never would. She said he wanted nothing to do with us, and would likely go to great lengths to ensure I'd never find him.

I hated going through all of this alone.

I made it home and flung myself on the couch in front of the TV. Valentine laid right at my feet. Sweet girl.

Everything in TV land looked fine. Too bad nothing in my world looked remotely right.

I was dead set on getting that water sample to Mrs. Barnett tomorrow, but the idea of going to school was not sitting well with me.

A knock at the door startled me. No need to ask who it was. Even if it was someone I knew, I didn't know that person anymore. I inched toward the door. "Hey Owen, it's me, Lance. You there?"

It was refreshing to hear my best friend's voice. I turned the lock and begged the universe to let me see Lance without anything around his neck. No such luck. He and his girlfriend Meagan both stood on my porch with shackles and chains.

"Hey dude, we've been worried about you. Are you alright?"

I stared at him. He returned the favor. Meagan squeezed Lance's hand uneasily. There was always a slight tension between her and me, I guess because, deep down, I resented her for stealing my best bro.

"Can we come in?"

I was afraid of that.

"Sure." I opened the door and walked away. The stomach-churning sound of chains dragging on the floor followed me.

Lance took charge of the situation. "Meagan, why don't you hang out here while Owen and I go upstairs and talk a minute?"

I didn't allow chained people in my room, but he didn't know that. Meagan flashed a charming smile then respected his wishes by taking a seat on the sofa. I hated to admit it, but she really was cute, minus her metal trappings, of course.

I went up the stairs ahead of Lance and he clamored up a few steps back. I sifted in hyper-speed through the events of the last two days and tried to settle on what I would and wouldn't disclose. I sat on the corner of my bed, and he relaxed on the floor.

"So, did you skip practice to come see me?" I asked.

"Coach said it was fine. He wasn't happy yesterday when you missed practice, but when you were absent again today and no one had heard from you, I think he was more worried than mad. Are you gonna be okay for the game tomorrow night?"

How do you play a basketball game with the sound of chains slamming the court and cords flinging in your face? "I don't know. I'm really not doing well."

"Are you down or something?" Lance was clearly worried that I'd be the thirteenth suicide. He was right to worry.

"Yeah, but it's not what you think. It's worse than you think, actually."

"What do you mean? Did your mom do something?"

"No. I did something, something totally dumb."

"What?"

I hesitated for a moment, then spilled my guts to him, revealing every deranged detail of my recent experiences. I described how Jess and I went to the woods and found the mysterious water. I told him I drank it, and it made me sick, and I thought I was going to die. He asked me if I was feeling better now, so that's when—after I asked him to promise not to freak out—I told him more—about the chains and the cords and the graffiti everywhere.

Lance searched my face, no doubt thinking I'd been smoking something.

"You're serious?"

"Lance, please believe me." A tear fell down my cheek, a display of emotion that embarrassed us both. He stood but said nothing. I wiped my face with my sheets.

"You're not making any sense, Owen."

"I know, but I need you to believe me anyway. Do you?"

"Help me understand. Who do you see these chains and stuff on?"

"Everyone." I left off the part about not seeing it on the little boys. That was too much to explain right now.

"So, what about me?" He smiled. "Do you see something on me?"

His expression stiffened when I didn't say anything.

"Do you?"

I sensed this would be a defining moment. "Yes, I do— on you, Meagan, Jess, my mom, people I don't know, too."

He glared at me like I'd just socked him in the face.

"Owen, you need to go to the hospital. You got a hold of some bad crap, and it's seriously tanking your mind."

"I know—I thought that too, but then something happened this morning with my mom." I suddenly wished I hadn't started down that road, but it was too late.

"What? What happened?"

I explained about seeing the chain cuff with the name David Allen Barrett and my mom's reaction when I asked her about him.

I hoped he was about to help me put together some clues and throw out some possible explanations, but instead, he put his hands on his hips and mocked me. "So you see chains on me right now?" I wanted to punch the grin off his face, but I understood his skepticism. He was barely wading into the madness while I'd been drowning in it for two days. I figured the best way to respond was to be completely honest—a virtue that tended to elude me quite often.

"Yes. You have a shackle around your neck and three chains attached in the back."

"And I've got cords coming out of my head, too?" he said sarcastically.

"Yes. I can't see how many though. You'd have to turn around."

"Owen, you can't seriously believe that!" He was indignant, then so was I.

"Did you hear what I said? I see it with my own eyes! And I hear it, too. And the name on my mom's chain—"

"There's nothing there! Nothing's hanging from my neck or coming out of my head." He grabbed his scalp, then pointed at me. "You're an idiot!"

I hated being called that, but I refused to get upset.

"Owen, get some help. I'll tell Coach you've had a migraine or something. Just go and let someone figure out what's wrong with you. Seriously."

I couldn't hear his footsteps down the stairs over the racket of his chains. I looked out my window and saw him drive off with Meagan, then I shrunk back into my bed. My best friend didn't believe me.

I had to get that water tested, but how in the world would I go to school tomorrow? Who would I talk to?

What would I see?

4. Young Victims

My mother stayed in her room all morning. I put her eggs on a plate in the microwave. It seemed like it had been forever since I thought about schoolwork. I was too busy mulling over the absurdities of the past couple of days and trying to decide if my life was ruined beyond repair.

I sat at the breakfast table and stared at the clock. I dreaded the thought of going to school, much less getting there early. If I left at ten after seven, I'd have just enough time to give my sample to Mrs. Barnett, then get to first period. No need to factor in time for picking up Jess anymore. She and I weren't on good terms.

I scrolled through my friends' status updates on my cell. Lots of people were planning to attend Jamie Longmire's funeral today. I suddenly felt like a jerk.

As dreadful as my life is, at least I'm alive.

I think.

I heard my mother clanking around and interpreted that as a cue to get going. I promised myself I would do everything I had to get done today without over thinking it. I didn't want to give fear time to arrest me.

"Just get in the car and drive."

I locked myself in my car, then fidgeted for a moment with my rearview mirror. I recognized a certain steadily-increasing sound.

"Unbelievable!" The female jogger I blamed for triggering this whole psychotic upheaval jogged right in front of my house again. I was sure it was her. I'd never, ever forget her face, or her metal scraps. I turned to look at her. As expected, she carried along four chains and multiple grotesque cords.

I faced forward and took heart. Seeing her made me queasy and still struck me as evil personified, but it didn't send me into a panicky whirlwind this time. I needed that boost of confidence for what I was about to endure.

I turned onto Grant Road and could already see the sign people swarming around my school, only this time there were chains and cords all over the place. I was less prepared for the scene than I had hoped. Anxiety grabbed hold of me.

"I can't do this!" I was helpless to tame the trembling in my hands. I pulled off the road and gasped for air. The weight of uncertainty sat like an unmovable boulder on my chest.

"Why am I seeing this stuff?"

The only thing more ferocious than my fear was my unquenchable desire to find answers—logical, reliable answers. And hopefully a cure. What I wasn't willing to do was sit back and stay lost in confusion.

I eased my way back onto the street and gave one of those "thank you" waves to a driver who graciously paused long enough to let me in the flow of traffic. Never mind that she had hardware groping her neck.

I tried to calm myself. "Everyone looks like impish freaks, but they're acting normal. No one's out to kill you." My body wasn't buying it, as evidenced by my sweaty palms and erratic breathing.

I managed to pull into a parking spot. That felt like a real accomplishment. I gave myself one last pep talk before peeling my fingers off the steering wheel and reaching for my backpack and specimen bottle.

"Treat people like you don't see a thing. Get the liquid sample to Mrs. Barnett. Get through the day. You can do this."

My buddy Jared tapped on my driver's side window and sent me into cardiac arrest. I pulled it together as quickly as a psychotic person can. "Hey Jared." I opened my car door and whispered my mantra: "Treat people like you don't see a thing. Get the liquid sample to—"

"You're playing in the game tonight, right?"

"Um, I'm actually feeling pretty sick. I don't think I can play." Okay, so I *could* carry on a conversation while surrounded by metal-clad monsters. That was good to know.

"Dude, Coach is gonna kill you."

That was a real concern of mine. Seriously. "I know. I'm gonna talk to him and try to explain."

I kept my eyes pasted to the pavement as Jared and I walked up the steps outside my school and into horrorville—the hallway by the front office. The clashing of hundreds of chains dragging every which way overloaded my senses. And it was freezing.

"Hey, are you okay?"

I gave the best assurance I could muster and looked him in the face for a fleeting moment. "Sure. I just don't feel good, that's all. I'll be fine." I tried to pull off a grin, but my cheeks were too cold.

Jared gave me a brotherly pat on the back and walked away, but not before I saw four chains dangling from the shackle around his neck and five cords lagging from the back of his head.

I dodged through the crowd and kept my face planted toward the floor, stepping over countless chain links before arriving at my old chemistry classroom. Mrs. Barnett was conversing with a student. It's a strange thing to see your favorite teacher entrapped in metal. I was torn—I wanted to free her, but I was hoping she could help free me.

She glanced in my direction and lit up with familiar delight. "Owen, how are you?" Her joy shifted to concern the longer she looked at me. No sleep, a belly shiver, and evil hallucinations do tend to take a toll on one's appearance.

I wiped my icy nose. "I'm alright," I lied. "I have a favor to ask of you. Do you have a way to examine this substance for me?" I handed her the demon water.

"What is it?"

"I think it's just water, but could you run some sort of lab test and tell me if there's anything odd in it—toxins or something?"

"I don't have the ability to do that here, but I'm sure my husband could do an examination at his lab, providing he has the time. He works for Jamison Chemical."

"That would be awesome. Um, how long do you think it will take?"

"I can give it to him tonight, and I'm pretty sure I could have some results for you by Monday."

That's four days away. I'll probably be dead by then. "That's fine. I really appreciate it."

"Where did you get this?" She took a lingering look at the bottle's contents. I counted three cords spiraling straight down through her curly hair.

"My dog has been sick for a couple of days, vomiting and all. I saw her slurping up water the other day out of an empty flowerpot in our backyard, and I thought maybe something in it is making her sick."

I liked the idea of keeping the primary focus off me and onto an organism that couldn't be questioned.

Her perplexed expression made me anxious to leave. "Thank you. I've gotta get to class now. Please don't forget to give that to your husband. Thanks again."

I tried not to look nervous as I backed out of the classroom but probably didn't succeed.

My journey to first period was challenging. I closed my eyes as often as I could, for as long as I could, but still didn't escape seeing chains. And what a heinous racket.

I took my seat in English Lit and stared out the window like always. I craved normalcy more than food and oxygen combined. The two knuckle heads next to me struck up some pathetic conversation about who drank the most beer at some pizza place. I tuned them out.

It took great restraint to keep from jumping out of my skin when the girl seated in front of me, Amy, kept leaning back, waving all five of her cords just under my nose. I could clearly see a word etched into one of them— "anxious." Then I read another cord—"vain." I marveled at the ridiculousness of my circumstances. *I'm seeing cords jetting out of people's heads that have labels on them—troubled attitudes, or something. How totally preposterous.*

Amy complained to her friend that a guy named Jimmy took advantage of her. From the sound of it, she gave him the only thing he wanted—her body, of course—and he gave her the one thing she didn't want: a breakup text.

Amy had just one chain that coiled onto the floor less than an inch away from my left shoe. I considered dropping something on purpose as an excuse to take a closer look at the icky open cuff but elected to just lean in and stare. No one was paying any attention to me.

There it was, clear as day on the outside of the cuff:

jimmy thomas lieberman

This had to be psychosomatic—my brain merely projecting a vision of a first name I just heard and taking creative liberty to add a middle and last name. And maybe the name I saw on my mom's chain was some cosmic coincidence. My disturbed brain crafted a name of a person who she happened to know.

My pragmatic mind had a hard time accepting those notions, but what other possibilities were there?

Mrs. Manchester began giving instructions for an upcoming book report. About the time I typed "Jimmy Thomas Lieberman" in a notes app on my cell, a putrid smell wafted in my direction. I looked all around, but no one else seemed to react to the aroma invasion. The stench got stronger. I put my hand over my nose. The guy next to me did a "what's up?" hand motion at me.

In an instant, my eyes were diverted to the closed door. I must have moaned out loud because several heads snapped in my direction. This was beyond anything I could ever conjure up, toxins or no toxins.

Its feet were stained dark with sludge and filth, and its rotten toenails looked human-like but projected several inches past each boney toe. An unsymmetrical conglomeration of black fabric shrouded its form and raveled just above its scrawny ankles. What looked to be hip bones protruded beneath its slovenly attire. The thing was emaciated, anorexic, starved to death but somehow still clinging to life.

After passing effortlessly through the closed door, I witnessed the hideous being take steps, yet glide through the air as if escorted on some hellacious conveyer belt.

I clutched the sides of my desk and leaned away as far as I could, shoving my chair into the desk behind me. The thing awkwardly jerked its shaved head so that its inflamed, depraved eyes glared toward me. It slithered closer and closer on a one-way path to murder my soul. I didn't dare continue to observe its face, but I did make one bone-chilling observation before forcing my eyes down. As if boasting, it wore the word "shame" across its forehead. It was some sort of branding, as though burned into its decomposing flesh.

The closer it got, the more I discerned that this somewhat human-looking presence could not possibly have originated from a mother's womb. Its skin was wrinkled and gray like cinderblock and eroding in spots on its shriveled hands. The smell of perspiration and decay was unbearable.

Without stepping in a new direction, the creature's frame jerked forty-five degrees and began its daunting descent down the aisle on my left. It had to be at least eight atrocious feet tall. I closed my eyes and tucked my chin in my chest, fully expecting to endure a merciless assault.

Seconds past. I sensed it had stopped just short of me. I heard the disturbing sound of unintelligible whispers and timidly lifted my head. Although mumbling something, the thing wasn't breathing. It had no need for air.

The stench was rancid, like road kill smoldering in the sun, while I sat shivering in my seat.

Mrs. Manchester's voice grabbed my attention. "Let's review the steps for constructing an A+ book report. You guys do know what an A+ is, don't you?" My classmates' laughter was bizarre. How could they be amused while this monster stood in our midst?

It stood motionless, peering down at Amy. Sweat dripped from its dirty chin, and I wondered how something could have such a masculine jaw line and feminine cheekbones. Its parched lips were drawn back, not in a grin but like a panting beast about to strike. It didn't blink—not one time. Its clothing was soiled and damp and reeked of vomit.

"Oh my God."

In one erratic movement, the repugnant thing dropped to the floor. I held my nostrils shut and watched in shock as it extended its left arm, placing its disjointed wrist into the open cuff at the end of Amy's chain. Its hand was scarred and grossly malformed. I held my breath as it ceased movement, yet the cuff drew closed and locked in place. I shuttered at the ringing reverberation.

It entered my mind to warn Amy, but she wouldn't believe me. I didn't believe me.

The creepy manifestation resumed an upright position, hoisting the two-ton chain off the ground without a hint of effort. Although I don't claim to have been able to read its mind, with my entire being, I sensed it festered with hatred toward Amy, despising the mere sight of her.

Its movements suddenly became spastic and rushed. It leaned in over her head. With its cuffed arm and fist exalted in the air, it used its other hand to draw Amy's cords to its gnarly face, then scanned the words on each cord as if frantically seeking out a certain one. The filth under its unkempt fingernails was sickening.

Its teeth were absurdly white though pointed in every unnatural direction, and it had twice as many as any creature I've ever seen.

Finally, one scraggly cord met its approval. The thing extended its elongated fingers so that the cord sat lifeless in the center of its palm.

As if pulled by some wicked magnetic force, the cord began to burrow into the bottom of the intruder's hand. The foul thing rapidly pulsed its fingers, coaxing the cord to penetrate deeper into its wrist. I let go of my nose and covered my mouth with both hands, repulsed by the slurping sound.

Amy's executioner raised its eyes and surveyed the room like a paranoid assassin. I felt cowardly doing nothing to intervene but was sure I was powerless to stop the assault.

In the midst of my horror, my teacher had the audacity to call on me.

"Owen, what's another composition mistake we want to avoid?"

I dropped my hands from my mouth, but my jaw remained open. I couldn't possibly comprehend her question, much less answer it. Heads turned in my direction, and I searched for any indication that someone could see the beast by my desk. But they couldn't.

My mind crashed—a cognitive control, alt, delete. Nothing was firing. None of my classmates looked familiar.

"Owen?" my teacher said, prodding me for an answer.

"Just . . . say . . . anything." I heard myself speak, but the words bypassed my brain and slurred off my tongue.

"Well, that's true. We don't want to use random statements in our report that just take up space but carry no relevant purpose or description." Mrs. Manchester miraculously ascribed meaning to my mindless uttering. "That's a great way to score a failing grade. Carla, what's another mistake we want to avoid on this assignment?"

The defiled creature raised both hands in the air and began meticulously winding the chain and cord around its wrists, removing all slack. It then jerked its arms into its hollow chest, and something dusty and shadowy jarred inside of Amy. I could only see it for a second.

The disturbing figure seemed oblivious to my watchful eye. It continued mouthing something at Amy, which I heard as intermittent, echoing whispers, a hissing mumble that sent an electric chill down the curvature of my spine. I couldn't understand its words, but I knew, without a doubt, they were malicious.

Amy raised her hand and responded to a question. She remained unaware that a hostile enemy was somehow accosting her with its poisonous words and death grip.

Mrs. Manchester retreated to her desk, and a relatively lucid thought occurred to me. *What if I capture a picture of the thing?* I grabbed my phone and pointed the lens right at it.

Should have known. It didn't show up on my screen. Neither did Amy's cords or chain. I interpreted that as proof that none of this was really happening. It was all a mind trick, a meaningless mirage.

My heart skipped a beat when the bell rang. I fumbled my phone, and it crashed onto the floor, right behind the giant's grimy heels. I didn't dare grab it.

Amy was the one being tortured, but I was the one in agony. She stood to her feet and chatted with the girl across the aisle, then casually walked toward the door. The living dead was connected to her—one with her—making every move in sync with its prey.

They walked out of my sight.

How do you get up and walk to your next class after witnessing such a thing? I shook myself. I'd never believed in God, devils, angels, ghosts, goblins, or haunted houses—surely there was a reasonable scientific explanation for what I just saw that had nothing to do with the supposed existence of spiritual beings.

It was time to accept that I needed help, medical help for my deranged, ailing mind. Something was in that water that was causing hallucinations. That had to be it. Mrs. Barnett's husband would discover exactly what it was, and then I'd get treated with some sort of remedy and get my old life back.

But in the meantime, I had to get up. Students in Mrs. Manchester's second period class were pouring in. So were their chains. I retrieved my phone, then concentrated on putting one numb foot in front of the other.

"Just get through the next few days. Everything will be okay by Monday," I said to myself.

I entered the hallway with my head down. Someone called my name. It was a basketball buddy of mine—another shackled friend.

"Owen, you gonna play tonight?"

"Sure." I gave zero consideration to his question.

"Awesome. See you later, man."

He was a nice guy. In that moment, seeing his chains and cords evoked strange feelings in me. Now that I knew they could be used against him, utilized as torture tools, I felt even more sorry for him.

I cast off restraint and allowed myself to look around and take in my environment. I wondered where Amy and the huge creepy thing had gone.

I turned to walk down the main hallway that runs through the center of the school, then froze. Someone slammed into me from behind, but I didn't budge. Moving among the flow of students were three towering rag-clad giants.

I couldn't take it, not a second longer.

I hightailed it out the door and sprinted through the rain to my car. Someone called my name, but I wasn't about to look back. I gave no thought to speed limits, stop signs, or yielding to other drivers. I got home and ran to my room, then gave myself permission to break.

I sobbed.

I wailed.

I yelled.

I clawed at my face and neck and punched the ice in my stomach.

I have no idea how long that went on. I only know what little sun existed was setting when I began regaining some sense of control. I heard my mom say something about dinner and a game of scrabble, but I ignored her.

I wasn't locked up in a mental institution, but I was trapped in a four-walled cell nonetheless—a mental state of confusion with madness pressing in on me from all sides. In the midst of the chaos, one reoccurring thought prevailed above all the others: *I'm likely seeing evil that isn't there . . . but what if everyone else is actually blind to the evil that really is?*

It was improbable, irrational, and, quite honestly, scary as hell. But I couldn't refute it.

Monday could not come fast enough. I had to know what was in that water.

5. Ominous Clues

The weekend was a blur of conflicting discoveries and hiding out. A quick online search revealed that Jimmy Lieberman was a real person, a junior at my school, and he was definitely the guy Amy was talking about in class. Her social status said she was "in a relationship" with him. Not surprisingly, his status said "single."

"His name was written on the cuff of her chain because—" And that's as far as I got all one thousand times that I set out to complete that statement.

I stayed home from school on Friday. Coach came to my door along with one of the school counselors. I thought they'd never stop knocking, but they finally left. Jess came by on Saturday, but my mom told her I was resting and sent her on her way.

Lance sent me a text on Saturday afternoon: **Heard Jess is going to prom with Dan Mitchell. Thought u were**

going w/ her. Whats up? I guess he chose to forget the awkward falling out we had.

Given my crazed condition, I was seriously relieved to hear that I was off the hook and didn't have to endure prom. But Dan Mitchell? He was one of the two knuckle heads who sat next to me in first period and bragged about his sexual conquests. *Good choice, Jess.* I couldn't help but worry about her.

It was Sunday night, and I was hanging my entire future on Mrs. Barnett's explanation of what parasite or poison was in that water. I emailed her to see if she would just tell me the results right then, but she nonchalantly replied, "Busy now. Let's talk Monday."

I dreaded returning to school. I not only feared seeing the creepy creatures, but I loathed the idea of making more observations that I couldn't explain—observations that pointed not to insanity, but to clairvoyance or something. How was I seeing names of real people?

I left my bunker of a bedroom and headed to the kitchen to fix a bowl of Apple Jacks. I did a double-take when I saw the word "guilty" inscribed above the living room window. That wasn't there the day before. The ice churned in my gut. I kept walking toward the pantry, exploding with frustration at my inability to make sense of the never-ending sightings.

Monday morning's drive to school was as expected— unnerving. The only exception was that the sky was clear and the sun was shining. It was actually a beautiful day. *Perhaps the scary things don't come out on sunny days,* I thought.

I'd obviously watched too many vampire movies because I saw—and smelled—two of the horrifying, creepy things within seconds of entering my freezing school. One of them was linked up to a guy just like I'd seen with Amy. The mere sight of it sent me into a panic, but I was dead set on getting to Mrs. Barnett's classroom. I finally made it.

"Hi Owen. I've got some interesting results for you," she said with an uplifting smile.

Finally, some answers. "Great, I'd love to hear it." It was the most enthusiasm I'd shown in a week.

"Where did you say you got this water?"

"It collected in a bucket in my backyard." Crap. I originally told her it was in a flowerpot. Oh well. She didn't seem to notice the discrepancy. "What did you find?" I asked. "Something lethal? Is it contaminated?"

"Actually, not at all. The lab results indicate that this water is abnormally pure."

As she continued to speak, all the blood left my face and took my hopes with it. She said something about an excellent pH level and a seldom seen abundance of minerals.

"Are you sure, Mrs. Barnett? Did your husband check for rare contaminants and parasites?"

"Trust me, if there was anything in that water, his lab would have found it."

"So the water is pure enough to drink?" I was flabbergasted.

"Sure it is." She kept smiling. My smile was long gone.

"I don't know what made your dog sick, but it wasn't that water."

She handed me a printout of the lab results and looked over her shoulder to acknowledge another student needing her attention.

I've heard people say that right before you die, your whole life flashes before you. In that instant, that happened to me, only it was my future. I would never graduate from college, never be a doctor, never travel the world, watch a game at Wrigley Field, or have a family of my own. Without a cure for my new visionary existence, a normal life seemed out of the question.

I stumbled out of Mrs. Barnett's classroom without expressing the slightest hint of gratitude. My mind raced. I had no plan B. The only place to go was first period, and that seemed like a terrible idea. I went anyway.

Dan's comment momentarily slapped me out of my hypnotic funk, just as he intended. "I'm gonna party with Jess all night after prom," he said, boasting to his equally obnoxious friend.

I took a long look at him, from the bolted shackle around his neck, to the eight cords plunging out of his head, all the way down to the ten or so chains coiled around his feet. If I could have lifted one of those chains, I would have strangled him with it.

Amy sat down in front of me. She was alone, as in not escorting an iniquitous presence. She seemed fine, like nothing had happened.

Mrs. Manchester passed around a sheet of paper and asked us to write down the name of the book we selected for an upcoming book report. I wrote down the title of a book someone else four names up had picked.

I did the usual between classes—rushed to my next classroom with my head down, trying to avoid the myriad of disturbing sights jumping out at me. I noticed words written on several walls and even on a few lockers—

unsettling words like "despair" and "wrath." And there were Creepers among us. That's what I began calling the tormentors in my unstable mind. I could smell their nauseating odor even when they lurked beyond my line of site.

My alarming paranormal observations were tempered by the mundane. My teachers piled a ton of makeup work on me. It was nearly impossible to concentrate, but I experienced a welcomed sense of comfort while doing schoolwork. I guess because it reminded me of my former carefree life.

It was time for lunch, and I was surprisingly glad to see my friends. I didn't like what I saw, but I liked who I saw. I grabbed a few things from some vending machines then sat in my usual spot next to Conner, Jared, and my other basketball buddies, all the while contemplating my next step now that my "toxic water theory" was debunked.

No one dared ask me why I missed last Thursday's game. Even though Lance was acting like nothing had erupted between us, I wondered if he had told people about my demented accusations. They seemed leery of me.

My bag of Cheez-It crackers was nearly gone when I glanced across the cafeteria and saw a Creeper closing in on a girl like a vulture swooping down on a carcass. I watched the Creeper shrink to the floor then hoist himself up again with a chain fastened to its wrist. Between nervous glances in every direction, it fumbled through cords, then picked one.

The grotesque ritual began. It fluttered its fingers while the cord burrowed beneath its skin, lodging deep into its forearm.

It occurred to me to sit there and do nothing, but that was getting old. What did I have to lose? The worst that could happen is the Creeper would kill me, and that would be a gift. I think my friends already believed I'd lost my mind, so why worry about what they would think?

"Owen?" Jared said, attempting to jar me out of the daze I was in.

"I'll be right back." I stood and took one last sip of my Dr. Pepper, then made the trek across the cafeteria. As I drew closer, I could see "hopeless" on display across the Creeper's filthy forehead.

I walked right up to the girl and ignored the fact that she was surrounded by friends. It was obvious they were freshmen, and they were seriously taken aback by my arrival at their table.

"Hey," I said, suppressing all instinct to run far in the opposite direction of the nearby Creeper.

She glanced over her shoulder then looked back at me, wondering if I was really talking to her.

"I'm Owen." I reached out to shake her hand. She eased her hand toward mine, still skeptical of my presence. Her friends were giggling at this point.

"I'm . . . Misty." She didn't sound convinced of her own name.

I tried not to look at the Creeper. It didn't seem concerned that I was there. Its garbled tribal-like whisper was disturbing, to say the least. I reminded myself that there was no need to talk loud to compensate for the noise. I was the only one who could hear it.

"Can I talk to you, Misty?"

She responded to my question by taking a wide-eyed glance at her equally stunned friends. One girl prompted the others to all get up and give us some privacy. *Perfect.*

I sat down directly across from her. "Are you okay?" My tone was more fatherly than friendly.

"Um . . . sure. Yeah. I'm fine." She grinned, revealing a mouth full of braces.

"I know we don't know each other, and this is gonna sound crazy, but . . ." *How do I explain this?* I kept trying. "I'm wondering if you feel down or something, maybe hopeless?" As the word "hopeless" rolled off my tongue, the Creeper's branded head jerked and twisted in my direction. I almost wet my pants.

"Uh . . ." She didn't know what to say. "I'm doin' okay."

I leaned in. "Are you sure, Misty?" I was making her uncomfortable, but under the circumstances, I felt it was called for.

She looked down and bit one side of her lip. "I'm okay, I guess." She was even less convincing this time.

"Misty, I know this is a very weird thing for me to say to you, but if you start to feel hopeless today," the Creeper's head snapped at me again. *Oh my God.* ". . . please ignore it. Don't listen to those feelings. They're not real. There is hope." I needed the very advice I was giving.

"Promise me you won't give in to feelings of . . ." *Do I dare say it a third time?* ". . . sadness." The Creeper didn't budge. "Will you promise me that?"

She was quick to wipe the tear from her cheek, but another one escaped on the other side. She really was hurting, but she wouldn't dare say so. That's what we all do for some reason.

"I'll do the best I can," she said while standing to her feet and crumpling her lunch sack. She stared at me, expecting me to say something more, but the towering Creeper behind her stole my attention. I wanted to hit it with something, but hell would freeze over before I dared pick a fight with it. I felt like I had "coward" branded on my forehead.

"I'll talk to you later." I didn't know what else to say. I walked away.

I didn't hear a single thing my calculus teacher said. My whole paradigm had turned upside down in the last few hours. I went from desperately wanting help to desperately wanting *to* help. How totally strange.

Before today, I questioned if what I was seeing was real, but now, it was hard to believe otherwise. A resounding "what if" drowned out the clanking of chains for the rest of the day. *What if I'm not crazy at all?*

During sixth period athletics, my coach called me into his office and gave me what can only be described as a bipolar lecture. He raised his voice in dismay, then spoke sympathetically while asking if I was okay. This back-and-forth interrogation went on for the entire class period. I finally convinced him I'd been really sick, which was sort of true, and I couldn't play in this week's game either. It was our last match of the season, and we had no shot at playoffs, so he let me off the hook without too much grief.

I'd always considered my coach to be the strongest man I knew, but seeing him dragging around three chains and four cords ruined that.

I stopped off at my locker before heading home, and there was Jess, right across the hall. I thought she would come talk to me, but Dan stepped up and diverted her attention. I couldn't stand the sight of her flirting with him. I wasn't so much jealous as I was annoyed. It may have been illogical, but I was starting to measure people's character by the number of chains and cords they had. People like Dan and my mom had tons. People like Misty and Mrs. Barnett had just a few.

I didn't want Jess around him.

I concluded I had bigger issues to worry about and headed toward the parking lot. Just as I was about to exit the building, something bogus caught my eye. I spotted a girl who had no chains or cords. Instead, she had this brilliant, gold looking glow-of-a-thing emanating around her feet and onto the floor around her.

I did an about-face and followed her. With each step, the illumination remained, as if lighting her path. Her long blonde ponytail swished back and forth. I recognized her, but it took me a few seconds to remember her name, Ray Anne Greiner. She and her twin brother Justin lived in the neighborhood right next to mine. I hadn't talked to her since middle school.

I was just about to say something to her when she darted in the other direction, unaware that I was tracking her. I stood in stunned silence watching her bounce up to a friend and start talking her ear off as they walked up the stairs.

No chains? No cord? A glow? How is that possible?

I drove home mulling over the unbelievable series of events that unfolded that day. My emotions were all over the place—frustration, anticipation, fear—all overshadowed by an exhausting sense of defeat.

I came home and turned on the TV right away. I loved how I never saw anything abnormal on television. The harder I tried not to look at the accusatory word written above the living room window, however, the more it invaded my mind—"guilty."

Around six o'clock, I made mac-and-cheese and fish sticks and waited for my mom to wake up. She was the only person I knew who would takes naps from dinner time to bedtime.

I tried doing my calculus make up work but only got halfway through one assignment. *Why can't everything in life be as simple as math, every problem solved with a corresponding formula?* I kept thinking about Misty and Amy.

Then Jess.

Then that glowing girl Ray Anne.

Over and over.

By nine o'clock at night, I figured my mother would sleep until the morning. I would normally watch TV this time of night with the living room lights turned off, but—sad to say—I was now officially scared of the dark. Such a manly feeling.

I piled two throw blankets on top of me, knowing full well that wouldn't warm the icy chill clawing at my stomach. Valentine was sprawled out on the floor right next to me doing her favorite trick—lazy.

Something suddenly piqued her interest. She sat straight up and made that inquisitive doggy face, the one where I could tell she was listening as hard as she possibly could. She stared intently toward the stairs.

I laughed for the first time in I don't know how long when she growled and flared her gums, revealing polished white teeth. "Maybe if the vet hadn't cleaned your teeth the other day, you'd be a little more intimidating. What do you think you're growling at this time, huh?"

I tried to pet her, but she moved away from me. She started barking, and the strip of fur along her back stood on edge.

"Valentine, calm down." I wasn't laughing anymore. She was freaking me out. "Stop it!"

She ducked her head and ran to the side of the couch, then resumed growling at the stairs.

The sound of chains dragging was a sure indication that my mother was stirring. I heard her bedroom door open. Valentine barked. "Be quiet, girl. It's just Mom."

A familiar rancid stench filled the room. I knew that smell.

It was normal for our stairs to creek a bit. It was not normal for the wood to sound like it was buckling under the weight of my petite mother. I jumped up. Valentine scurried behind the couch.

I could see her feet, then her robe, and finally her dejected face as she reached the last few steps. "Mom!" I couldn't contain myself. A Creeper was just inches behind her, taking each step in stride with her. She looked miniscule in comparison. It was bound to her through a chain and cord. "Accuser" was right there, on display across its hideous forehead.

"Tell that dog to shut up," my mother said over Valentine's fierce barking.

"Mom!" I called out again in a panic.

"What?" She'd been drinking and crying, as usual.

"Are you the one doing this to my mother? Are you the one who makes her cry all the time?" I lost it. I was pointing and raging right at the massive mongrel. It didn't notice.

"Owen, what's the matter with you?"

I spilled my guts so fast I couldn't catch my breath. "I haven't wanted to tell you this, but I've been seeing things, Mom. Things that people aren't supposed to see. I don't know. I just see all these scary, horrible words and chains and . . . and . . . I thought I'd lost my mind, but I'm starting to think I haven't. And—I'm not trying to scare you—I'm really not—but, Mom, there's this huge, awful . . . thing attacking you right now! It's attached to you, and it hates you. It hates all of us!"

I might as well have made a fist and socked her in the stomach. She was horrified, but not for the right reasons.

"Son, I . . . you've gotta . . . I think . . ."

"I know it sounds like a lie or something I'm just making up, but please Mom, I'm begging you. Please believe me. I wouldn't lie about this. I wouldn't even know how to make this stuff up!"

I pointed to the living room window. "Do you see that? Do you see what it says above the window?"

"I don't see anything. Owen, I need you to—"

"Okay, fine, you can't see it, but someone—something— wrote on our wall. It wrote the word 'guilty.' It's right there. Do you believe me? I need you to believe me!" I could feel my face raging red.

My mom froze for what seemed like fifteen minutes. I'm guessing it was actually a few seconds.

"Owen, if you're seeing things . . ."

Please let her say she believes me, I thought.

". . . you need help. You need to go talk to someone. I think you need to go see a priest or something."

Those were fighting words, especially coming from her. She avoided religion at all cost. Her comment wasn't a real suggestion but a sarcastic jab at me. She was still clinging to the false assumption that I was dabbling in drugs.

"A priest? Are you kidding me? The last thing I need is some religious nut job adding his delusions to my already unbelievable life! What I need is . . . I need . . ."

How awful. I had no idea what I needed. I collapsed on the couch then looked right at the filthy Creeper. How dare that monster come into my home. I sprang back onto my feet and charged toward my mother, abandoning every ounce of common sense.

"Accuser!"

What was I thinking?

It tilted its wicked head back at an outlandish angle, a maneuver no human being could ever master, and glared directly at me. Its lethal eyes squinted, not to block out light but as an unmistakable gesture of volatile hatred toward me, toward all things living.

I knew I was outmatched. It was an unbeatable foe. I couldn't stop it from having its way with my mother. Her disbelief was just what it needed to work its black magic on her abused and tattered soul.

My mom didn't say another word. Neither did I.

I walked right past them both and went up the stairs to my bedroom.

For one fleeting moment, I wasn't scared.

I was completely outraged.

81

6. Unbelievable Proof

I stared at my blinds, waiting for the first hint of sunlight. The unmistakable stench was gone. Surely that meant the Creeper was gone.

I dreaded seeing my mother after last night's fiasco, and I imagined she felt the same way about me. Still, oddly enough, I had a new sense of hope this morning. As dejected as I was about the "perfect" water sample results and seeing my mother bound to a Creeper, Ray Anne's shackle-free existence was encouraging. Maybe there was a way I could free my mother, too. And Jess. I'd free Lance and the rest of my classmates, too, if I knew how.

I had to find Ray Anne. She was now my official plan B.

The sign people didn't scare me today. Don't get me wrong. It was freaky to behold a loud-mouthed mob of crazies surrounding my school. But I didn't feel threatened by them anymore.

I wish I could say the same about the Creepers. Once again, the mere sight of them overwhelmed my senses.

They were everywhere, drifting among us, looming above our heads in the crowded hallways.

Although the Texas heat had finally returned to Cypress, the air still felt chilled to me. My friends gave me a hard time for dressing like it was the middle of winter. I told one obnoxious girl, "If there weren't icy, evil creatures everywhere, I'd wear shorts, too." She laughed. I didn't.

Now that I was walking the halls with my chin up, intentionally taking in my sadistic surroundings, I noticed two more people who illuminated like Ray Anne and had no shackles or chains. Unfortunately I didn't know either of them. I almost talked to one guy, but the only thing I could think of to say was, "Hey, do you know why the floor around you glows?" Dumb idea. I kept quiet.

I looked all day for Ray Anne but didn't see her. I was walking out to my car when I glanced in the direction of the makeshift camp grounds and was instantly angered. There was Jess, hugging all over Dan. And there was Dan, harnessed to a Creeper. It goes without saying that all Creepers are raunchy, but Dan's foul companion was named "Lust." How fitting.

"Jess, what are you doing?" My disapproval was evident.

Dan had that familiar smirk on his face. Jess obviously didn't feel the liberty to let go of him and come talk to me.

There was nothing I could do. She wouldn't believe me if I told her she was dating a guy attached to a hellion spirit, no doubt reinforcing Dan's plan to use her and discard her in one fleeting moment.

I took the long way home to clear my brain, but I should have known that would never happen. My mind was swollen with anxiety. I thought about getting into my mom's liquor cabinet but decided against it. Surely the only thing worse than seeing Creepers was being drunk and seeing Creepers.

Around six-thirty in the evening, I got a text from Jess: **Plz come outside.**

I opened the door. She stood at the end of my driveway, by herself, thank God.

We sat in the shade in my front yard. I didn't say a word, not to be stubborn, but because I couldn't possibly explain the latest events of my life to her, much less my most recent observation about the loser she was now dating.

Jess broke the silence. "I guess you heard I'm going to prom with Dan."

"Yeah. Great choice."

"Well, what was I supposed to do? You don't want anything to do with me, and he's been begging me to go to prom with him for months. It's nothing serious. We just hung out last weekend and have been getting to know each other better."

"Oh, he wants to get to know you alright."

She blew off my concern and changed the subject.

"I know you've been sick and all, but you never did explain why you ran from me the other day or what's been going on with you."

Her tone was kind. I sensed she'd been missing me. I wanted to spill my guts to her, to tell her everything. But I was afraid. If she didn't believe me, it would pile on even more frustration.

I shifted the topic of conversation back. "Jess, I don't blame you for moving on. I just wish you would reconsider who you're moving on with and how fast things are moving. Dan is up to no good. He's always going on and on about all the girls he's fooled around with. He doesn't really give a crap about you."

"He already explained to me how he used to be all about hooking up with girls, but he says it's different with me. He really respects me."

"You don't believe that, do you? That's just his way of manipulating you. You've spent, like, one weekend with him, and he's already saying that he's a changed man? Give me a break."

"I know what I'm doing, Owen. He's liked me for a long time. At least he hasn't rejected me."

I couldn't believe it. I was the bad guy now, and Dan was the knight in shining armor. How absurd.

"Jess, I never had any intention of ditching you to go to prom with Cindy Rutherford. And I'm sorry I ran from you the other day." I eased back onto the grass and stared up at the sky through the tree branches. "Please just know that it's not you. I'm going through something very difficult right now."

She laid down, too. "Why can't you just tell me about it?"

One, I already tried, and you didn't take me seriously, and two, you'll call me crazy, and it will wreck me.

"Because it's something I have to work through and figure out on my own."

"Is there anything I can do to help?"

I sat up and peered down at her tan face. "Stay away from Dan Mitchell."

She closed her eyes and smiled. "You're just jealous."

I couldn't help but smile back, which annoyed me because this was no laughing matter. "I'm not jealous. I'm seriously worried about you."

"I can take care of myself."

There she was, encircled by two chains and four cords boasting about how she doesn't need any help. She kept her eyes closed, making this an ideal opportunity to take a closer look at her entrapments. She assumed I was playing with her hair. I knew right where to look on the cords to see what was written. "Unforgiveness." "Self-loathing." "Insecure." "Defiant."

I felt like an intruder, like I just snuck a peek at her diary. I knew her well enough to recognize that those were all thoughts and attitudes she battled on a reoccurring basis—personality weaknesses specific to her, I guess. Observing them so tangibly on display made me pity her.

I wanted to see the names written on the cuffs of her chains, but they were both down by her feet.

"Your shoes are coming untied. I'll get it."

She chuckled while I covertly untied then retied her laces. I could see the name etched on one of her cuffs.

bill herbert thompson

Her dad's name? That was weird. I snuck a look at the other cuff.

jeff joel thompson

Who's that? A relative, I supposed.

I crawled back to my spot in the shade next to Jess. I hesitated at first, then blurted it out. "Jess, has anyone hurt you?"

She sat straight up. Clearly, my question hit a nerve.

"What do you mean?"

I sat up, too. "I'm just wondering if there's someone you haven't been able to forgive."

She looked straight ahead and spoke softly. "Well my dad has done some things . . ." her words broke off. I sensed she wanted to tell me, but it was too painful. How crazy—we both longed to confide in each other but were too scared.

I assured her she could tell me anything.

She abruptly looked my way, then lit into me. "Why would you ask me that? Don't you think that's slightly personal? One minute you don't want anything to do with me, and the next minute you want me to tell you my deepest, darkest secrets?"

She had a point. I suggested a truce. "What if you come clean with me about what you're hiding, and I'll do the same?" She thought a moment, then voiced her counter-offer. "Okay, but only if you go first."

I was nervous but willing, under one condition. "I'll tell you, but you have to promise me something," I said.

"What?"

"Don't call me crazy."

"I won't. Just tell me."

"Okay. You know how I told you that after I drank that water I started feeling weird and . . . seeing things?"

"Yeah?"

"Well, I'm still feeling weird and seeing things. Really scary, terrible things."

She turned onto her side and leaned on her elbow. "What did the doctor say?"

"I didn't—" Oh, yeah. I told Jess I went to the doctor. "He didn't have much to say." She didn't question my contrived response. I resumed telling the truth. "I thought the best thing to do was get the water tested, so I did, but the results showed absolutely nothing abnormal. Mrs. Barnett's husband did a professional examination at his lab."

"If you're seeing things, why haven't you, like, gone to a psychiatrist?"

"Well, it's complicated, Jess. At first I assumed I was hallucinating, that I was totally delusional and in need of serious psychological help. But now I'm not so sure. Some of the things I'm seeing actually seem to add up."

"What do you mean?"

I didn't feel a green light to tell her about the chains, names, or cords, much less the Creepers. I tried to keep it vague. "I can see certain things about people—what they're struggling with and who they're struggling with, I think."

She leaned back and narrowed her eyes in disapproval. "So there really was a reason you asked if I have unforgiveness toward someone. You think that's my issue?"

It was *one* of her issues, but I wasn't going to pile it on. "Well, yeah," I said as gently as I could.

She stood and slapped the grass off her legs, then raised her voice. "So what about you, Owen? What's your issue?"

"Mine?"

"Yeah. You're so aware of what everyone else needs. What about you?"

"Well, actually there are a few of us who don't appear to have any issues." I realized that sounded arrogant, but it was true.

"How convenient. Looks like you're already a doctor, aren't you? You know everyone's problems and exactly how to fix em'."

She stormed off toward her car. I didn't get a chance to tell her that I actually had no idea how to help anyone. I started to go inside but took one last look at her. She was driving away but slammed on her brakes and yelled out her open passenger-side window, "You're crazy, Owen!"

I couldn't believe she went there. At the risk of sounding like a chick, that really hurt. I was livid.

I was about to go inside when I had a change of plans. Although fuming, I thought there was a chance I could remember where Ray Anne Greiner lived. I was confident of her street and figured I'd be able to pick out the house when I got there. Maybe she'd be outside or something.

I decided to walk. I felt my jaw clinching shut the whole time. I was so mad at Jess. How could she say the one thing to me that I begged her not to say? That "defiant" cord was right on. I told her my personal story, but she shared nothing with me. That wasn't fair either.

I thought about sending her a text, but I had nothing to say except "I hate you," so I decided not to bother. The longer I walked, the angrier I became.

It only took about fifteen minutes to get to Ray Anne's street. It was easy to pick out her house; I recognized her brother's car.

There were several small children playing in the cul-de-sac, and I marveled at what I saw. Like the two boys I'd seen before, they didn't have shackles or anything abnormal, but when they faced me head on, I could see a blinding, small concentrated golden light near each child's heart. It was like looking at a brilliant star. Something about it was beautiful—not just the way it looked but the way it made me feel.

It was similar to the illumination I'd seen on Ray Anne and the two other kids at my school, only the light on the children was far brighter and filled one tiny spot instead of glowing all around their feet. It was breathtaking. I snapped a picture with my cell, but it came out completely normal—no shimmering lights.

After standing there mesmerized for a while, I directed my attention again to Ray Anne's house. I had hoped she would come outside perhaps, but she didn't. Spontaneity is not usually my thing, but the sun was setting, and I desperately wanted to talk with her.

I knocked on her door, and her mother answered. She emanated light, too. *Interesting.*

"Hi. Is Ray Anne home?"

"Yes, she is. May I tell her who's here?"

"Of course. I'm Owen Edmonds." I reached out and shook her hand. I thought perhaps I'd feel some sort of sensation making contact with a glowing person, but I felt nothing whatsoever.

I heard some whispers and shuffling, then Ray Anne finally came to the door. She was obviously surprised to see me. And still glowing.

"Hi Owen."

"Hey Ray Anne." I felt like a complete weirdo. "I know we haven't really talked much since, what, the seventh or eighth grade?"

"Uh, I guess so."

"So, what are you up to tonight?" A lame question yields a lame answer. I already knew that.

"I'm, um, finishing making up a dance for the Spring Show and doing laundry."

She's on the dance team with Jess. Lovely.

"When is Spring Show?"

"The end of next month."

"Awesome." We both looked down at the doormat and fidgeted in the awkward silence. I took a deep breath and made a bold move. "Hey, do you have plans Friday night? Would you like to go out with me—just as friends, I mean—to catch up on old times?"

She was puzzled by my impromptu invitation but responded graciously. "That sounds good. What do you have in mind?"

"I could pick you up, and we could go grab dinner or something. My treat."

"Um, okay. But just so you know, my parents are gonna want to meet you. Even though it's not, like, a date or anything, they'll want you to come in and visit a minute before we go. Is that okay?"

"Of course." A bit old fashioned, but I could respect it.

We exchanged cell numbers and then talked a little more about how awful things had gotten at school. She was easy to talk with and delightful to look at, not only because she was cute but because her neck was shackle-free and there was nothing but shiny blonde hair coming out of her head. I tried not to stare, but it's kind of hard when someone's emitting a glow.

It was dark by the time I left. I was terrified of running into a Creeper. I hadn't planned to be out after sunset.

A kid rode by me on a skateboard wearing an "I survived a day at Lincoln Forest High" T-shirt. I used to scoff at that silly statement. Now it felt more like my life motto.

I turned onto my street and—wouldn't you know it—a rancid stench enveloped me. A menacing Creeper lurked in a driveway about eight houses away. I had to walk by it if I was going to get home. I didn't like that at all.

I stood there and spied for a few minutes, observing its jerky movements. A man pulled his car into the driveway right next to the Creeper. He was on his cell and fumbled with his keys while walking toward the front door. The Creeper followed him, then hunched down and selected a chain. By the time the man entered his house, the stalker was rummaging through his cords, looking for a particular one. The door closed. They were both inside. How sickening.

I sprinted toward my house and contemplated the implications of what I was seeing. As best as I could tell, these hateful beings took advantage of a person's messed up relationships and crappy attitudes to torment and manipulate them somehow. I couldn't figure out exactly how it worked, but I believed they tricked people into feeling or acting in a destructive way. Like, the Creeper with "hopeless" on its forehead wanted Misty to feel hopeless, and the one sporting "accuser" on its face accused my mom of who-knows-what until she felt horrible and self-destructed, all without them knowing it.

It was cruel but clever.

Think about it. To destroy an opponent, what better strategy is there than to go stealth? Do your most damaging work under the cloak of invisibility? And even if some cursed soul like me happens to discover what's really going on, the truth is so outlandish and farfetched no one would believe it. My stories sounded more like the plot of a bestselling fiction than a real life dilemma. And I was sure that was exactly the way they wanted it.

I couldn't understand why they despised the human race, but I was absolutely positive they did. I considered that perhaps they were out to take over Earth, to extinguish humanity and populate our planet with their superior species.

I didn't allow myself to think about God often, but as far as I was concerned, the Creepers served as concrete proof that God didn't exist. There was no divine, loving mastermind overseeing our lives—just hateful invisible thugs dominating humanity.

And even if there were some celestial Creator floating around somewhere, I couldn't count on the people I *could* see. I wasn't about to start asking for help from a supposed God I'd never seen—a God who sat back and did nothing while his, or her, creation was decimated by evil.

The tension gnawing at my mind was miserable. I went upstairs, brushed my teeth, and went straight to bed. Not surprisingly, I had a terrifying nightmare about Creepers breaking into my house.

The next morning, first period was awful, not just cause Dan was there, but because that nasty "Lust" monster was still latched to him. Disgusting.

Dan flapped his gums like always, looking for every opportunity to rub it in my face that he was talking to Jess now. Whatever. At least I didn't have an eight-foot ogre chanting spells into my soul.

I'd finally learned to beware of thinking I'd seen all the freaky third dimension stuff I was going to see. Between first and second period, I noticed three Creepers huddled together in a corner. They paid no attention to me as long as I didn't speak what was written on their foreheads. I wondered if that was, like, their names or something? Maybe. Oddly enough, all three of the Creepers gathered together had the same name—"Violence."

They looked at each other as if communicating—more like strategizing as fellow soldiers in the same bloodthirsty battalion—but they verbalized nothing. They would nod now and then, affirming one another's thoughts, I suppose. It was beyond eerie.

One of them opened its massive palm, then used a jagged fingernail like a pen and appeared to write something on the surface of its hand. It then held up its palm, allowing the other two Creepers to read the message. An awkward flick of its wrist caused the message to fling off and float to the floor.

The group dispersed, but I kept my eye on the supernatural note. It sailed through the air, carried around by the students' oblivious movements in every direction through the hallway. I followed it all the way past the science wing and into the language arts pod. Finally, the bell rang, and, with the exception of one other student, I was alone in the hallway.

I caught up with the note. I dropped to my knees and took as close a look as I possibly could without touching it. What I saw reminded me of when my friends and I would paint our palms with Elmer's glue, then when it dried, peel it off to reveal a thin sliver of what looked like dead skin, only there were numbers and letters inscribed on there: 0602sqm.

I used my index finger to touch the very edge. The mystery material deteriorated the instant I made contact. I pulled my hand away.

A girl I didn't know turned down the hallway.

"Hey, can you come here, please?" I asked as politely as I could.

I pointed to the note. "Do you see that? It's not a piece of paper. It's something else, and it has numbers and letters. Do you see it?"

"Yeah. What is it?"

"You see it? Are you sure? What does it say?" Could there finally be some proof of my sanity? I held out hope.

She got on the floor with me. "I think it says zero, six, zero, two, then S-G-M."

"Yes, that's exactly what it says!"

"Okay?" She got up and dusted the dirt off her knees. "What is it?" she said with zero enthusiasm.

My surge of excitement was quickly tempered by reality. What was I supposed to tell her? A Creeper wrote this note on its hand then flung it to the floor. Yeah, right.

"It . . . uh . . . someone dropped it," I said.

She leaned over to pick it up. I freaked out. "No, don't touch it! It will dissolve."

"Whatever," she said, then meandered off.

My pulse was racing. I probably couldn't use that note to prove much to anyone else, but it served as solid evidence of something crucial to me. What I was seeing was real.

Completely real.

I took a picture of it with my phone, and there it was in my photo stream, clear as day.

"What are you doing, Owen?" My ninth grade homeroom teacher caught me on the floor. With all the excitement, I couldn't remember her name.

"I just dropped something. I'm going to class now, Mrs., um . . ."

She rolled her eyes and told me to hurry up.

I left the note and ran to my class.

I struggled to wrap my mind around my latest finding. "The Creepers are real. I have proof. They're real," I said to myself.

I had to learn more about them. Why did they want to hurt us? What was their ultimate mission?

As much as I hoped to discover a way to defeat them, I feared that was impossible. Creepers were clearly at the top of the food chain, the most vicious of hunters with no one big or brave enough to hunt them.

Or so I thought.

7. Supernatural Help

I tossed my backpack on the couch and impulsively sent both Lance and Jess a text: **Can u come over today?**

I was still mad at Jess, and my friendship with Lance was definitely strained, but against my better judgment, I felt compelled to tell them about my latest finding. I knew they weren't likely to believe me, and I was probably making a serious mistake, but I wanted to show them the picture of the Creeper note anyway. Perhaps if I pled my case to them yet again, they would at least consider my claims. And now I had something to show them, not just tell them.

Lance responded: **Coming.**

I didn't hear from Jess, but fifteen minutes later, they both pulled up in front of my house at the same time. I would have preferred to talk to them separately, but oh well.

Lance was confused that Jess was there, and she was equally surprised to see him.

The three of us sat in my living room. I let my guard down. "Thanks for coming over. I told you both that I've been seeing some very strange and scary things lately. Neither of you believed me, but I understand. I'd have a hard time believing me, too, if I was in your shoes. Jess, yesterday you called me crazy." I tried to conceal how much it infuriated me. "I asked you guys to come over because I want to show you something—proof that I'm not crazy at all."

I took out my cell and pulled up the picture of the Creeper's note. "Do you see that?"

Jess took a look. "What is it?" she asked before passing the phone to Lance.

"It's a note. But not just any note. I know this is gonna sound unbelievable, but please, please take me seriously, okay?"

They both nodded, but I doubted their sincerity. I sensed I was about to make a fool of myself once again. I had to give this a try though.

"This isn't easy to explain, but here goes. There are these creepy, huge things that walk around our school—everywhere really. They latch onto people and try to brainwash them or something. I don't know why I can see them and you can't, but I saw three of them grouped together today in the hallway, and one of them wrote this note, then tossed it to the floor." I wasn't about to tell them it used its fingernail and somehow wrote on its skin.

"I chased the note down and took a picture of it. I tried touching it, but it dissolved the instant my finger made contact—not the whole note. Just the part I touched.

Anyway, I wanted to show you guys this so you would know I'm not making all of this stuff up."

Lance gave me my phone back. He and Jess stared at one another, and while I don't claim to have the power to read minds, it was obvious what they were thinking—*Owen's psychotic condition is far worse than we realized.*

"So, talk to me," I said. "What do you think of this new evidence?"

Lance cleared his throat. "Owen," he paused for an eternity. "I'm really, really concerned about you. This isn't funny. You need to get help, dude. This is scary."

Jess nodded in complete agreement with his diagnosis.

"But what about the picture? That note is proof that this isn't all in my mind. Can you please try giving me the benefit of the doubt? I wouldn't lie about this."

Jess looked down while insulting me. "You want us to believe that some invisible zombie-thing wrote that note? Why would we believe that? That's so crazy."

I guess calling me crazy once wasn't enough. I could see this was going nowhere.

"Just forget it. Seriously. Don't worry about it. Thanks for coming over. It's all good." Not really, but I wanted them and their metal appendages to leave.

I walked them outside and hoped they would drive off and forget everything I just said. Unfortunately Lance wasn't done talking. "Owen, promise me you'll go talk to someone, a doctor or therapist or something."

"Okay." Another lie.

I sank into the sofa and tried not to drown in the flood of internal conflict.

What if I am imagining things that don't exist?

What if I'm the only one who sees what's really happening to humanity?

What if I do need to be locked up in a psych ward?

What if I discover a way to free people of their shackles?

What if I really am crazy?

I did the only thing I knew to do—flip on the TV and try to escape my distorted world for a little while.

Jess sent me a text: **I hope my comments this afternoon didn't hurt you. I just don't know what to make of your stories.**

Honestly, neither do I, I texted back.

My mother came home from an evening out with her boyfriend and went straight for her liquor stash. Ever since I tried to tell her about the Creeper two nights ago, she'd been completely avoiding me.

I did the best I could to finish some homework, but it was super hard to focus on anything other than the supernatural stuff.

I decided to type up a timeline of events, beginning with the evening that I drank the water and developed a nonstop belly freeze. It was hard to fathom how much had happened in just nine days. As I logged all that I'd seen, I had to admit, it was absurd. At the same time, there were certain pieces of the preposterous puzzle that actually fit together. Unfortunately, I still had a lot more questions than answers.

I went to bed thinking about the Creeper's note and drove myself crazy assuring myself over and over that I'm not crazy.

I woke up Thursday morning reluctant about tomorrow night's dinner plans with Ray Anne. As much as I wanted to talk with her and try and figure out why she was exempt from the shackle and all, I was bothered by the inevitable—hearing one more person tell me I'm psychotic.

I also wasn't looking forward to the drama once Jess found out I went out with Ray Anne. Even though it wasn't going to be a real date—and despite the fact that Jess was already on some fast-track relationship roller coaster with Dan—she would freak when she heard about it. And she would hear about it. Gossip spread among the drill team girls like mold on a rotten potato.

What an odd life, worrying one minute about endangered souls and the next, about petty rumors.

I pulled into the school parking lot and tried to ignore the sign people. Two of them were connected to Creepers. I found it ironic, them warning us about our evil school while bound to evil.

I got to first period and was relieved to see Dan flying solo, not out of concern for him but because I dreaded smelling that nasty Creeper funk the whole class period.

Walking the hallways was always a challenge. There were more of the mean words written all over place this week than the last, marking up the hallways, lockers, bathroom stalls—you name it. Some of them appeared to be fading while others looked freshly penned.

Finally, on my way to third period, I beheld what was responsible for the cruel graffiti. I witnessed a Creeper raise its skin-and-bones arm and use its grimy pointer finger to write the word "hate" above the entrance to the library. It was so weird to point my cell camera at the library and see no Creeper or markings, then put my phone down and see both clear as day.

How did it write with its finger? I chalked it up as another frightening, brain-twisting mystery.

Admittedly, my emotions were all over the place lately, but as I made my way to the cafeteria for lunch, I was bubbling over with just one feeling—a major sense of injustice. None of this seemed the least bit fair. I wanted to make a sign of my own and protest the Creepers' presence and my classmates' ignorance. I mentally debated which was worse, to see wickedness at work or not see it at all? Both felt like a death sentence.

I got my usual snacks out of the vending machines, then took a seat at my lunch table. That's when I saw Misty again. That same Creeper from the other day, "Hopeless," was following a few feet behind, shadowing her every move. I gasped when it motioned toward another Creeper, beckoning it to come near.

Are two Creepers gonna attack her at once?

I couldn't imagine it. I was already indignant and outraged by the suffering I'd seen. I couldn't stand for this.

I had no plan of action, yet I charged in Misty's direction. I saw the Creeper's name and must have said it out loud: "Rejection!" The snarly thing contorted its head and peered right at me for a brief heart-stopping moment, then went right to work with its putrid partner, shrinking to the floor and slamming their wrists into two open cuffs.

I couldn't separate the visible from the invisible. I raised my voice. "Stop it! Leave her alone!" I didn't realize that my shouting caused a hush to fall over the cafeteria. I carried on with my futile tantrum. "You have no right to do this! Stop it!"

Misty's eyelids were plastered wide open, and her face was white as a corpse, not because she saw and feared the two Creepers behind her back, but no doubt, in response to my deranged behavior. I picked up an aluminum can off the nearest lunch table and hurled it at the beasts. Soda flew everywhere, but the can passed right through the preoccupied Creepers.

I heard someone call my name, but I was in a state of shock, I guess, and couldn't reply. I don't recall what else I yelled, but I know that words flew out of my mouth machine-gun style and, as far as everyone else was concerned, I was shouting into thin air.

My threats were useless and utterly ignored. The Creepers strummed through the cords drooping from the back of Misty's head and made their strategic selections. As the detestable ritual continued, the assailants moved in perfect sync with one another, enticing the lifeless cords to dig into their pulsating hands. The Creepers' sweaty heads thrashed in every direction. They suddenly looked afraid, but of what? They certainly weren't intimidated by me.

I heard a man's voice call my name again, but I was powerless to acknowledge him—not because I was fixated on the Creepers but because, in that instant, I beheld the single most breathtaking, fearsome, unconceivable sight I'd ever, ever seen.

He was huge, at least five feet taller than the Creepers, and a blinding, crystal-white radiance enveloped the space around him. I would have covered my eyes, but I was too astounded. Although I could only stand to glance for brief seconds at a time, I could see that his massive physique was sculpted to perfection. He wore immaculate white garments and gave off a magnificent scent that overpowered the Creepers' putrid stench. He moved with unprecedented grace, yet was clearly a warrior, a supernatural being prepared for the fiercest of battles.

Human words cannot describe his flawless complexion nor the passion and fury exuding from his eyes. A thin, solid gold crown encircled his glorious head, beaming beneath his wavy brown hair as if to signify authority far greater than any measly earthly power.

"Owen!" I felt a firm grip on my arm, but I paid no attention. I was witnessing another dimension, beholding a life form that exceeded the most exquisite of fairytale heroes.

My knees buckled, and I shrank to the floor when I saw another mighty being of equal stature and strength appear on the opposite side of Misty. The Creepers went ballistic. They jerked, twisted, and squirmed in a desperate frenzy to free themselves at once from her cords and chains.

I watched in amazement as the two astronomical allies took steps toward Misty, closing in on the Creepers. Surely I was not the only one who felt the earth shudder. They had no weapons in their hands. Their massive hands were their weapons.

Now unbound from Misty, the Creepers planted their shamed faces on the floor, not in sorrow or heartfelt submission but out of inevitable defeat. They dared not utter or hiss a word.

As their victors towered over them, I watched the Creepers writhe in anguish. The mere presence of the superior beings unleashed torment and suffering upon them. It was a beautiful, barbaric sight.

The splendid beings backed slightly away from the Creepers, clearing the way for them to escape. And oh, how they ran.

I dropped my head back to stare at the ultimate avengers, but I was interrupted by the sensation of pain in both arms. I felt my body spin around in the opposite direction. It took me a moment to realize two men had an unyielding grip on my upper arms. I don't know if my feet drug the floor or I took steps. I do know that by the time they laid me down in the nurse's office, Principal Maxwell was on the phone with my mother.

The nurse scrambled to take my temperature and blood pressure. It was no surprise to me that my body temperature was low and my blood pressure soared. That's what happens when you carry around a blizzard in your belly and stand inches away from supernatural rivals.

"Is he okay?" I heard Lance ask the nurse if I was alright, but I didn't hear her response. I guess my secret was out. Everyone saw me explode. What a debacle.

I wanted so badly to get up and go find Misty. I wanted her to know that she was the center of an epic fight, the sought-after treasure by two fierce opposing forces. And I wanted her to know that the good side won today. They won without even having to raise a fist.

Principal Maxwell knelt down and spoke uncomfortably close to my face. "Owen, I just got off the phone with your mother. She's on her way."

I was relieved when she backed off, but then a school counselor got right back in my face. "Owen, how are you feeling?"

"I don't know."

"Are you aware of what just happened?"

I wanted to ask her the same thing.

"What were you doing, Owen?"

I couldn't crack now, not after what I just saw. I had to keep it together and downplay the seriousness of the situation so they wouldn't banish me to a treatment center.

"I just let the stress get to me, that's all. I haven't been sleeping much lately. I've been worried about my college plans and worried about my friends with all this suicide stuff. I just lost it for a minute. I'll be okay."

She looked at me with adoring eyes. "Bless your heart. Why don't you stay home and rest tomorrow and relax over the weekend, then come see me on Monday morning?"

Whew. I dodged that bullet. I wasn't sure what to expect from my mother though. As far as she was concerned, this was the second episode this week, and she was already leery of me. Who knows; I feared she might pull up to the school with a straight jacket in hand.

I laid on the stiff, plastic-covered bed and stared up at the ceiling tiles, trying to comprehend what I had just witnessed. It was larger than life. It was like watching death versus life.

I reached up and wiped my eyes. Why was I feeling so emotional? It wasn't because I just completely humiliated myself in front of everyone, and it wasn't because I was afraid of what my mother would say. It wasn't because I was sad, really.

Deep down, I knew what was stirring my heart, but I didn't want to go there. I smothered the thought, pinning it down for as long as I could. But soon, it was out in the open, echoing with clarity across my mind.

I've always believed we're all alone—each of us left to ourselves to fight the onslaught of life's trials and challenges in our own limited strength. But now I knew better. We're not completely forsaken or alone. Something—someone—truly cares about us.

That realization choked me up.

And it freaked me out.

A bothersome thought haunted me. *What if there is a God?* I dismissed the idea. I had to stick with what I could see and deem the unseen unreal. Admittedly that felt slightly hypocritical, but the reality was I hadn't seen God. I saw good forces triumph over evil forces today—that's it. That was a big enough stretch for a die-hard skeptic like me.

My mother spent a while in the counselor's office, and then we were released to go. I assured her I was feeling good enough to drive my car home, and she was quick to agree. She didn't want to be confined to a car with me, I guess.

I went straight up to my room, got my laptop out, and added to my timeline. "What do I call them," I wondered. I settled on the term "Watchmen."

My phone lit up with text messages. Everyone, including Jess, wanted to know what in the world happened to me. I figured it would help diffuse the situation to reply and assure them all that I was fine and there was nothing to worry about.

I was surprised to get a text from Ray Anne. She must have been pretty horrified to hear that the guy she' s going out with on Friday night just completely flipped out in front of the whole school. She asked me if I was okay, and I responded with an apology and a promise: **Im sorry I**

acted like an idiot today. I hope u still want to hang out tomorrow. I swear I will not cause a scene :)

She confirmed our plans. I was nervous, but looking forward to our evening together. I had a hunch she could help me piece some things together.

I just hoped I could keep my promise and not freak out and embarrass us both over something I might see.

8. Eventful Evening

I woke up on Friday morning feeling conflicted about staying home from school. On the one hand, I was relieved I didn't have to face everyone after my breakdown yesterday, but on the other hand, I wondered if the Watchmen would make another appearance and I would miss it.

Maybe it's just a guy thing, but I really wanted to see them get into a physical match with the Creepers. I have no doubt the Watchmen would put a major beat down on them. I would just love to see it.

Around three o'clock, I got a text from Jess: **U want to hang out tonite?**

I don't know which was more confusing—making sense of the paranormal life forms that kept appearing, or trying to figure out why females do what they do. Why would she want to hang with a "crazy" person like me?

I didn't take the time to consider her invitation because I already had plans with Ray Anne. I was hoping to keep that on the down-low, though. I took the easy way out.

Sorry. I have to help my mom do some stuff around the house tonight.

I did help my mom move some heavy boxes and reorganize the garage a few weeks ago, so it wasn't a blatant lie. It was just one of those mini-lies, I think.

She responded right away: **K. Will u call me this weekend?**

I told her I would and resisted the urge to take a pot shot at Dan. I wanted to say something tacky about her needing to spend a little time with a real man like me, but I let it go.

I jumped in the shower to get ready for my date—more like fact-finding mission. It was hard to tell if I was nervous because I was going out with a girl I didn't know very well or because I no longer trusted myself to be rational. I didn't want to tell her too much, but I feared I would. And I hoped, while in her presence, I could ignore the supernatural stuff, but feared I couldn't.

I styled my hair to perfection and splashed on some cologne, then headed out the door. My neighbor was pulling into her driveway. She was bound to be in her mid-fifties, but she dressed like she was sixteen. I couldn't get into my car in time to avoid her.

"Well don't you look like a dream. Where ya goin' tonight?"

Maybe it shouldn't have surprised me that she had lots of chains—like, as many as my mom—and a head full of cords, but it caught me off guard. "I'm just going out with a friend. Have a good night." I slid into the driver's seat and slammed the door. The sight of her sickened me, and I found myself really looking forward to seeing Ray Anne's glowing appearance.

I pulled into her driveway and fought back the nerves building in my gut. Adrenaline and a belly freeze don't mix. As I knocked on her door, I remembered what she said about meeting her parents. Hopefully I would pass whatever drill they put me through.

Ray Anne welcomed me inside with a sweet smile, and I was relieved to see she hadn't lost her shimmer. I stood near the couch and tried to figure out what to do with my hands so that I looked natural, not like the nervous buffoon I felt like.

Her parents entered the living room together, both glowing—literally.

Hello Owen. I'm Trevor Greiner." Ray Anne's dad gave a firm, confident handshake.

"It's great to see you again." Her mom hugged me. *Unexpected but nice, I guess.*

They sat down on the couch and motioned for me to sit in the chair across from them.

"So, tell us about yourself," Mr. Greiner said. For one millisecond, I entertained offering a candid response: *I'm a psycho who sees spirit beings that no one else can, and I'm on a mission to figure out why your family glows.*

I went for a less shocking, more fitting response. "Well, I'm a senior, I'm on the basketball team, and I always drive the speed limit." We all laughed, except Mr. Greiner.

He continued with his inquiry. "So how did you meet Ray Anne?"

"We were friends in middle school. I just thought it would be a good idea to reconnect." I hoped they couldn't sense any ulterior motive.

"What are your plans tonight?" Mr. Greiner asked.

113

"If it's okay with you, I'd like to take Ray Anne out for dinner."

After a few more minutes of small talk, he leaned in toward me, now maintaining a no-nonsense expression. "Owen, you look like a nice young man. I just want you to know that I'm entrusting you with one of the most precious people in my life. I have faith in you that you're going to act like a gentleman and treat my daughter with decency and respect tonight."

"Oh, yes sir, I will, of course." I really did have nothing but good intentions toward her.

As Ray Anne and I headed out the door, Mr. Greiner gave her a hug and me a heavy pat on my shoulder. I don't think he trusted me one bit.

I decided to take Ray Anne to the Kemah boardwalk. It was over an hour away, but there are lots of restaurants to choose from, and the long drive would give us more time to talk.

Our conversation on the way there was surprisingly comfortable. Neither of us brought up my episode at lunch the day before. We kept making each other laugh, which was cool. I noticed she had beautiful, muscular legs, but I tried not to stare or let my thoughts digress. I was definitely feeling the weight of Mr. Greiner's hand on my shoulder.

By the time we arrived and found a parking spot, the sun was setting, making Ray Anne's glow appear all the more spectacular.

The neon-lit rides along with the buzzing restaurants and live music created an energizing social scene, but it made me jumpy. Crowds were now a concern of mine. We were still a ways from the frenzy of people, and I could already see Creepers in the mix. Yuck.

I also saw the word "sick" slopped on the side of a restaurant in huge lowercase letters. That didn't help my nerves.

I suggested we have dinner at the Aquarium, and I could tell she was happy about that. It's a neat place. Not cheap, but a great atmosphere.

After waiting nearly an hour, we were seated at our candle lit table. It was right next to one of the massive aquariums, and several sharks kept swimming by. It was awesome, and, if I'm being honest, slightly romantic.

The restaurant was dim, causing Ray Anne's luminescence to reflect off the floor and onto her face. It was intriguing.

The only downer was I could smell something horrible. I was sure it was a Creeper and not the restaurant. I tried to ignore it.

We looked through the menu and discussed what foods we each do and don't like, but our conversation was interrupted by the disturbing sound of a woman raising her voice. I looked over my shoulder and observed a heavyset lady shouting at a man who I assumed was her husband. And there was that filthy Creeper I was smelling, attached right to her. The ambient lighting provided just enough illumination for me to read its forehead: "hostility."

I turned back around and looked at Ray Anne. She was fully engrossed in their volatile conversation, as evidenced by her open mouth.

I heard the lady shout even louder. "I don't know why I put up with you!"

The man across from her stood and yelled back, "What's wrong with you?"

I turned over my shoulder again and glared at the Creeper. "You just love destroying lives, don't you?" I thought to myself.

The couple stormed away from their table, and the waitress chased them down.

"Could you pay your check and then flip out?" Ray Anne said, dripping with sarcasm. Once again, she made me laugh.

After a minute or so, everyone went back to minding their own business, and our waitress took our order. I was sipping on my drink when Ray Anne made an unexpected statement. "I can't imagine being attacked by one of those vicious things."

I nearly spit out my tea. "You see them, too?"

"The sharks?" She pointed to the aquarium. My heart sank, and I worked to regain my composure.

"Oh, yeah, it would be awful to face one of those in the open seas." She picked up on my disappointment.

"Are you alright?"

"Absolutely." I put on my game face and changed the subject. "So what does your father do for a living?"

"He's a football coach at a Title One school in the Houston school district, a high school with basically all low-income students. He's worked there for over fifteen years."

"That's neat. He seems like a nice guy. Your mom seems really nice, too." I almost told her how lucky she is to have two caring parents, but I decided not to go there. I didn't want to have to explain how weird my mom was and how my dad had never wanted anything to do with me.

Our conversation continued to flow, and although it was casual and lighthearted, I made an interesting observation. Jess and other girls I'd been around would always take jabs at me, incessantly trying to compete with me or something. But Ray Anne wasn't like that. She would compliment me when I told her something about myself. It was different. I really liked it.

Our meal was delicious, and so was our dessert. We cut a piece of key lime pie in half and each devoured our portion. I guess Ray Anne was feeling pretty comfortable with me at that point because she started asking more personal questions.

"So why did you come to my house the other day out of the blue and ask me out?"

I bit my bottom lip and sorted through dozens of possible responses, hoping to quickly settle on a good one. That didn't happen. "I saw you at school on Monday and thought, 'Hey, she was a nice person when we used to talk in middle school. I should see how she's doing these days.'"

She looked suspicious of my answer but let it slide. "So what exactly happened in the cafeteria yesterday?" I could feel my heart begin to race. I wanted to tell her so badly about how my world had been invaded by the paranormal, but I didn't want to blow it before I had a chance to figure out what makes her and her family different. I aimed for middle ground.

"Something unexpected started happening to me last week, and sometimes I handle it better than at other times. That's all." I should have known that would only compel her to probe more.

"What do you mean 'something unexpected'?"

You know that feeling when you're strapped into a mega coaster and it's about to change from clanking uphill to freefalling down a massive drop? That's precisely how I felt. I let go of my fork, put both palms flat on the table, and leaned in toward her. "Ray Anne, if I tell you something unbelievable, something frightening and absurd and . . . just totally bizarre, would you believe me? And if you don't believe me, would you at least just not call me crazy?"

Her response was unexpected. She glanced around the restaurant for a moment, seemingly deep in thought, then looked back at me. She actually gave serious consideration to what I asked of her.

"Yes," she said with total confidence. I feared I was setting myself up for a major let down, but I was actually tempted to believe her. I was just about to speak again when our waitress showed up at our table. She thanked us for coming and dropped off the change.

"How about we head outside?" I said. She agreed, and we made our way down to the boardwalk. It was bubbling over with people, and by people, I mean shackled folks, and also small children with that wonderful star-like glow near their hearts. Of course there were Creepers, as well as people enslaved by Creepers. Then, every once in a while, I spotted a liberated soul who radiated like Ray Anne.

I was looking for a quiet place to sit and continue our talk. I second guessed my decision to confide in her, but she was already expecting me to tell her something important. I finally spied a bench in a grassy area in the distance. We made our way there and sat facing out toward the boat docks. Everything looked navy blue in the moonlight, except Ray Anne, of course. The sidewalk below her feet was glistening with that soothing gold light.

I looked up at the sky, but there wasn't a single star. I wanted something to fix my eyes on while I spoke. Ray Anne stared at me, waiting patiently for me to talk. I was back at the top of the coaster. I took a deep breath and proceeded with cautious abandon.

"Last week I was out in the woods, and I drank a sip of this weird underground rushing water and it made me feel sick. I got this awful cold feeling in my stomach, and I went home and collapsed on the floor, and I thought I was literally going to die. When I woke up the next morning, everything had changed."

I thought about stopping there, but I was in over my head.

"What do you mean? What happened?" She slid to the edge of the bench, nearly holding her breath in anticipation.

I watched the boats bobbing in the current and began telling her the uncensored truth. In a matter-of-fact manner, I explained how I saw the jogger lady with a shackle and chains and cords and how later that day I saw everyone with the same thing. I told her about the first Creeper I encountered and how it attached itself to a girl in my first period class and then what happened when my mom came downstairs attached to one. I went into detail about the group of Creepers, and the note, and how I wasn't the only one who saw it. I then shared how two of my friends didn't believe me when I showed them a photo of the note.

I told her about the amazing star-looking thing kids have. I also described what happened the day before at lunch— how two Creepers tried to attack Misty, but these freakishly large and breathtaking warrior beings showed up out of nowhere and intervened.

As if I hadn't dumped enough craziness on her, I disclosed one more of my outrageous observations. "The reason I asked you to have dinner with me is because there are a few of us who don't have a shackle or chains or cords. Instead there's this beautiful glow-like deal around their feet. I don't see any kind of glow coming from me, but Ray Anne, that's what I see when I look at you, and also your family. You're one of the rare ones. You don't have the stuff Creepers use to attack people, and I want to know why."

I sat back and waited for Ray Anne to pull her cell phone out of her purse and call her dad to come get her that instant.

"Show me the picture of the note."

Was she actually taking me seriously? I pulled my cell phone out of my back pocket while trying to conceal how nervous I was. I enlarged the image of the note, then passed my phone to her. She stared at it for a long time, pulling it close to her face, then holding it far away like some expert detective. Finally, she handed it back to me.

"Owen?"

Oh God. Here comes the hammer, I thought.

"It's difficult to absorb everything you just told me, and I'm sure you understand that it's really hard for me—or anyone—to believe such a thing. But I don't think you're crazy, and I'm sorry no one has been willing to try and believe you. That's what I'm gonna do. I'm gonna try to believe you. I want to be a good friend to you and be here for you the best I can while you go through all of this."

She put her hand on mine and kept talking. "I'm sure the more I think about everything, I'll have a lot of questions for you, but if you'll be completely honest with me, I'll hang in there and walk through this with you."

The aching lump in my throat was about to burst, but breaking down in front of her was not an option. Her response was so kind and gracious that I struggled to believe it. It hit me right in the heart and overwhelmed my emotions. Finally, I had someone I could go to, someone I could confide in without being insulted. What an indescribable relief.

"So, what's going on in your world?" I said. She found my question amusing, just as I intended.

It was getting late. We decided to walk back to the car and head home.

Ray Anne wasn't ready to change the subject yet. "Do you think you should have that water tested or something?"

I explained that I already had, but I could hardly finish telling her about it when she interjected more questions. "Why did you drink the water in the first place?" "Do the Creeper things know you can see them?" "What does the writing look like?" On and on she asked me one thing after another, and I supplied as much detail as I could.

We were almost to her house when she mentioned that she was thirsty, so I pulled into a convenience store. She insisted that wasn't necessary, but I assured her, buying her a drink was the least I could do considering how well she handled hearing my scary secrets.

We were picking out sodas from the refrigerator at the back of the store when two Creepers passed right through a wall. They were both named "Terror," which was fitting.

By the time I noticed Ray Anne walking toward the register, it was too late to grab her. I didn't blink or breath while she crossed smack dab in front of the Creepers.

I couldn't believe it. The filthy things went out of their way to avoid her. They leaned away from her as if the light surrounding her was toxic to the touch.

She glanced back at me. "Are you coming?"

The Creepers sliced back through the wall behind the register, out of sight.

I approached the cashier and pulled out my wallet to pay. "This one's on me," Ray Anne said. I normally would have insisted on paying, but I was still in a shocked funk of sorts.

"Did something just happen?" she asked.

"Yeah. I'll explain when we get in the car."

I opened the passenger door for her to get in. That's when a different kind of hell broke out.

"Owen, what are you doing? Guess you had a change of plans tonight!"

Jess's car was two parking spots away. She yelled loud enough for us, and everyone in a one-mile radius, to hear.

"Hey, I um . . ." There was nothing to say. I was busted.

"So I guess you didn't stay home to help your mom?"

Ray Anne looked confused. Jess looked ready to pounce.

"I'll give you a call later, okay?"

"No, it's not okay! You think you can just lie to me?"

It felt cruel, but I didn't know what else to do. I ignored Jess, got in my car, and pulled out of the parking lot. I couldn't believe she happened to show up at the exact store we were at for all of five minutes.

I had such a wonderful night with Ray Anne. I was disappointed it was ending like this. I wanted to talk to her about what just happened with the Creepers, but I figured I needed to try and smooth over the whole Jess thing instead. "I'm really sorry about what just happened."

"Did you lie to her about going out with me tonight?"

"I did stretch the truth a little, but only to keep from starting a lot of drama. That obviously blew up in my face. I should have just come clean with her. I don't have anything to hide. I just didn't want rumors starting, that's all."

We didn't say much until we pulled into her driveway, and I walked her to the door.

Ray Anne turned toward me, and I thought she was going to kiss me. No such luck. "You know how, before you shared everything tonight, you asked me to please not call you crazy?" she asked.

"Yeah?" I took in a deep breath and held it, anticipating a crushing insult.

"Well I'm gonna ask something from you."

"Okay?" I exhaled.

"Don't ever lie to me. I can overlook a lot, and I know no one is perfect, but please, don't ever, *ever* lie to me, alright?"

I thought about how, earlier in the evening, she had given my request serious thought before answering, and I wanted to show the same consideration. I've always lied when I needed to, not to intentionally hurt people, but to get out of a jam or whatever. Could I really promise not to lie to her?

I truly believed I could, and I wanted to make that commitment. "I won't lie to you, Ray Anne. I promise I won't."

She went inside, then faced me again before closing the door. She flashed an adorable smile, and it made me feel all tingly inside, in spite of the ice in my stomach.

I walked back to my car unable to wipe the grin off my face. She had to be the sweetest girl I'd ever met.

I really meant what I said about not lying to her.

Little did I know that in just three days, I'd have no choice but to break my promise.

9. Epic Mistake

I would have liked to hang out with Ray Anne again on Saturday, but I didn't want to appear desperate, so I didn't dare initiate any plans. We texted back and forth a few times, then talked on the phone for a little while that afternoon.

I told her what happened at the store, how the Creepers avoided her like the plague. She had even more questions for me, and again, I answered the best I could.

I felt a two-man team forming. I finally had an ally working with me to try and solve the mystery unfolding before my eyes—literally. I could tell she was skeptical but really trying to make sense of things, nonetheless.

I asked her a lot of questions, too, but wasn't able to come to any reasonable conclusions about why her family was shackle-free.

I took the easy way out and apologized to Jess in a text message. She didn't respond. I figured it was best to let her anger subside a bit before trying to speak to her in person. I did notice all of her recent online posts were about the beauty of honesty and the disgrace due anyone with the audacity to tell lies. *Hmm, I wonder who all of that is directed at?*

I really did feel bad for hurting her, but then again, she didn't hesitate to hurt me and call me crazy, not once, but twice. She technically had it coming to her. At least that's what I told myself.

I figured Sunday afternoon would be uneventful. I was just finishing up washing my car in the driveway when my basketball buddies Jared and Conner showed up at my house.

"Hey!" Jared called out from the passenger seat of Conner's Ford truck. "You wanna go shoot some hoops with us, white boy?"

I didn't feel I had it in me to focus and actually score baskets, but it seemed like it had been forever since I'd played. I really missed it. I wasn't sure how I would run up and down the court alongside two guys dragging chains, but I agreed to come along anyway. I threw on some shorts and my favorite Under Armour tennis shoes, then jumped in the truck.

We went to our usual spot, Franklin Park. It was a hot, gorgeous day. It felt amazing to have a basketball in my hands. I had forgotten what a stress reliever it is to play ball.

We never kept score, but we always knew who won, if you know what I mean. I didn't come out on top, but I cut myself some slack. There word "rebel" was written on one of the basketball goals, and it kept distracting me. And just as I predicted, so did Jared and Conner's clanking chains and flailing cords.

We returned to the truck, and Conner pulled some sports drinks out of a cooler. I was gulping mine down when Jared mustered up the courage to ask me a loaded question.

"So Owen, what's this we hear about you seeing all this weird, supernatural stuff?"

It was all I could do not to squeeze the bottle in my hand into a tiny ball of plastic. Lance had obviously blabbed to them. Some best friend he was turning out to be.

"What do you mean?" I tried playing dumb to buy some time while I gathered my thoughts.

"We heard you've been seeing chains and stuff on people and these, like, zombie creatures or something," Jared said. He and Conner looked at each other and laughed. Clearly they didn't believe any of it. Still, I didn't feel the need to deny it.

"Yeah," I said, nonchalantly. "I've been seeing some pretty freaky things, things that would scare both of you guys to death." I took the last sips of my drink and waited for their next inquisition.

That's when things took a serious nosedive. My friends went from joking about my claims to downright taunting me. At first, I shook off their insults, but the more they kept it up, the more infuriated I became.

"We heard you drank some mysterious water, and that's when you started having bionic vision," Conner said, all the while laughing hysterically at my expense, right in my face.

127

"Scoff all you want," I said. "You girls don't have the guts to drink it."

"Are you kidding me?" Conner said, moving way too close to my face. "We're not scared to drink it. Take us there, and we'll show you."

As angry as I was at them, I couldn't imagine serving them a cup of the living hell I'd been living lately. I told them they were full of crap and insisted we leave the park and call it a day.

I wish I could say they drove me straight home and that was the end of our conflict. Unfortunately the two of them kept talking trash, so much so that, before I knew it, I was contemplating taking them to the woods and serving them a swig of spirit water.

I reached a breaking point when Jared made a cutting remark about my hallucinations being alcohol-induced. He was one of a handful of people who knew about my mother's addiction. He should have known better than to accuse me of being a drunk.

You know that voice in your head that scolds you when you're acting like an idiot? I totally ignored it. All I could think about was the sweet vindication I would soon get if they drank the stuff and could see like me.

"Take us to the water, and let us settle this," Conner said, all the while cracking up like the whole thing was some stupid joke.

My concern for my friends' wellbeing took a backseat to my pride and desire for vengeance. I led them right to the wooded spot, fully aware that I was being one-hundred percent self-centered.

We got to the area at dusk, and I started digging. They were slightly taken aback by the sound and feel of the rushing water underfoot, but they remained jovial.

I used their empty drink bottles to scoop out some of the warm water. Jared clutched his container while searching my face for the slightest hint of humor. "You guys are taking me for a wild ride, aren't you?" He suspected this was all a big prank Conner and I had conjured up.

"I really do wish we were kidding," I said.

"Go for it." Jared urged Conner.

"You go first," Conner said.

"How about you both drink on the count of three," I said. They couldn't argue with that.

"One—"

They moved their bottles closer to their lips.

"Two—"

Conner took a deep breath and stared me down.

"Three."

They both drank.

No one moved or said a word for several seconds, then Jared hurled his bottle across the woods. "Man, nothing happened."

I looked at Conner. He was still grinning. "You're a liar, bro," he said while throwing his empty bottle at my head. "There's nothing mystical about that stuff."

"I told you I'd drink it." Jared said, puffing up his chest.

"You only did cause I did," Conner said.

They were getting all worked up, then Jared stopped midsentence and grabbed his midsection. "My stomach hurts."

"Mine too," Conner said. "It feels really cold or something. And my head hurts."

"That's just the beginning," I said, feeling an odd mixture of both shock and relief that the water affected them the same way it did me.

"What do you mean?" Conner looked pale all of the sudden.

"When I drank that water, I didn't start seeing things right away. I got an awful chill in my stomach first. It was the next morning when I actually began seeing all the frightening stuff."

"What?" Jared was visibly alarmed.

"That ice you feel in your belly, I still have that, even now," I said.

"Why didn't you tell us about that?" He was furious.

Conner got in my face. "I can't believe this, Owen! You knew we were gonna get sick, but you let us drink it anyway?"

I felt a tinge of remorse but mostly relief. Finally, this time tomorrow, everyone would have to take me seriously.

"What have you done to us?" Jared said in a panic, bracing his stomach with both arms. I wasn't willing to tell him that in my self-absorbed desire to have company join me in my misery, I just allowed them both to destroy their lives.

"Look, you asked for this, it happened, now we have to focus on preparing for what's next." I felt no need to coddle them. "You might as well learn what a Creeper is now, before you see them in a few hours.

"A What?" Jared said while crouching to the ground, holding his pounding head with both hands.

I filled them in. "Okay guys. Pretty soon you're gonna start seeing the most horrible things you've ever laid eyes on, and you'll smell them, too, but don't freak out. As long as you don't say whatever word is written on their foreheads, they won't pay attention to you."

"What in the world are you talking about? That's crazy." Conner didn't believe a word I said. He just wanted the ice in his belly to go away.

I tried to put a positive spin on things. "Hey, I went through this all by myself. At least we have each other."

Jared narrowed his eyes at me in utter disgust. Admittedly, I deserved it.

"Okay, here's the plan," I said. "Let's all go home, and you guys try and rest. It won't be easy because your stomach is gonna seriously ache and your head is going to throb, but just try and sleep, and then come straight to my house in the morning. Don't talk to anyone or so much as look at anyone. Just come directly to my house at, like, six o'clock in the morning, and I'll walk you through things. We can work together to figure this out. It's gonna be okay."

The gravity of what I just did was starting to sink in.

Jared plunged his finger down his throat but couldn't make himself vomit. "Tomorrow's Monday," he said. "I can't miss school. I have to exempt out of finals."

Poor guy. Pretty soon, he wouldn't care about such things.

"I understand. Just come to my house in the morning, got it?" I hoped they were on board with my plan. It was hard to tell.

They looked pitiful standing there holding their stomachs. I tried to offer some assurance. "For what it's worth, I totally know how you're feeling. Seriously, I understand. It really

131

is gonna be okay." I told another one of my infamous half-lies. I actually preferred to call them half-truths. Jared and Conner weren't gonna die or anything, but things weren't exactly going to be okay either.

I offered to drive, but Conner insisted he could get us all home and make it to his house by himself. We drove right past a Creeper as we entered my neighborhood, and I cringed at the thought of Jared and Conner having to deal with seeing them, too, shortly. At the same time, I reasoned, at least they wouldn't be blind to them. "Who knows, maybe they'll thank me later," I thought.

Not likely.

As Conner slammed on the brakes in front of my house and I got out of the truck, I reminded them both to come see me first thing in the morning and to not tell anyone what had happened. I also said they could call me as many times as they needed to that night, but I don't think they took much comfort in my offer. It was obvious to me that they weren't at all convinced they were going to start seeing weird stuff. They were just infuriated by how sick they felt.

I made one final suggestion right before they drove away. "Guys, whatever you do, don't look in the mirror in the morning. Just get dressed, and come over." I imagined beholding their own shackled reflections would scare them beyond belief.

The hours dragged on and on, and I thought Monday morning was never going to come. I texted them both at 6:00 a.m.: **U okay?**

It made me really edgy when neither of them responded. Had they gone to the emergency room? Called the police?

Was an angry mob on its way to my house, led by their outraged parents?

My thoughts ran wild, especially when, at a quarter until seven, I still hadn't heard from either one of them. I paced back and forth and contemplated driving to their houses. I didn't know exactly what to do, so I did the usual—flip on the TV and try a little distraction therapy.

The news was on, and I was just about to change the channel when I noticed the reporter was broadcasting live from the parking lot of my school. The sun was barely up, and already the sign people and campers were acting as loony as always in the background.

"It appears that two more Lincoln Forest High School students have taken their lives," the reporter said.

"What? Who?" I stood inches away from the TV screen with my hands cupped over my mouth, waiting to hear.

"Both of the young men's parents discovered their sons' lifeless bodies early this morning at their individual homes. Although the cause of death has yet to be determined, authorities fear it was a double suicide."

"For crying out loud, tell us who!"

"High school seniors Jared Sanders and Conner Roshkey were active members of the school's basketball team and, according to fellow classmates, were close friends. Although many details are not being disclosed at this time, we do know that one of the boys was found lifeless in his bed while the other appears to have died on the floor within a few feet of his bed. This news comes as a total shock to school officials and the community."

"No! There's no way!"

I got to the toilet just in time to throw up. Surely I heard her wrong. Jared and Conner couldn't possibly be dead.

I clawed at my face. I pulled my shirt off. I punched the floor.

"What happened? Did they kill themselves or—"

I curled up on the bathroom floor, withering in self-hatred.

"Did that water . . . did I . . .?"

I flung myself over the toilet again but had nothing left in my stomach. I dry heaved. My throat was on fire.

"I did this! I can't believe I did this!"

My mother appeared outside the bathroom. I fell at her ankles and sobbed.

"What's the matter, son? What happened?"

She dropped to her knees and grabbed my shoulders. "Tell me."

"Jared and Conner. They—"

I didn't have to finish. She knew my friends were dead. She hugged me harder than she had in a very long time. "Oh, son, I'm so sorry. I'm so very sorry. Their poor parents."

She eventually let go, and I sat motionless for who knows how long.

My phone rang, but by the time I found it on the floor and grabbed it, I had missed the call. It was Ray Anne. She texted me. **Did u hear about Conner and Jared?**

I couldn't possibly tell her what really happened. I couldn't tell anyone. There was no way either of those guys took their own lives. It had to have been the water.

I felt like their blood was smeared across my face and dripping from my hands. I wanted to run away, to hide.

I had to leave. I was completely disoriented as I searched for my keys.

"Where are you going, Owen?" I didn't have a clue and couldn't answer my mother.

I finally found my keys on my dresser and ran to the front door. I only had on a pair of jeans and socks, but I didn't notice. I flung the door open, then gasped.

"Are you Owen Edmonds?"

Two police officers stood on my doorstep.

10. Terrifying Observations

"Son, I asked if you're Owen Edmonds."

I might have denied it had my mother not chimed in. "Yes, this is my son Owen."

One of the police officers looked to be in his mid-thirties, and he was shackled, but the other was an older man, and he glowed like Ray Anne. The shackled one spoke again. "I'm Officer Smith, and this is Officer McFarland. We need to ask you a few questions. May we come in?"

My mother nervously welcomed them inside. I clung to the sofa, and the two cops remained standing. My mom went scurrying around the living room picking up empty wine glasses as if they were coming to arrest her for being an alcoholic mother.

The glowing one, Officer McFarland, began questioning me. "Owen, have you heard about what's happened to Jared Sanders and Conner Roshkey?"

Think Owen, think. Don't say anything stupid.

"Yes. I saw it on the news just a while ago. It's really hard to believe." Most murderers have to pretend like they're grieving, but not me. I was genuinely remorseful. The officers didn't seem concerned with how I was feeling, though.

"When did you last see Jared and Conner?"

"We all went to shoot hoops yesterday."

"What time and where?"

"I guess it was about four o'clock in the afternoon when they picked me up. We went to Franklin Park."

"How long were you there?"

"A couple of hours, I guess. I really wasn't paying attention to the time."

"Did either of them display any odd behavior or say anything to you about plans to harm themselves?"

"No, sir. They seemed just fine to me."

"Owen, Conner's truck was seen parked at the edge of the woods on Spring Cypress Road yesterday evening. Do you know anything about that?"

"Um, yeah. We went to the woods after we left the park."

"What for?"

"We wanted to jog on the trails."

My mind was scrambling. In the intense pressure of the moment, I couldn't decide if it was in my best interest to disclose the water-drinking incident or conceal it at all costs.

He took a step back, then stared directly into my eyes. "So you went and played basketball for a couple of hours, then wanted to go for a jog?"

Oh no. That sounded ridiculous, but it was too late to change my story.

"Yeah. Jared and Conner wanted to race." That was the best recovery I could muster.

The shackled cop responded to a call on his cell, then came and stood inches away, peering down at me. "Wanna tell me why you sent both boys a text at 6:00 a.m. this morning asking if they were okay?"

"Yesterday I suggested they come over to my house early so we could all go have breakfast at IHOP before school. When they didn't show up, I asked if everything was okay. I had no idea they were . . ."

I left it at that. My fabricated story was growing and mutating with each response and would likely be debunked any second.

I was relieved when Officer Smith received a page on his radio summoning him elsewhere. He handed me his business card and assured me they'd be back in touch soon. Both officers finally left. I felt sure I had seriously flunked their interrogation.

I quarantined myself in the bathroom and eventually got in the shower. The more I thought about it, there was no doubt in my mind that neither Jared nor Conner committed suicide. The cause of death was undetermined because there were no outward signs of injury; the water had ravaged them from within. I was sure of it. The water I scooped out and told them to drink on my count of three snuffed out their lives.

I didn't mean to kill them, but they were dead because of me, nonetheless. I was guilty of manslaughter. That's a tough one to swallow.

It occurred to me to go to the police and confess everything, but I was way too scared. If I hadn't lied to Mrs.

Barnett about where I got that water sample, she could vouch for me now, assuring the police I believed the water was clean. But I did lie to her, and to go back now and try to explain the situation to Mrs. Barnett would only expose what a liar I am, bumping me up on the list of suspects.

To make matters worse, I told several people that the water in the woods made me deathly ill—specifically Jess and Lance. How would I explain my decision to police to serve it to Jared and Conner? I was clearly acting with malicious intent, and I was sure a prosecutor could spin that into a believable motive for murder.

I decided it was best to keep my mouth shut.

Call it a hunch, but I had a feeling prison would be crawling with Creepers. Getting locked up was not an option.

I had absolutely no idea why the stuff didn't kill me. I only knew I was responsible for the deaths of two of my friends, two young guys with their whole lives ahead of them. The guilt and grief were excruciating.

I got out of the shower, threw on some mismatched clothes, then got under the covers and basically stayed there for a week.

I had no desire to speak to anyone during my self-imposed house arrest, well, except for Ray Anne. She asked if I had any thoughts about the cause of death concerning Jared and Conner, and I said I had no idea.

Unfortunately I couldn't stop people from coming to see me. The cops came by and asked a whole lot more questions. I did the best I could to give reasonable answers and deflect their suspicions, but I was sure they were picking up on the rotten scent of my deception.

That counselor lady from my school who likes to talk obnoxiously close to my face came to see me twice. She let me know, in no uncertain terms, that no matter how my grades plummeted or my absences stacked up, any senior who stayed enrolled—or alive—at Lincoln Forest High until the end of May would graduate. That was nice to hear since I had no intention of doing any more schoolwork.

We discussed my feelings, my grief, and all my newfound phobias as a result of the school year's traumatic events, but I just played along. I would have liked to let my guard down and confide in her, but those days were over. I couldn't tell a single soul what was really going on in my head in the aftermath of Jared and Conner's deaths, and that included Ray Anne.

She and I spoke on the phone for a while every day, and I kept up my charade with her. Yeah, I broke my promise not to lie to her, but I figured it was actually the noble thing to do. If I told her about my involvement with Conner and Jared's deaths, she would be legally liable. My dishonesty was protecting her, I told myself.

My seclusion brought zero comfort. On Sunday night, exactly one week after I led my buddies into the woods to guzzle down killer cocktails, I felt just as horrible as the moment I learned that they were dead.

Jared's funeral was tomorrow and Conner's, the following day, on Tuesday. Staying home wasn't an option. I killed them; the least I could do was go pay my respects. And skipping out on their funerals might make the police more suspicious.

How in the world would I sit there and keep it together while their parents and everyone else sobbed and questioned over and over, "How could this happen?"

I knew why it happened, and the hideous answer was me.

One minute I wanted to beat myself to death out of pure self-hatred, and the next minute I was worried about keeping my butt out of prison. What a nightmare.

If I thought my future was wrecked before, now it was seriously annihilated. My dream of becoming a doctor went from majorly threatened to a definite no way in hell. Saving lives is not an acceptable career path for a murderer in hiding.

I didn't know what my future looked like, but I felt confident it would be dark, lonely, and one hundred percent miserable.

It looked like our entire student body came out to Jared's funeral, along with the rest of the city. Things almost got violent when the sign people had the nerve to show up outside the funeral home, shouting their mean-spirited chants and senseless accusations. Some of Jared's relatives nearly decked them. I, for one, would have cheered.

The press was there, of course, in full force.

There was a section reserved for all the basketball team members, so my mother and I sat there. A crowd of people spilled over into the foyer, out the door of the building, and onto the street.

I tried not to look at Jared's casket. It was open, and that seriously bothered me. I diverted my eyes to the rolled up program in my hand, my shoes, my mom's overstuffed purse on the floor, the flowers lining the sides of the room—anything but his lifeless body.

The ceremony was gut-wrenching, just as I anticipated it would be. They showed a slideshow of Jared's life starting with baby pictures, all the way through snapshots taken at his eighteenth birthday just over a month ago. It was unbearable watching Jared's little sister sob.

I was also dealing with the ghastly stench of a Creeper hovering in the back of the room. I turned to glimpse over my shoulder but instantly snapped right back around. I could have sworn it was staring directly at me. I didn't see its name. I tried to put it out of my mind.

By the time Jared's uncle shared some final words, I was on the edge of my seat, ready to get out of there. I was aggravated by what happened next. The ushers signaled for one row at a time to stand, then, in single file procession, motioned for each person to walk up to the casket. I thought I was going to hyperventilate.

It was my row's turn. I scrambled for ideas, ways to get out of having to look at him, but I couldn't come up with anything reasonable. I took steps forward while keeping my gaze fixated on the dark red carpet. I could see the casket out of my peripheral vision. I was almost there.

My heart literally ached. It throbbed as if someone had bludgeoned and bruised it, then set my chest on fire.

As much as I dreaded seeing Jared's embalmed body, this was an opportunity to say some final words, and if anyone had an obligation to say something, it was me. The compulsion to speak welled up inside of me. I'd have to whisper, but I was determined to say what needed to be said.

I stared at the mass of flowers draped over the bottom half of the casket as my mother burst into tears, no doubt a reaction to gazing one last time at Jared's youthful, lifeless face.

She stepped away.

I closed my eyes and slid forward. I spoke as softly as I could. "Jared, I know I don't deserve your forgiveness, but— "

My eyelids parted, and I jolted backwards and nearly fell. The atrocious sight of Jared's mutilated body sent me into hysteria. I couldn't peel my eyes away. I stumbled toward the casket and slapped the palms of my trembling hands over my gaping mouth.

It was unsettling to see his chains and cords coiled meticulously around his neck, encircling his shackle, but what took my breath away was his midsection. It was gone, like, completely caved in. It looked like a grenade had detonated in his gut, shredding right through his suit and stomach. And it left a filthy hole, not lined with blood or body parts, but with what looked to be some sort of dirt or dust.

I glanced around the room, trying to keep my composure. Why hadn't anyone warned me about his appearance, particularly my mother? Why was the casket open in the first place?

"Owen, are you okay?" My mom reached up and wrapped her arm around me, leading me toward the door. People were staring.

"Mom, why didn't you tell me he was . . . that he looked so . . ." I didn't know what to call it.

"I know son." She started crying again. "It's so hard to see him lying there like he's just sleeping. He looks so handsome."

"Mom, he looks terrible!" The harshness of my tone startled her. "What happened to him? Why did he have that huge hole?"

Her eyebrows pressed together. "What are you talking about?" She was embarrassed by the scene I was causing.

"Mom, he had that disgusting—"

I couldn't believe it. It suddenly dawned on me. It was one more thing that only I could see. How cruel.

"Just forget it." I shut my mouth and resumed walking toward the door. I shoved past the crowd, giving no thought to whom I pushed.

We finally made it outside and navigated through the mass of people. I glanced back to see if my mom was still behind me. She was, and so was it. That Creeper had tracked me all the way out of the building.

I hurried to the car and locked my mother and me inside. As my mom pulled onto the street, I glanced in the rearview mirror through my passenger-side window. The Creeper stood right where we had parked, watching our car pull away. This time I saw its depraved name.

"Murderer."

Oh, hell.

I went straight to my room and grabbed my laptop, all the while looking over my shoulder. I pulled up my timeline and made my strangest entry yet.

Monday, April 9, Jared's dead body has gross gaping hole. Chains and cords appear to have been removed and spiraled around his neck. Cuffs at the end of chains are gone.

I also wrote about how that Creeper followed me. It must have known about my crime. Perhaps my guilt led it right to me like bloody chum beckoning a shark.

I was convinced there was no way I could go to Conner's funeral tomorrow. I'd tell my mom, and anyone else who asked, that I just couldn't handle the intensity of it all. I hoped it wouldn't be a red flag for the police, but I had no choice. I wasn't about to subject myself to that environment a second time.

I was just getting ready to text Ray Anne when my mom came into my room and dropped a bomb on me.

"Conner's aunt called. They need one more pallbearer tomorrow, and they thought of you. I told them you would gladly do it."

"By pallbearer, you mean one of the guys who carries the casket?"

"Yes. It's the least we can do." She turned to leave, dragging her chains along.

"No freaking way!" I said.

She looked back at me with what was becoming a familiar expression of shock mixed with anger and demanded to know why I refused.

"Mom, you saw how I reacted today. It's all too much. I can't do it!"

She crossed her arms and then proceeded to give me a mouthful of unsolicited advice. "Life isn't always easy, son. And we don't get the luxury of taking the convenient, painless way out and running from difficult situations."

146

I jumped to my feet and spoke my mind for a change. "You're going to lecture *me* about not taking the easy way out? You, the woman who spends every day drowning her secret sorrows in alcohol and useless men?"

My words slapped her across the face, and she despised me for it.

"I don't know who you think you are!"

"Well I don't have a clue who you are! You won't tell me anything. Your past, your exorbitant income, my grandparents—I'm the only person I know who knows nothing about even one grandparent." I hesitated to keep going, then trespassed into forbidden territory. "You won't even talk to me about my own father."

She gasped then wailed as she spoke. "How dare you! I've told you everything you need to know, Owen."

"Have you?"

That was it. She tore into me. "How many times have I explained to you that I had a horrible upbringing and miserable relationship with my parents? I wouldn't dream of bringing you around them. And I've told you over and over that your father walked out on us when we needed him the most, when you were just an infant. What more do you want to know? Come on!"

"For starters, why don't you have a single picture of your family or my dad?"

"Like I said the last ten times you asked me that, it was too painful to hold on to all of that stuff. I purposely got rid of it and started a new life, with you." Her voice softened.

I only recalled asking her about photos once, maybe twice before, and I found it hard to believe that anyone would get rid of every shred of their childhood and young adult years.

"I feel like you're hiding something, Mom."

"Well you should know."

"What's that supposed to mean?"

"You don't think I've noticed the way you've been acting lately? That you're hallucinating and delusional? It's obvious to me you're on drugs, though we both know you'd never admit it."

Few things made me as mad as when she accused me of that.

"Getting smacked out of your mind is *your* way of dealing with life, not mine, remember?"

Her cheeks flushed red with furry. "You're a liar!"

"I'm not gonna let you do this to me anymore, Mom!"

"Do what?"

I was fuming. "Turn the microscope on me in order to take the focus off of you!"

"Just stop it! I'm leaving. I have plans with Frank." She stormed out of my room. This was the woman who just told me we don't have the luxury of running away from difficult situations.

"What a hypocrite."

Unfortunately it took all of two seconds for my words to fall right back on me. While I obviously was not caught up in any secret drug addiction, I was trapped in a complex web of secrecy and lies.

I heard the front door slam. Valentine was barking her head off. I looked out my window, and my mother was still crying. But I couldn't give that another thought.

That daunting "Murderer" was hovering at the edge of my driveway, peering directly up at me through my bedroom window.

11. Hidden Fight

I woke up Tuesday morning terrified to look out my blinds for fear that rancid Creeper was still stalking me. Valentine sat at the foot of my bed, panting and drooling like always, but with her eyes fixed on my window. That didn't help my nerves one bit.

I decided to shower. I'd look outside after that.

My mom and I did the usual—acted like there was no vicious falling out between us and gave each other lots of space. She spoke with Conner's aunt last night to find out if the casket would be open or closed, and she said it would be closed. Given that bit of information, I decided to go ahead and attend the funeral and endure being a pallbearer. I gave my mother just one stipulation; I wanted Ray Anne to sit with us.

Yes, I wanted her near me because I really, really liked her, but I also had a much more selfish reason. She repelled Creepers, and I needed some repellent right about then.

I got dressed, then stood at my window, daring myself to look out. I didn't want to count to three. That brought back bad memories. I decided just to go for it.

I didn't see anything.

It bothered me that Valentine was still fixated on my window, though.

I walked outside and was sure I smelled the putrid Creeper stench, but I didn't see one anywhere. I lowered into the passenger seat of my mom's car and began fiddling with the air conditioner. She was on the phone, I'm guessing with her boyfriend.

We were at the end of our driveway when I glanced up at our house.

"Oh my God!"

"What?" My mom slammed on the brakes and nearly jumped out of her skin.

"It's nothing. Never mind." I tried to stay calm.

"Don't scare me like that."

"Sorry."

If she could have seen what I saw, she would have completely understood why I panicked. That Creeper had climbed up our house like a venomous spider and was clinging to the exterior brick next to my second-story bedroom window. As if that wasn't horrifying enough, it had written the word "liar" just above the glass.

I was relieved to get away. I spent the entire drive lost in my thoughts, wondering why the filthy Creepers were so obsessed with words, particularly written words. I couldn't figure it out.

My plan was to bring Ray Anne to my house later to hopefully run off that nasty "Murderer." The image of it clinging to my house made me cringe. I wished I knew how to call on some Watchmen to come exterminate the thing, but I had no clue how to find them. In the days following their appearance, I found myself increasingly resentful. *Why aren't they intervening and helping more often? Where did they go?* I wondered.

Conner's funeral was at a huge, plush church. Just like the day before, masses of people came to show their support. We met up with Ray Anne in the lobby along with her twin brother Justin and their mom. We all sat together. It was nice to be around some glowing, chain-free people. I saw a few more of them here and there as I looked around.

I tried to put the image out of my mind of the Creeper lurking outside my window. Was it there all night, crouched just a few feet away from me while I slept? My cold belly was nauseated.

Some preacher guy walked up onto the stage and spoke. He was young and hip looking, and truth be told, probably making a fortune off that enormous church. He was also glowing.

Hmm, I thought. *Maybe this whole thing is about being one of those religious church-goin' types.* Certainly Ray Anne's family fit that description. I hoped that wasn't the answer, though, because the concept of religion didn't sit well with me.

Two girls sang the saddest song I've ever heard, then Conner's relatives shared stories about him. All three females next to me were bawling while Justin did an impeccable job holding in his emotions. I struggled. Conner was my friend, after all, and his death felt slightly personal.

One thing is certain—funerals suck, especially when the occasion is your fault.

The preacher took the stage again and opened his Bible, but I found it difficult to pay attention to what he was saying. For one thing, Jess was there, sitting next to Dan, staring me down the entire time. I tried to ignore her, but it wasn't easy. We still hadn't cleared the air since the whole convenience store debacle.

Second, I kept looking at Conner's distraught parents. For just a moment, I actually considered confessing my crime to them and begging their forgiveness.

I couldn't do it, though. I was too big of a coward, I guess.

I was hoping the preacher would finish soon so I could get the whole pallbearer thing over with. It seemed disgustingly ironic that I would be one of the guys escorting Conner's dead body to the hearse seeing as I escorted him to the fatal water in the first place.

I was fidgeting in my chair and preparing to stand soon when the trendy preacher said something that seized my attention and made the hairs on my neck stand on end:

"Allow me to remind you what the Bible says in Ephesians, the sixth chapter and twelfth verse. It says that in this life, our fight isn't with other human beings, but rather, against the wicked spiritual forces in the heavenly, unseen world—the rulers, authorities, and cosmic powers of this dark age. That's why verse thirteen tells us to put on God's armor, so that when the evil day comes, we can resist and withstand the enemy's attacks, and in the end, we'll hold our ground."

I knew Christians believed in the existence of spiritual beings, but in light of my recent experiences, hearing him put it like that really hit home.

I turned to my mother. "Did you hear that? He just said there's such thing as spiritual forces."

"Shhh."

I should have known better than to try to discuss a biblical concept with her.

The preacher asked us to bow our heads and pray. I cooperated, but my mom didn't. He said amen, then I came forward along with the other pallbearers.

I expected the weight of the casket to smother me with grief, but oddly enough, it didn't. I think hearing what the preacher said about withstanding the enemy's attacks elicited a slight change of emotion, a new drive in me.

Yes, I was deeply sorry about what happened to Jared and Conner, specifically the part I played. But I had a renewed sense of determination to discover how to defeat the Creepers and help my mom and the rest of my classmates— the ones who were still alive, anyway.

I didn't expect to find that kind of motivation at Conner's funeral. I guess that's what religious people call a "blessing."

I pushed past the news crews and caught up with Ray Anne as she was leaving. I casually asked her to come over to my house, as opposed to begging. She said she would go home and change, then head on over. Before I walked away, her mother invited me over for dinner that evening along with my mom. I thanked her and hoped my mom would be willing.

I should have known my mother would already be in the car. I don't know if there's a word in the dictionary for people who have a phobia of setting foot in a church, but if so, my mom's picture belongs beside it. It's not my scene either, but she's even more opposed.

I had a knot in my stomach when we turned into our neighborhood. It morphed into a bowling ball as we drove down our street. We pulled into the driveway, and I looked up and saw the relentless Creeper standing tall and proud on my rooftop, only now it had an equally crude companion.

I cupped my hand over my eyes to block the sun, then took a good hard look at the destructive duo. Next to "Murderer" stood "Accuser." Either it was the same one or had the same name as the one that recently attached itself to my mother.

"Mom, I'm gonna go for a walk, okay?" I wasn't about to go anywhere near our house, at least not without Creeper kryptonite, also known as Ray Anne.

"Now?"

"Yeah. I just need to clear my head."

My chain-clad mother meandered right up to the front door without the slightest awareness or concern that two sly and slovenly Creepers towered overhead.

It wasn't like me to want to talk to a religious leader-type person, but I wanted to meet with that preacher as soon as possible. I was hoping he could explain more about his understanding of the spiritual beings he read about in the Bible this morning. As I walked hurriedly in the direction of Ray Anne's house, I pulled up the church website on my cell, then gave them a call.

The receptionist said the minister's name was Pastor Newcombe and transferred me to his administrative assistant. I explained to her that I wanted to meet with him right away, but she said that the Senior Pastor didn't have any openings in his schedule for at least five weeks. She asked my age, then suggested I meet with the Student Pastor instead, a guy named Scott. I would have much rather met with Pastor Newcombe, not someone I'd never seen before, but I reluctantly gave her my number so Scott could call me. For all I knew, he'd turn out to be shackled.

When I got to Ray Anne's, I texted her and told her I was outside. She came out, and as we walked back toward my house, I got her caught up on things. Not everything, of course, like my involvement with Jared and Conner's deaths, but about Jared's terrifying appearance in the casket the day before, how the "Murderer" followed me home, and how two Creepers were on my roof at that very moment.

She said she'd come to my house with me but wasn't willing to climb onto my roof. I liked that she managed to keep her sense of humor through all of this. I wasn't laughing much lately.

I brought up what Pastor Newcombe said about the spiritual forces, and she explained that she'd heard and believed those scriptures all of her life. I asked her if she knew anything about the armor he mentioned, and she confirmed the obvious; it was spiritual armor, not something you physically put on.

Although my interest to learn more about those particular Bible verses was now stirred, I felt my religious tolerance meter escalating toward overload when she brought up Jesus Christ.

"Ray Anne, with all due respect, I don't believe in religion—none of that. It's all manmade and shallow."

"But a relationship with Jesus Christ isn't about religion. It's about—"

"Seriously, I get really annoyed when I feel like someone is trying to convert me."

She stopped walking, then gave a pretty compelling speech.

"Okay, Owen, here's the deal. I've already committed to be a friend to you during what you keep describing as the scariest time in your life, and like I said I would do, I've kept an open mind and been willing to consider all the bizarre stuff you've told me. That openness has to go both ways, though. You have to be willing to let me talk about things that take you out of *your* comfort zone, too. Don't you think that's only fair?"

I responded to her question with a question. "Are you sure you want to pursue a nursing career cause I think you'd make an excellent lawyer?"

She laughed, then waited for a real answer.

"Okay. I'll do my best to be more open minded. You're right. It's only fair."

"Also, don't you think it might be helpful to consider biblical claims as we try to figure out why certain people glow?"

I loved that she spoke about glowing people without the slightest hint of sarcasm, like she really believed me.

"Maybe. I just don't think I could ever . . . never mind."

"You could never what?"

Is it just me, or do females have an innate ability to coax information out of the deepest recesses of your soul?

"I just don't think I could ever become religious. Don't get me wrong. I don't mind doing good things for people and all, and I could probably manage to sit through church once in a while. But I could never see myself being a person who prays and goes around talking about God all the time like his existence is a reality or something. If that's why you glow, because you believe in all of that, then there's no hope for me and seriously no hope for my mother."

She stopped walking and placed her hands on my shoulders, looking up at me. "Owen, if religion isn't your thing, then you and I are gonna get along great," she said with a beaming grin.

I didn't know what she meant by that, but I let it go. I was weary of talking about religion. Apparently she wasn't.

"So, why do you think you and your mom are so opposed to issues surrounding faith?"

I didn't have to think long about that one. "About the only thing I know about my mother's parents is that they drug her to church every time the doors were open, then abused and neglected her at home. Her dad was actually the pastor of the church, but he was a cruel man. I've been raised knowing that religion is a farce, a smokescreen people hide behind to make them feel better about themselves.

"And also, I'm the type of person who needs proof, sensible evidence that revolves around more than faith-derived hopes."

I suddenly realized I may have just wounded her with my words, but instead of getting defensive, she said how very sorry she was to hear about my mother's difficult childhood. I really appreciated that.

"Thanks Ray."

"Did you just call me Ray?" She started laughing.

"I guess. What's the big deal?"

"Well, it's just that my little brother always called me Ray, and I loved it."

"Your little brother?"

"Yeah. He passed away when he was five. I was seven at the time. He died of cancer."

"That's awful. I'm so sorry to hear that."

"Thanks. We still miss him very, very much. Okay, I've been thinking, and how about we start keeping a list of all of the students you see at our school who glow?"

She shifted gears so fast I could hardly keep up. "Um, okay."

As we made our way down my street, we were downwind from the Creepers, and I could smell their nasty stench. Ray Anne continued talking.

"I'm thinking it might be helpful to all meet up at some point soon, you know, for all the glowing people to talk about things."

"You mean to have me humiliate myself by telling even more people about my deranged life?"

She laughed and was right in the middle of making yet another suggestion when we arrived at my driveway. The two Creepers were still on my rooftop, now pacing back and forth.

"Is something happening?" she asked.

"Yes. The Creepers are still up there, and they're visibly bothered by your presence."

"Really? Stay here." She motioned for me to stand still while she proceeded to walk all the way up my driveway. I couldn't help but think that her bravery was largely due to the fact that she couldn't actually see the hideous creatures.

The closer she got, the more frenzied they became. They finally scurried to one side of my roof, then jumped off, only they didn't drop straight to the ground. They did this eerie thing where they arched and contorted their backs and floated down. I'd never seen anything like it, but I guess that goes without saying.

The minute their filthy feet made contact with the grass, they scurried away from my house and out of sight.

Ray Anne turned and faced me. "What's happening now?" As freaky as that experience was, I couldn't resist the urge to pull a prank.

"They're walking up to you! They're about to grab you!"

Her eyes got huge, and she braced herself. "Lord, help me!" she said at the top of her lungs. It was hilarious.

I finally came clean. "I'm just kidding. You scared them off. They ran to the corner of the roof, then did this weird floating thing all the way down. They're gone now. That was awesome."

"Remind me to stay home the next time Creepers come crawling all over your house." She was only mildly mad. "You're sure they left?"

"Absolutely. You sent them packin'."

"Thank God!"

We hung out at my house for a while and then my mother drove all three of us to Ray Anne's for dinner. I didn't know what to expect from my mother. Intimate social settings were not her thing. She'd be much more comfortable at a crowded bar or hard rock concert, I'm sure. I think she felt obligated to go though since they were nice enough to invite us. This was sure to be interesting.

Mrs. Greiner ushered us into her home like a modern-day June Cleaver. She literally had on pearls. I looked over at my mom and could tell she was uncomfortable in their home, not because it was unwelcoming or messy, but because it was so welcoming. My mother was allergic to kind-hearted women. I have no idea why.

There was quite a spread on the table. Ray Anne seemed to think nothing of it, but to me, placemats, cloth napkins, and a full set of silverware felt ultra formal.

Mr. Greiner barged into the room like a cannonball, talking way too loud and with far too much enthusiasm for my mother's nerves. "Well hello! I'm so glad you could join us." His smile was on par with Santa's.

We began taking our seats around the dining room table. When Justin entered the room, my senses became overpowered by an outrageously tantalizing, unfamiliar scent. He plopped down in the chair next to mine, and I leaned slightly toward him, wondering if he was the source of the supercharged cologne. He didn't smell like anything, though.

About the time Mr. Greiner made a comment about his wife's irresistible twice-baked potatoes, that unbelievable fragrance hit me again.

"What?" Ray Anne was seated across from me and observed that I was deep in thought.

"Nothing." I didn't feel comfortable announcing that, as best I could tell, when a glowing family is all together, they give off a really invigorating scent. I'd tell her later.

I knew my mom was slightly out of her element when Mr. Greiner offered to lead us in a prayer over the meal, but when they all joined hands—clutching ours as well—I knew she was ready to bolt out the door. I found it amusing.

The food was delicious. Once we got passed the heavy-hearted discussion about Jared and Conner's funerals, there was lots of small talk. I was relieved the way my mom kept contributing to the conversation. The subject of prom came up, and she busted out, "Owen, you already have a date, right?"

"Um, no. That fell through."

"Ray Anne, do you have a date?" She asked.

"No ma'am, I don't."

Her mom jumped in at that point and explained that several guys had asked Ray Anne to prom, but she turned them down for one reason or another.

I couldn't believe what was happening. My wild-child mom and "Mrs. Manners" were actually giggling back and forth and plotting something together. I guess my mother volunteered to say what they were both thinking. "Owen, why don't you and Ray Anne go to prom together?"

"But it's just two weeks away. I don't have a dress," Ray Anne said. Of course her mother swooped in and saved the day.

"Didn't you spot one at the mall you really liked? Why don't you go buy it?"

I didn't see the look of delight on my mother's face very often, so I guess I should have cherished the moment, but I didn't. It wasn't the idea of going to prom with Ray Anne that bothered me. It was the prom itself. A stiff tux, a cheesy DJ, and a crowded dance floor crawling with Creepers isn't exactly my idea of a fun evening. I had already gotten out of having to go once, and here I was, trying to avoid it again.

The fact that our moms brought the idea up really irked me. Couldn't we decide for ourselves if we wanted to go to prom together without their "motherly" intervention?

"What do you think, Owen?" My mom wasn't about to let me off the hook.

Given the situation, there was only one thing I could say. "Sounds great."

Ray Anne's mother literally clapped, and my mom belly laughed with an unfamiliar glee. Whatever.

Seconds later, Ray and I were out the door and on our way to the mall to buy her a dress.

Guess I should have known we'd cause a scene.

12. Appalling Answers

Ray Anne drove us to the mall in her brother's car. Actually, she corrected me, it was *their* car to share. He just hogged it most of the time.

I told her about the amazing scent her family gave off at the dinner table, and she thought that was completely absurd.

As we walked into the mall, I tried to mentally prepare myself for the crowd of people—more to the point, the petrifying prevalence of Creepers. Just as I anticipated, they were everywhere, brushing through the multitudes and slithering around connected to various people. One poor soul had two Creepers attached to him. Apparently no Watchmen were coming to his rescue.

To my relief, Ray had a specific store in mind, and we headed straight there. Like cockroaches scurrying away from a blinding light, I got a kick out of watching the Creepers scatter to avoid crossing paths with my luminescent new prom date.

We walked into a mirror-clad place with fancy dresses draped from one end of the store to the other. I spied a plush seating area and made myself at home there. I was still feeling really down, but I tried to conceal my sulky mood from Ray Anne. Two funerals in two days weighed heavily on me.

Ray Anne held up a red sparkling dress and flashed a sweet smile. "This is the one I like."

"It's nice. I like the shiny things on there," I said.

"Those shiny things are called sequins." She laughed.

And that's how I became a guy who knows about sequins.

A cute, brown-headed boy who looked to be six or seven years old flopped down in the chair across from me. He had that brilliant star-like glow in his chest, so of course I stared.

His shackled mother asked him to sit there and hold her shopping bags while she went into a nearby dressing room.

"No!" He had the nerve to shove her bags off his chair and onto the floor, spilling the contents. She scolded him while picking everything up, then, looking exasperated, firmly instructed her son a second time to sit down and hold her things. He huffed, then wrapped his skinny arms around the bags. She disappeared into a dressing room at the same time as Ray Anne.

"Jordan?" The lady called out to her son.

"What!" he responded with all the attitude his pre-pubescent voice could muster.

"I just want to make sure you're still sitting there with my bags."

I was appalled at what the brat did next.

"I'm sick of holding your stupid stuff," he said while launching his mother's merchandise straight up in the air. For the second time, her belongings littered the floor.

I expected his mother to come flying out of the dressing room and tear into her unruly son. I didn't expect to see two revolting Creepers trespass right through a wall and make a beeline toward the obnoxious kid.

"Ray Anne!" I called for her help, but she didn't grasp how badly she was needed. She told me to hold on. She'd just started putting on the dress.

Not knowing what else to do, I jumped to my feet and stepped in front of the boy, as if I could somehow shield him from their double-team assault. Yeah, right.

I guess the kid didn't like me standing so close. He had the audacity to give me a swift kick in the butt. I caught my balance just in time to turn around and witness him undergo a terrorist attack of supernatural proportions.

A Creeper named "Thief" plunged its atrocious hand into the boy's small chest and literally ripped the shimmering light right out of him. The ball of illumination was then crushed into some sort of dust in the Creeper's grip. It gradually opened its misshapen fingers, releasing the ashy substance to the floor. It reminded me of the dirty stuff I saw on Jared's ravaged body.

The boy's mom finally came careening out of the dressing room. Despite having on a white formal gown, she got on her knees and began scooping up her belongings, all the while demanding that her son get down there and help. Her enraged voice echoed through the store, and by now, a handful of shoppers were rubbernecking.

That's when the other Creeper, "Condemnation," hunched over and gathered the gritty grossness off the floor into its already gross hands. I wondered what it could possibly want with the dusty remains its partner had just discarded.

Once in hand, it spit on the dirt, then massaged the polluted concoction through its bony fingers. What it did next was so off the charts freaky that I grabbed and squeezed the arm of a complete stranger standing nearby. As the boy stood up, the Creeper flung the muddy sludge off its hands and onto the child's throat, at which point the stuff started moving and molding around the kids' fragile neck.

Within seconds, it formed a shackle.

"No way!" I couldn't keep my thoughts to myself.

It turns out I had grabbed onto a young lady who worked at the store, sending her into a panic.

"Let go of me!" she said, yanking away from me. Now even more people were starring.

"Oh, I'm so—" I was about to apologize when I saw the "Thief" walk behind the boy and grab hold of the back of the oblivious kid's freshly-fashioned shackle. The Creeper began a jerky pulling motion. Each time it tugged, it let out a blood-curling shrill—not because it was straining but in sheer delight.

When I saw that it had somehow pulled a chain out of the back of the boy's cold metal collar, I called for Ray Anne again. "Can you please get out here?"

This time she sensed the urgency in my voice. "Oh, okay. I'm getting dressed now."

My eyes were glued to the boy, which made his mother uneasy, so she glared right back at me.

"Do you have a problem?" she said. I was engrossed watching the foul-smelling "Thief" run its calloused hands through the boy's wavy hair, then begin forcedly rubbing the back of the small guy's head in a circular motion. It uttered something, then two cords protruded, wiggling and contorting like disgusting worms. They grew right out of the kid's scalp.

"Ray Anne!" I yelled so loud that I startled everyone in the vicinity. That same rattled employee was now on the phone, probably with security. We needed to get out of there.

"Give me just a second," Ray Anne said. "I'm coming. Is everything okay?"

Yet again, I didn't answer. The Creepers' unpredictable behavior consumed my attention.

The one named "Condemnation" clasped its hand around its wrist, then spastically twisted back and forth, eventually pulling off a cuff that somehow formed on demand. The Creeper crouched down and attached the metal cuff to the end of the boy's bulky chain as if merely twisting yarn into place.

The repulsive perpetrators surveyed their environment with trepidation, no doubt fearing the arrival of a band of Watchmen. Still, they continued their raunchy raid.

Using their index fingers, one Creeper wrote on the boy's cords while the other etched something onto the cuff that was now lagging from the kid's chain.

Then that was it. The two delinquents disappeared behind the same wall through which they first manifested.

I wanted to get the heck out of there, but I had to see the cords up close first. I walked right over to the boy and took a lingering look.

self absorbed

rebellious

His mother pointed in my face. "Get away from him!"

"Hey, your son kicked him in the butt." I have no idea why some lady I've never met felt the need to stick up for me. Unfortunately she only spurred the protective mom to yell louder.

Ray Anne finally exited the dressing room. I grabbed her arm, and the dress in her hand flung to the floor. "We have to leave," I said.

She remained composed while pleading for an explanation.

"I'll explain later. We just really need to go."

The boy's mother called me a jerk and hurled more insults at me as we exited the store. A mob of people had stopped and were staring at us from every direction.

As if sensing I was especially vulnerable, that revolting Creeper "Murderer" stepped forward out of the gawking crowd and narrowed its eyes straight at me. To my relief, though, it quickly retreated backwards, no doubt in response to Ray Anne's presence.

We hurried to the car and locked the doors, then blasted the air conditioning. As we sat in the mall parking lot, I tried to recount the whole horrific story for Ray Anne, but I talked so fast my words slurred together. She was having a hard time following me, and as usual, she asked a million questions.

I eventually managed to explain everything to her satisfaction, and the two of us sat awestruck for a while.

We finally had some answers. We now knew how people got their shackles, chains, and cords. But I seriously despised our discovery.

"Think about it, Ray. It's only a matter of time before the sweet, brilliant light—the innocence children carry in their hearts—gets snatched and snuffed out."

While I was sure that kid had to be a bigger nuisance than most other children, I was also sure that every child, at some point, gives in to rebellion. I mean, who hasn't copped an attitude with his mother?

It was hard to accept that a shackled existence was the inevitable consequence for mankind's insubordination—an inescapable destiny that awaits every person on earth who lives long enough to defy authority.

"But not everyone is shackled," Ray Anne said. "There's obviously a way to get free."

As she drove us off the mall parking lot, I aired my offense. "Where were the Watchmen just now? They have the power to stop all of this, but they did nothing."

This experience supported my preexistent paradigm for life, and I felt the need to vent about it to Ray Anne. "Either there's no God, or there's a God who's failing miserably at governing the universe. I'm unsure about a lot of things, but not that."

She tried to speak, but I didn't give her a chance. "What kind of cruel, pathetic, narcissistic being creates life, then sits back and watches his creation get pulverized by superior enemies—enemies that, *by design*, outmatch us? Why weren't our eyes created so that we could naturally see them? Why don't we have the physical strength to kick their—"

"So God *made* that child talk back to his mother? It's God's fault the kid acted out, right?" Ray Anne was just as vocal with her opinions as I was.

"What kid doesn't talk back to his mother, Ray? Haven't you done that at some point?"

"Of course, but all that proves is that we're all inclined to do evil, and you can't pin that on God."

I was quick to respond. "If he exists, he made us this way!"

Ray Anne got quiet, and about the time I was reveling in the idea that I had deflated her argument, she countered. "What if God gave us a choice, Owen? What if this whole thing is about what we choose—*who* we choose?"

"There's no sense in talking about this any longer because God doesn't exist, anyway," I said. "We're wasting our breath. I want concrete solutions, not opinions, theories, or 'what if.' "

She was about to challenge me yet again, but her phone rang. Ray Anne's mom wanted to know how the shopping trip went. Ray chose her words carefully. "Yeah, I didn't buy the dress after all. The mall was crazy tonight. I'll come back and get it later." I could hear her mother's disappointment seeping through the phone.

"It'll still be there, Mom. It's okay. Seriously, I'll come back, maybe tomorrow."

She hung up, and I began to worry that perhaps I had spoken too harshly. I didn't want to run off the only friend I had. Besides, she was quickly beginning to feel like more than a friend to me. Honestly, I wanted to kiss her so bad it hurt.

We pulled up to a red light, and she took the lead clearing the air. "Look, I know our conversation got a little heated just now, but if you can take it, so can I." She held out her hand. "No hard feelings?"

I smiled and shook on it. "No hard feelings."

Now I really wanted to kiss her.

She parked in front of my house, and I apologized for ruining her shopping trip.

"Yeah, well, that's what I get for going to prom with a guy who sees into the spirit world." I laughed and marveled at how cute she was.

I went to bed reluctantly replaying the awful scene from the mall over and over in my mind. I also thought about Ray Anne's comment about each of us having a choice, but that only frustrated me. What choice did any of us have? I sure didn't choose to see the supernatural freak show that had completely engulfed my life.

I finally drifted off and had a horrible nightmare about being in the woods with Conner and Jared. I held two loaded guns in my hands, both aimed at their decaying heads. It was awful.

I was relieved to wake, only to realize it was the middle of the night, and I was gagging on the Creeper stench. I feared that "Murderer" was lurking in my room, perhaps hovering over my head or trudging up a wall.

I thrashed around in my bed, frantically looking in every direction. I didn't dare go to sleep these days without my closet light on, so, for the most part, I could see. I didn't spot a Creeper anywhere, but I gasped at the sight of the word "insane" written across the inside of my closet door.

"That wasn't there when I went to bed."

It really stunk in my room, but I clung to the hope that the nauseating funk was merely the aftermath of its presence. I noticed that Valentine wasn't in her usual spot on the edge of my bed. I spied her in the shadows, hunkered down in the corner of my room. Her eyes were unflinching and fixed in my direction.

"You okay, girl?" She didn't move.

I was too terrified now to stay in my bed and way too scared to get up.

"Come here, girl." Valentine responded with a low-pitched growl. Adrenaline shot through my veins.

That's when it hit me. I felt sure I knew where the "Murderer" was lurking. There was only one way to find out.

I cautiously leaned over the side of my mattress, then prepared to draw back the bed skirt. I was in the process of daring myself to peek under my bed when I spied something strange on the floor.

I bellowed out a series of profane words while springing toward my bedroom door in a single bound. A mucky foot with festering toenails was poking out from beneath my bed.

I flew down the stairs to the living room. There was my mom, sprawled out on the couch, wasted. I took careful steps toward her. That's when my heart nearly stopped for the second time in the span of less than a minute. A Creeper emerged from behind the couch.

Its name was "Torment," and it was in the process of connecting to my mother. I remained frozen until an unmistakable sound demanded that I react. The stairs popped and cracked, nearly caving under the weight of what had to be that "Murderer" headed my way.

I grabbed my mom's keys off the coffee table and darted out of the house. I felt like a deadbeat leaving my incoherent mother in a den of devils, but she was too drunk to get up and come with me. And she wouldn't believe me, anyway.

It was four o'clock in the morning. I couldn't call Ray Anne at that time of night. All I knew to do was drive around.

"Why is that Creeper after me?" I didn't have chains or cords, so I wasn't sure what it could have done to me. Then again, I didn't glow, and I clearly had no ability to repel it.

I gave zero thought to where I was going but ended up driving past my school. That's when I saw gangs of Creepers, slithering all over the place. The savages climbed the walls, scurried along the rooftop, huddled in groups in the parking lot, and converged on the front steps.

They slipped in and out of the building, evading the exterior as if it didn't exist, and lingered all the way into the eerie makeshift campgrounds behind the school.

It was a disturbing scene. I pulled over and watched, trying not to despair over the reality of how these creatures had invaded my world and infested my life.

I banged my forehead against the steering wheel, feeling sorry for myself and agonizing over humanity's plight. The foul odor crept right through my sealed windows.

It was probably a good forty-five minutes later when, one by one, the Creepers began staring in the same direction, then huddling and hunkering down.

I followed their gaze into the grassy field across from the school. And there they were—a dozen or so Watchmen. I flew of out of the car and climbed up the hood and onto the roof of my mom's BMW.

Wow. They were even more magnificent than I remembered. Their colossal bodies and brilliant illumination were glorious to behold. Their bulging muscles were a stark contrast to the Creepers' atrophied frames.

The Watchmen stood nearly motionless, their lustrous white garments fanning in the breeze, ushering their one-of-a-kind fragrance in my direction.

Their dazzling faces held stern expressions as they glared at the Creepers with disdain. I hoped they would move in and annihilate them, but instead, they began looking up toward the sunrise. Some closed their brilliant eyes while others peered out into the stars. I didn't understand it.

By dawn, most of the Creepers had retreated out of sight. I needed to leave. I didn't want to be there in my pajama pants when people started showing up for school. A few sign people were already arriving on the scene.

It was difficult to drive away. I could have stood there and gazed at the Watchmen for the rest of the day. I hated to let them out of my sight.

Had I known what was about to go down, I would have begged them to stay and insisted they come inside my school.

13. Thwarted Intervention

I was driving around in my PJs with no phone, no wallet, and no courage to enter my hijacked house. I parked out front and sat there. I had to go inside. My mom was in there with the assailants.

It occurred to me to go to Ray Anne's and beg her to come with me, but I worried that would be asking too much. I had exposed her to enough supernatural warzones in the last twenty-four hours.

I opened my front door about an inch. The contaminated smell slapped me in the face. My mom was hunched over on the couch watching TV. She spotted me.

"Hey Mom." I flung the door open and walked inside as if everything were fine and there was no Creeper brooding behind her back.

"Where were you?" Her speech was slow and muffled.

"I ran an errand." Thank God she didn't notice I took her car. That would have sent her into a tirade.

"Please go do something with that obnoxious dog of yours. She won't shut up." My mom blew her nose. Not surprisingly, she'd been crying—and already drinking despite the early hour.

Valentine was barking at the top of the stairs. I dreaded going up but told myself that if "Murderer" was going to brutalize me at some point, now was as good a time as any.

I made it to the upstairs hallway unharmed. My dog's aggression remained directed at the living room. I hoped that meant the "Murderer" was long gone out of my room.

I went straight to the bathroom and pulled Valentine in there with me.

While showering, I jerked the shower curtain back about every ten seconds for fear of what loomed on the other side. Valentine laid there on her belly, exhausted from a sleepless night. I was counting on her to warn me if an intruder breached the door.

I survived the shower. It was time for the real test. I had to go in my bedroom and get dressed.

I wanted to go to school, not just to get out of my Creeper-ridden house but because I suspected something major might go down. Two opposing cosmic forces had converged on my high school campus, and I hoped to figure out why.

I grabbed Valentine's collar and timidly opened my bedroom door. I basically shoved my dog inside, then watched her reaction. She hopped up on my bed and plopped down. I took that as a good sign.

I picked up my baseball bat and used the handle to raise the bed skirt. I had to look. There was nothing but a few random objects under my bed.

My closet door still displayed the Creeper's graffiti—"insane." That was nerve-wracking.

I was dressed and in my car in sixty seconds flat. The adrenaline high kept me wide awake. By the time I got to school, the Watchmen were gone, but the Creepers were still there, tons of them hunting in every direction.

I zipped up my jacket and headed toward my first period class. I noticed there were Creeper notes all over the place, sailing just above the floor, then landing in random corners and in the gap underneath some lockers.

I took pictures—lots of pictures. The notes all had numbers and letters like before, mostly that same combination, 0602SGM. Others had a different number and letter pattern, and some had a line through the text, like the information was dismissed for whatever reason.

I took a seat at my desk and sent Ray Anne a few of the images. She texted back: **So Freaky!**

There sat Dan with his two-tons of cords and chains, grinning at me from ear to ear like a fat hyena.

"What?" I was in no mood for his antics.

"Jess is a sweet, sweet girl," he said while winking at his equally-annoying buddy.

"Tell me you didn't do anything stupid, Jess," I thought to myself. I sent her a text: **Once again, I'm sorry about lying to you the night I went out with Ray Anne. Meet me before 2nd period OK?**

She didn't respond.

I looked for her after class, but it was nearly impossible to locate her with all the towering Creepers infringing on the hallways and stinking up the place.

"Hey Owen! You lookin' for me?" Ray Anne hopped in front of me and stopped me in my tracks. I was happy to see her.

"Yep!" I didn't think it would be polite to tell her I was actually searching for Jess.

"So now that you mentioned there were lots of notes floating around today, I've been noticing them everywhere. They look like trash or something. No one's giving them a second thought. They're too busy hanging Stella Murphy's graduation party fliers everywhere, I guess.

"Anyway, I tried touching one of the notes, but it turned to that, like, powdery mush, just like you said it would. I wrote down what was written on a few of them—"

Ray Anne's voice faded into the background. I saw Lance and Meagan hugging at his locker. My cold stomach churned. A Creeper was attached to Meagan. All Creepers are disgusting, but this one was exceptionally concerning. Its name was "Suicide."

I was grateful Ray Anne was with me. I interrupted her. "Hey, listen, I'm sorry to cut you off, but I've got to tell you something. You see Meagan over there?"

"Yeah?"

"She's linked up to a Creeper named 'Suicide.' "

"Oh, well, we've got to do something!" It was such a relief that I could count on Ray Anne, not only to believe me, but to be genuinely concerned.

"Let's get over there. Hopefully your presence will drive it away."

I walked up to Lance and greeted him as if the two of us were still best friends. He didn't return the favor. He gazed at the ground, giving me the epitome of a cold shoulder.

"Hi Meagan." Ray Anne stood right beside her, but the Creeper used Meagan like a human shield. It took several steps to the left, then Meagan did, too. Instead of it mirroring her, Meagan shadowed her parasite's every move without the slightest awareness, as if her subconscious mind was no longer her own.

Ray Anne tried inching closer, all the while looking at me for some sign of what was going on. I kept watching in frustration. Ray Anne's potency was no match for the Creeper. I assumed it had something to do with the fact that it was latched onto a human host. The thing clearly wanted to avoid Ray Anne, but it was not willing to let go of Meagan.

Where's a Watchman when you need one? I thought. Their continual absence ticked me off.

My friendship with Lance was all but ruined, but I had no choice but to try to warn him about his endangered girlfriend. "Hey, can I talk to you for a second?"

"Go ahead," Lance said with zero emotion.

"I'd like to talk by ourselves, if that's okay."

"Look, I've gotta get to class. Maybe we can talk at lunch, alright?" Lance had already turned his back and was walking away.

Even if I couldn't see the vile Creeper sucking the life out of Meagan, I still would have known something was wrong. Ray Anne agreed, she looked upset and visibly drained.

When lunch finally came, I passed up the vending machines and walked straight over to Lance. "Hey, you said we could talk now."

"No I didn't." He refused to look at me. "I said *maybe* we could talk at lunch."

"Look, I don't know why you're going out of your way to be a jerk to me, but I have to tell you something really important."

It took me by surprise when Lance grabbed my arm and pulled me away from our lunch table, forcibly yanking me as if he was ready to throw down or something. Once we were beyond earshot of our friends, he lit into me.

"Look, it's a well known fact that I think you've become psychotic, and it's also a well known fact that you were the last person to hang out with Jared and Conner."

"What are you trying to say?" I'd never seen Lance look so angry, particularly at me.

"I don't know what you did to them, but I don't think it's a coincidence that they both died the next day. You're not in your right mind. I wouldn't be surprised if it comes out eventually that you had something to do with their deaths."

His words punctured my conscience. I was speechless. He was spot on.

My mind went reeling. I diverted my eyes to the floor, a gesture that may as well have been a full blown admission of guilt. I didn't have it in me to try and fabricate a defense.

I was just about to throw in the towel and walk away when I saw Meagan approaching. I pulled it together. "Lance, you've got to listen to me. Your girlfriend is in danger."

"What the hell are you talking about?" He was in no mood to listen to anything I had to say.

"She needs help. I think she might try to harm herself, even kill herself."

He rolled his eyes. "I think I would know if my girlfriend was suicidal. Stay away from her. Stay away from both of us." He got halfway to our lunch table, then turned back toward me. "You're the one who needs help, Owen."

His comment caught the attention of our friends. They gawked at me like I belonged in a leper camp. How ironic. They were the ones being devoured by a paranormal plague. I was just trying to help.

I decided I would go sit on a bench outside until lunch was over. I craved the sun's warmth. But before I got there, Jess returned my text: **What do u want?**

R u ok? Where r u?

She responded immediately. **Stayed home today. Why do u care?**

I chose my words carefully. **Dan was acting weird. I wanted to make sure you're ok.**

She didn't text back.

I passed Lance and Meagan in the parking lot after school. They snubbed me. I pitied them.

I came home to an empty house and relied on my sense of smell and my dog's demeanor to determine if my home was safe or not. I didn't pick up on a Creeper scent, and Valentine was docile, so I proceeded inside and slowly sank into the sofa.

The word "guilty" inscribed above my living room window was now fading. That was a pleasant observation.

Ray Anne texted me, and we agreed to venture back to the mall in an hour or two to get her prom dress. I was surprised she wanted to bring me along, but she seemed to really want me there. I told her I was hanging at the house by myself, hoping nothing attacked me. She thought that was funny. I wasn't kidding, though.

I flipped on the TV and dozed off at some point but was startled by a knock at the door. I figured it was Ray Anne, but a quick glance through the peephole proved otherwise.

It was Jess, and she looked terrible.

I stepped outside and could tell she had been bawling her brown eyes out. Trails of black makeup tainted her cheeks.

"Jess, what's the matter?"

She shrugged her shoulders.

"What's the matter? Talk to me."

She turned and charged down my driveway in a lousy attempt to leave, but I stopped her. "Look, I'm sorry for what happened the other night, but I'm here for you. I really am. Why don't you just tell me what's going on?"

She and I took a seat at the edge of my driveway, and I tried not to react to the sound of her chains screeching against the pavement. I stayed quiet and waited for her to spill her guts.

"I'm so confused Owen." Her voice quivered. "I think Dan cares about me, but I'm not sure, and now it's too late, anyway."

She didn't have to elaborate. I knew what she meant. He was after her body from day one, and he obviously got what he wanted.

"It wasn't what I thought it would be," she said, crumpling a tissue. "I wanted it to be special, to feel close and loved, but instead it left me feeling lonely. And it brought back horrible memories." She buried her face in her hands. I assured her she didn't have to hide anything from me.

"No, I can't tell anyone," She said. "I promised."

"Jess, who did you promise? What did you promise? You can tell me."

She raised her weary head and swallowed her tears. Through an avalanche of emotion, she proceeded to describe how her dad's brother, Uncle Jeff, came to live at their house for three months several years ago when he was going through a divorce. Her parents welcomed him to stay in their guestroom.

It took her a while to say it, but she finally made a painstaking confession. "He didn't stay in his room at night. He came into my room. He took advantage of me, Owen. I was only twelve."

She became hysterical while explaining how she confided in her mother, and together, they told her father, but he accused her of exaggerating. He made her promise never to talk about it, to put it out of her mind and get past it.

"My mom has wanted to leave him ever since, but she says we can't afford to. My dad still hangs out with my Uncle like nothing happened."

She fell into my arms, chains and all, and I hugged her as tightly as I could. My heart broke for her. I wanted to find her uncle and rip him to shreds.

In that instant, something occurred to me. Two things, actually.

The name on one of Jess's chains was Jeff Thompson. Uncle Jeff, I now realized. And her dad's name was on the other one. That made more sense now. But there was a new realization: Jess had a third chain today. I had a sick feeling about whose name was on there.

While squeezing her anguished body, absorbing her tears into the sleeve of my shirt, I could see the cuff.

daniel quinton mitchell

Dan. How disgusting. That reprobate, sorry excuse for a man was now baggage around Jess's neck, a worthless weight she'd carry around for the rest of her life.

I had to pull back and let go of Jess. The chill of her chains was freezing my arms, but I continued my attempt at consoling her.

"Jess, I'm so sorry to hear—"

A Creeper passed through my neighbor's fence across the street and was staring right at us, making strides in our direction. I cleared my throat and jumped to my feet.

"Get up."

"What?" I'm sure Jess found my swift change in behavior confusing, but I didn't have time to coddle her.

"We have to get in the car, right now."

"I'm not going anywhere." Her defiant attitude was in full swing.

I feared it was that familiar "Murderer" coming to bully me, but it was close enough now that I could see its name was "Misery."

"Would you please get up?" I reached down and grabbed her arm, intending to pull her onto her feet, but she resisted and slapped my hand away.

"We're in danger, Jess. Please trust me. Stand up!"

"Oh, I get it. This is another one of your delusions." She scoffed while I panicked. "Misery" was closing in.

It was clear I wasn't going to get her obstinate butt off the ground. The Creeper stopped less than two feet from us. That's when I realized its comatose eyes were locked on Jess.

It began encircling us. I flung myself on top of her in a futile effort to shield her.

"What are you doing?" I was smothering her, sheltering her from the harmless warm breeze and pine trees, as far as she was concerned.

"Misery" continued stalking, encircling us. It finally stopped behind Jess, then lowered to the ground.

"Leave her alone!" My rebuke didn't hinder the Creeper one iota. It only served to aggravate Jess all the more.

"Stop it, Owen. You're freaking me out."

I knew of just one way to get its attention. I lifted my head and belted out, "Misery!"

The fangled-tooth freak snapped its head at me and came to a standstill for a moment, then went right back to inspecting Jess's chains. A lot of good that did.

There was nothing I could do but sit there and watch someone I cared about be violated. It didn't surprise me that the thing came to attack when Jess was down and out. That's what cowardly calculating opponents do.

I embraced Jess even tighter than before and watched as the Creeper zeroed in on a particular cuff. It was in the process of extending its arm and about to insert its wrist when it suddenly rose to its feet and took off.

I thought perhaps a Watchman was nearby. I turned to look, and there stood Ray Anne, no doubt shocked to discover Jess wrapped in my arms.

She looked devastated. "I thought I'd walk over here since we were going to go to the mall."

She took off jogging toward her house.

"Ray Anne!" I called out to her, but she didn't turn back.

"What did *she* want?" Jess said.

"Don't be rude. She just saved you." There was no use in trying to explain what I meant by that.

I stood there knowing I had really hurt Ray Anne. And knowing that really hurt me.

14. Group Attack

The environment at school on Thursday was just like the day before—cold and crawling with Creepers. The only thing worse than seeing Meagan still attached to that "Suicide" stalker was not seeing Ray Anne all day. She was purposely avoiding me.

I went straight to the mall after school to buy the red dress. I guessed at Ray Anne's size. The lady behind the register was less than thrilled to see me. She was the uptight sales associate I clung to the other day when that kid was being accosted.

The total was one hundred and ninety seven dollars. I whipped out the credit card my mom gave me to use in case of an emergency. Knowing I had wounded Ray Anne felt like an emergency to me.

I popped in another store and bought her a sparkly journal. I figured all girls like journals. When I got in my car, I turned to the first page and wrote, "I feel like these pages, empty inside. I want to keep writing our story. Please forgive me and allow me to explain."

Pretty impressive poetic expression, if I do say so myself.

I knocked on Ray Anne's door. I was disappointed when her brother Justin answered and even more disappointed when he said she wasn't available to talk. I handed him the dress and journal and asked him to please give them to Ray Anne. He set them on a nearby chair, then came back to the door.

"Are you okay?" He and I had never said much to each other, so I wasn't expecting his pointed question. I responded with the truth for a change.

"Not really. Your sister is mad at me, and she's the only friend in the world I have right now."

"What happened to all of your friends?" He and I ran in different circles, so I guess he hadn't heard what an outcast I'd become.

"They're just giving me a hard time lately." I chose not to mention that I also recently killed two of them.

"About what?"

"It's not worth talking about. Seriously. You wouldn't believe me, anyway."

He stepped outside and said, "Try me."

So I did.

"Lately I've been seeing things that other people can't."

"Yeah?"

I hesitated. "Are you sure you want to hear this? It's really strange."

He encouraged me again to keep talking.

"I see scary things everywhere, scary beings actually. They prey on people and mess with their minds and lives."

He responded like a doctor meticulously considering my symptoms. "Okay. Do you believe what you're seeing is real or imagined?"

"Of course, I thought it was all in my head at first, some horrific hallucinogenic state. But there's too many things that add up now. I feel sure it's real. Well, mostly sure."

"And you've told my sister about this?"

"Yeah. She seems to believe me. Also—this is gonna sound ridiculous—but your family gives off this light that actually repels the Creepers away. I call the things 'Creepers.' Anyway, Ray has really helped me out on a couple of occasions."

The expression on his face while contemplating my claims reminded me of his sister.

I was suddenly full of regret. Why did I open my big mouth? I sounded like a nut case. I couldn't read him. "You think I'm delusional, right?"

"Well, I don't know anything about Creepers, but I do believe in demonic power. There are plenty of stories in the Bible about evil forces, only people couldn't see them or anything. They could just see how crazy the demons made people."

I couldn't tell if he was saying he believed that I was seeing demons, or that demons were making me crazy.

"I don't know much about the Bible. I'm not into that sort of thing."

He laughed. "I think if I was seeing evil beings it would inspire a sudden interest."

"Well, I've never considered the Bible to be credible or worth my time."

"Have you read it?"

I wanted to repeat myself, but that would have come off as rude, so I simply said, "No, I haven't."

"You should read through the Gospels. There are multiple real accounts of demonic activity."

On numerous occasions, Ray Anne had also suggested I was seeing demons, but I considered that theory on par with an alien invasion or goblin infestation. They all lacked reliable proof. And since I didn't know what the Gospels were and I didn't own a Bible, it was difficult to take Justin's advice seriously. He somehow picked up on that.

"Do you have a Bible? I can give you one."

Before I could answer he went inside and came back with a thick, maroon-colored Bible. Ray Anne had offered to give me one multiple times, but I always managed to leave without it.

"Here, you can have it. I would suggest starting in the book of John."

I was more likely to throw the book *in* the john than actually sit down and read it, but I responded with words of gratitude, nonetheless. And I had to admit, I was growing curious about the demon stuff.

I waved goodbye to Justin, then tossed the Bible onto my backseat, all the while lamenting the fact that I had nowhere to go but home. I was dying to talk to Ray.

As I turned onto my street, I pondered why it was that glowing people, like Ray Anne and Justin, for example, took my observations seriously, but all of the shackled people I confided in dismissed me as deranged and my stories as psycho babble. *What's up with that?* I wondered.

A dark blue truck nearly took up my entire driveway, and I knew exactly what that meant: my mom and her boyfriend were all over each other on the couch. Sure enough, there they were, giggling like juveniles while my mom sat in his lap. Gross.

"Hey Owen!" She spoke to me like we had a thriving mother-son relationship.

"Hey." I spoke like I felt. Crappy.

"Do me a favor, sweetie. Run to Walmart and pick up the cake I ordered. It's Frank's birthday."

That's what I wanted to do with my evening—celebrate her shackled boyfriend's birthday.

"And grab some candles while you're at it."

Frank and my mother started laughing again. Whatever.

I blared my music and drove as fast as I wanted. I wondered how Ray Anne responded when Justin gave her the dress and journal and how long it would be before I heard from her. For a few fleeting moments, I was so focused on my desire to make up with Ray Anne that I didn't think about the supernatural world. The mental distraction didn't last long, though.

I came to a stoplight and glanced to my left. There were two ragged, shackled homeless people under the overpass, but that's not what made my skin crawl. It was seeing half a dozen Creepers swarming around them that made me feel sick.

I watched as the invisible bullies tormented, badgered, and even slapped the destitute man and weather-worn woman. In what looked to be an attempt to defend themselves, the two street people shouted at the Creepers. The distressed man reared back and threw a weary punch in the direction of one of his savage attackers, but it passed right through its dingy garments.

Someone honked at me. I hadn't noticed the light turn green. I proceeded through the intersection, musing over this new realization.

All my life, I pitied babbling street wanderers as a mentally deranged sliver of humanity that slipped through society's cracks. I assumed their insanity sabotaged all hope of coping with the demands of life, so they roamed the earth disconnected from reality. But that's not what I just witnessed. Those homeless people were under attack, and they could see the Creepers, or at least sense their presence.

I wondered, "What if those two street people gave up on a normal life and removed themselves from society because no one believed them, no one empathized with their plight or gave credence to their brutal Creeper-filled reality?"

As I continued to drive, I wrestled with a devastating conclusion. I would likely be under that bridge with them someday, suffering and swinging at Creepers alongside them.

The more I thought about it, the more I wanted to talk with those homeless people and ask some questions, but not without Ray Anne. I needed her light to drive away the Creepers if there was any hope of carrying on a conversation.

I fought my way to a parking spot in the crowded Walmart lot. I was used to seeing a mob of Creepers at my school and here and there around town, but this was ridiculous. The store was overrun with them. Who knew Walmart was the Creeper capital of the world?

I kept my head down and covered my nose the best I could while fetching Frank's cake from the bakery. I was on my way to grab some birthday candles when a blonde lady slammed her shopping cart into mine. I was in no mood to put up with a dingbat who couldn't steer a grocery cart, but I chilled out when I realized she was distracted by a gang— all of her children. There was a slobbering baby in the basket and three more little people bouncing around her. One tiny girl was throwing a tantrum. Her exasperated, shackled mom told her to be quiet, but the headstrong girl shouted for all the world to hear.

The lady looked upset. She had no choice but to momentarily leave her basket to go chase down her son, and that's when I decided to have a little talk with the stubborn girl.

"You better do what your mother says."

"I don't have to."

I leaned in and spoke right into her pouty, miniature face. "Oh yes, you do. Cause if you don't, an evil monster is gonna come charging down this isle and rip the light right out of your puny little chest, then crush it into a million disgusting pieces and plaster it around your skinny neck where it will stay and choke you forever."

Her eyes were glued wide open like I'd scared her to death. I guess I was a little too blunt. But I'd never claimed to be great with children, and my dreary mood didn't help. At least I told her the truth. Her mom returned, and I continued pushing my basket like nothing happened.

I grabbed some candles and got into the shortest checkout line I could find, then perused the chewing gum selection, all the while hoping Ray Anne would call me. When it was almost my turn to checkout, a heavy-set lady cut in front of me. Apparently the guy in line ahead of me was her boyfriend. As luck would have it, she was linked up to a Creeper.

Its back was to me, so I couldn't see its name. I only knew that it was way too close to me. Wouldn't you know it; the cashier stopped and called for a manager to come over and fix something. So there I stood, gagging with each passing minute. I looked around for a shorter checkout line, but didn't see one.

"God, it stinks." I thought I spoke under my breath. Apparently I didn't.

"Excuse me?" The woman in front of me spun around and challenged me right to my face.

"Did you just say that I stink?" She did one of those body rolls and jerked her neck with each syllable.

"Oh, no," I said. "I was talking about—"

What an idiot. I pointed to the Creeper as if they could see and understand that I was referring to it, not them. The problem was my finger was now pointing directly at her boyfriend.

"Oh no you didn't," she said.

For the first time in my life, I thought a woman was gonna beat me up.

She turned to the rather large man by her side. "Did you hear what that fool just said about you?"

He glared at me in disbelief, along with the cashier and the wide-eyed family behind me.

"No!" I tried to salvage the situation. "You guys don't stink at all."

"Yes they do." The little boy in line behind me felt the need to chime in.

The insulted man pointed in my face. "You better shut your son up!"

"He's not my son!"

"Hey!" The boy's mother was offended. "Who are you telling to shut up?"

"Just stop." I raised my voice. "This is crazy."

That's when the cashier intervened, though his foreign accent made it difficult to fully understand him. "Sir, please refrain from calling our customers crazy. No one is crazy here."

"I didn't call anyone crazy."

"Yes you did." The little instigator was at it again.

"Son, leave the mean young man alone."

"What? I'm not mean," I said.

"Yes, you are, sir. You are a mean one," the cashier said.

I was the only one who disagreed.

I'd had enough. I pulled some cash from my pocket and tossed it onto the counter. "Keep the change." I pushed my squeaky shopping cart out of the store as fast as it would go.

I chucked the bright-colored cake into the backseat of my car and drove home feeling paranoid that the disgruntled couple was after me. I didn't begin to calm down until I passed my neighborhood entrance. That's when I allowed myself to have a much-needed laugh. The look on that lady's face when I pointed to her boyfriend was hilarious— in hindsight, of course.

I set the cake on the kitchen counter, then excused myself and got back in my car. I'm sure my mother would have preferred that I stay and sing Happy Birthday to her boyfriend, but I didn't feel the need to play house with her man of the month, thank you.

It was getting dark. I decided to drive past Ray Anne's house. Yes, it was stalker-like of me, but I was desperate for an opportunity to explain to her what really happened with Jess, who, by the way, was once again not returning my texts.

Nothing new to report at Ray Anne's. She was still barricading herself inside.

I went ahead and drove back down the stretch of freeway where I had seen the two homeless people, but they were gone. That's when I pulled into a random parking spot in front of a shopping center. I rolled down the windows, killed the ignition, and just sat with my tormented thoughts for a while.

I eventually turned on my interior light and reached into the backseat for the bulky Bible. I flipped to the back to see if there was a glossary or something. Sure enough, there was a dictionary and concordance. I looked up the word "demon," and it said, "A wicked spirit sent from the devil. Sometimes demons lived in people, but Jesus could force them to come out."

I scanned down with my pointer finger until I landed on the word "devil," which was defined as, "Satan; formerly Lucifer; a spirit being; the enemy of God and human beings."

A spiritual enemy. I never would have believed in such a thing a month ago, but I was forced to consider it now.

There were references to look up stories involving demons, but just as I was getting ready to flip to one, my phone rang. It was Jess.

"Hey. Where are you?" she asked. I could tell in her voice that she was upset.

"I'm out. Where are you?"

"I'm parked in front of your house. Can you come home?"

"Yeah, but let's meet somewhere else." The last thing I wanted was for Ray Anne to happen to drive by my house and see me with Jess again.

We agreed to meet at Franklin Park. I wasn't excited about that location—it'll always remind me of the day I became a murderer—but I went ahead and conceded.

I pulled into the parking spot right next to Jess's car, but she wasn't there. The only lit area was the basketball courts, and she wasn't there either. Finally she called out to me, and I walked in the direction of her voice. I could barely see.

The warm breeze blew in my face, carrying a disgusting smell. I feared the obvious.

"Hey. Thanks for coming." Jess spoke with a stuffy nose.

She sat motionless on a swing, the silhouette of a hulking Creeper right behind her. I pulled out my cell and shined it on them both.

"Get that light out of my face," she said.

It was that same Creeper, "Misery." It got its vile hands on her after all.

I put my cell in my pocket and endured standing there in the dark just a few feet away from a Creeper.

"I'm sorry. I didn't know who else to call. I'm just feeling really—"

"Miserable?" I finished her sentence.

"Yeah, I guess."

I was willing to listen, but I had no advice for her. I knew the source of her misery, but I had no clue how to make things better. I couldn't free her no matter how much I wanted to.

I saw the Creeper hunch over and mouth something directly into Jess's ear. She started crying. "I feel like I can't go on."

The Creeper whispered again. "I don't have the strength to keep going," she said.

Again, the foul beast injected her soul with another lie. "My life is one big mistake." She struggled to catch her breath.

"That's not true," I said. "You're being told lies!"

"No I'm not. It's the truth—the ugly, miserable truth."

I couldn't hug her, not while she was linked up to a Creeper, so I did my pleading from an arm's length away.

"Jess, remember what you said to me in the woods, how sometimes you experience these intense feelings of sadness, or, like, depression?"

"Yeah?"

"Well there's a reason for that—an invisible, spiritual reason." I realized I was likely wasting my breath, but I had to try. "Misery is a spirit of sorts, and I see it. It just now snarled at me when I said its name. It's real, Jess. Please believe me. You really *are* being told lies!"

She wiped her face and stared off into the distance for a moment, then stood and took steps in the direction of her car. "Thanks for listening." She sounded grateful, but her reaction perplexed me.

"So, do you believe me?"

She stopped and turned around. "I want to, but I just can't. We're all handling the stress in different ways, and I guess you're choosing to invent delusions to try and escape reality."

How infuriating. I didn't have time to defend myself though. I bolted in the direction of my car, passing her up.

"Why are you in such a hurry?" she asked.

I had just spotted a Creeper staring at me from the basketball court and had a strong hunch it was that "Murderer" that had been tracking me for days.

I was also anxious to get home and do some research on demons. I hoped to find a few answers that would ultimately be a source of comfort. Unfortunately what I discovered was far from comforting.

15. Oblivious People

I stayed up until three o'clock in the morning learning everything I could about demons, looking up biblical references involving them and reading all kinds of stories online about people claiming to have seen or experienced demonic activity. Even after all the scary things I'd witnessed lately, the accounts freaked me out.

While many people described sensing the presence of evil beings, others testified to having been fully possessed by them, losing all control over their own bodies and minds. I'd never seen a Creeper attack escalate to that point, but I imagined it was possible.

What would I do if that "Murderer" tried to overpower me and exercise complete control? I had no way to stop it.

I finally crawled into bed, but even with my overhead light and bedside lamp on, I was too paranoid to close my eyes.

I was starting to think Justin and Ray Anne were right. Maybe the Creepers were actually demons, though I'd have a hard time calling them anything but Creepers at this point. I laid there dreading the thought of being attacked and, not just tormented, but possessed by them. I preferred that my head *not* spin 360-degrees and that my face remained intact, as opposed to contorting to look like a rat or snake.

I'm telling you, the stories were horrific. I'd never seen the Creepers do some of the things I read about, but I was sure they had the power.

What blew my mind was the possibility that the same invisible tormentors that violated humanity thousands of years ago—perhaps from the beginning of time—were still preying on people today. Our lives on earth come and go, but Creepers never stop hunting humans, no matter how many generations pass. How unfair.

Ray Anne texted me Friday morning, and although I was totally exhausted, I was elated to hear from her. She suggested we talk that afternoon, and I told her I'd stop by her house later.

The environment at school was typical—Creepers everywhere, their confusing notes littering the place—my new normal. Some people made a big deal out if it being Friday the thirteenth, but I could see with my own eyes that the infamous date was just a cultural superstition; it had zero significance among forces of evil.

Other than being bombarded by Stella Murphy who pressed me for a commitment to attend her beach house party the night of graduation, people pretty much left me alone. I didn't engage them either.

Thank God I decided to stop off at the upstairs water fountain after school, otherwise I would have missed him. There was an enormous Watchman standing in front of the window at the end of the hallway. This time I found the nerve to approach him. I wasn't about to miss this opportunity to plead for his help.

The smell was like an out-of-this-world mixture of expensive soap, men's cologne, and a scented candle, all smoldering together. I savored the stark contrast from the usual stench.

As I stood near him, I could hardly fathom the size of his armor-clad feet or the massiveness of his chiseled stature. The glistening crown on his head nearly grazed the ceiling. His chin was lifted along with his superhuman eyes as if he were gazing out into the universe.

I could only sneak brief glances at him. He was unbelievably bright. I was intimidated but determined to speak to him. I did my best to look up at him while making my case.

"Sir?" I didn't know how else to address him. "Certain people I really care about have these awful Creepers— demons, you might say—clinging to them, and I was hoping you could help me free them."

He didn't budge.

"Can you hear me?"

Still no response.

After multiple reserved appeals, desperation took over. "Please, I'm begging you. I need your help. We all do! Will you please help us defeat our attackers? I know you see

205

what they're doing to us. They're everywhere. I don't know what to do!"

When he still didn't flinch, I began flailing my arms and shouting, "Hey, I'm here! Do you see me? Please talk to me!"

The longer he overlooked my presence, the angrier and louder I became. "Why are you ignoring me? Why are you here if you're just gonna stand there and do nothing? Don't you see we're being tormented? Why won't you do something? Do you care about us at all?"

Nothing I did won his attention.

"Owen?" I turned around and faced Principal Maxwell along with a dozen or so classmates who stood gawking and laughing at me. "It's time to clear out of here and go home."

I was really surprised she didn't hand me a pink slip and insist I go talk to a counselor. I walked away majorly discouraged, continuously glancing back at the stunning, silent Watchman.

"Why wouldn't he acknowledge me?" I vented to myself all the way home.

At last, it was four o'clock. That's when Ray and I agreed I would come over and finally get to set the record straight. I wasn't expecting her to come to the door with curlers in her hair, but she was getting ready for her Spring Show dance performance.

We sat on a sun-bleached bench on her front porch. She spoke first.

"Here's the deal. You and I are just friends, and I know that. You're free to see whoever you want. The reason I got so angry the other day—and stayed angry—is because I felt like you lied to me. You told me you were just hanging out alone at the house, and then suddenly I found you hanging all over Jess."

Even though she said we were just friends, I got the sense that she didn't like seeing me in someone else's arms. I was glad about that. I wouldn't want her snuggling up with someone else either.

I dove right into a factual explanation of how Jess had stopped by my house unexpectedly and how a Creeper approached us and began stalking Jess. I explained that we weren't hugging. I was just trying to protect her.

"Ray, you walked up and saved the day. The Creeper ran. Seriously, I didn't lie to you. I promise." I could tell she was softening up.

"I guess I may have overreacted. I just don't deal well with people lying to me."

I assured her I understood, then told her how the "Misery" Creeper did eventually catch Jess, and how it was probably still linked to her at that very moment. I also told her about the homeless people trying to fight off a gang of Creepers and about the standoffish Watchman I saw just over an hour ago. Like always, she did her best to take it all in and follow my wacky tale of events.

As I stood to leave, I asked her, "Are we still on for prom next weekend?"

She took my breath away with one of those ridiculously sweet smiles of hers and said yes, we were still on. Then she asked me if I was coming to Spring Show, and I told her I wouldn't miss it. I felt my cold cheeks becoming warm. Just having her stare at me was enough to send me into orbit.

I went to Spring Show that evening knowing both Jess and Ray Anne would be performing. I brought flowers for Ray Anne and reminded myself I didn't owe it to Jess to bring her anything. She called me up when she needed a shoulder to cry on, but that was the extent of our relationship now.

It felt weird entering the auditorium by myself, without one single friend to hang with. Jess's dad waved at me, and I did my best to wave back, but I had lost all respect for him.

I wasn't sure what to expect when the curtains opened. How would Jess perform with a Creeper tied to her back? When I finally spotted her on the stage among the girls, "Misery" was no longer linked up to her. Unfortunately I spied the vulture in the back of the auditorium.

After the show, I waited with Justin and Mr. and Mrs. Greiner for Ray to come out of the dressing room. Once she met up with her family, that same awesome scent permeated the air, just like I smelled while having dinner at their house. She liked the flowers I gave her, and I loved the fact that things were cool between us again.

I actually slept fairly well that night for a change, with all of my lights on, of course.

I rolled out of bed on Sunday morning and spotted a bright yellow package on my bedside table with a milk chocolate bunny inside. My mom gave me one every year on Easter.

I got dressed and went for a drive. I pulled up across the street from the huge church where Conner's funeral took place, the church that was supposed to have someone call me back, but never did.

I sat in my car and people-watched, hoping to discover if there was any connection between going to church and being shackle-free. What I observed was a slightly higher number of glowing people coming in and out of the church than I normally saw, but lots of shackled people were there, too. They were all dressed in their Sunday best, giving zero outward indication that there was any significant difference from one person to the next, but with my paranormal vision, it was as blatant as night and day.

I had already previously observed that, in some families, not every member was shackle-free, but this stakeout really made that obvious. There were glowing people married to shackled people and shackled kids walking alongside their glowing parents, and then glowing kids whose parents were dragging chains. It was official: being a "light" was not an inherited trait.

The church marquee read, "Prayer changes everything."

Interesting.

On the drive home, in the privacy of my car, I decided to give the prayer thing a whirl. I wasn't so much motivated by faith—I still had none. It was curiosity that got the best of me.

"God, it's hard for me to believe in you, but I'm gonna give this a try." I felt like a moron, like I was bearing my soul to my steering wheel. "Will you please keep the Creepers away from my mom, Jess, Meagan—the people I care about and the others at my school? Thank you. The end."

I spent the rest of the evening watching TV, doing my laundry, and adding to my timeline of events. And I talked to Ray Anne on the phone for a long time.

By Monday morning, the intensity of the supernatural world was definitely stirring at my school. The sign people and campers were strange like always, but there were even more putrid Creepers. They clung to walls, intruded through closed doors, and clustered together in groups. They looked focused and restless, and there was no doubt in my troubled mind that they were preparing for something big, planning to execute a terrible plan of some kind.

I saw Jess in the hallway, and "Misery" had resumed its position, bound to her through a chain and cord. So much for prayer changing everything. Prayer hadn't changed *anything.*

Jess smiled at me from across the hall as if trying to assure me she was fine. Yeah, right.

There were lots of people linked up to Creepers. It was upsetting.

During second period, all the seniors were called down to an assembly in the auditorium so we could learn what to expect on graduation day. Oddly enough, I was getting accustomed to the sound of chains dragging the hallway floors and slapping up and down the stairs. Unfortunately the freezing sensation in my stomach bugged me every second of every day and all hours of the night.

I imagined that at other schools, students were hyper and excited during assemblies about graduation, but there was no positive energy among my classmates whatsoever. Our senior class had dwindled down to half the size it was our freshman year. Students were either dead or had moved to another school to escape the curse.

I spotted Ray Anne and took a seat next to her at the end of a row, then noticed Lance and Meagan were seated directly in front of us. The "Suicide" Creeper was no longer attached to Meagan, at least for the moment.

Ray Anne and I texted back and forth about prom. She lined out the plan—pictures at her house with friends, followed by dinner at Branson's Steakhouse, then on to the prom at the Reagan Hotel. I was looking forward to spending the evening with Ray, but still less than thrilled about the prom scene.

I came home after school and did something I hadn't done in ages—homework—all the while peering out the breakfast room window for fear that "Murderer" was trespassing onto our property.

My mom came home from work around six o'clock and extended an unexpected invitation. She invited me to dinner. We sat in a booth at Gringos Mexican Restaurant and somehow both got a major case of the giggles. It was great.

I wanted so badly to confide in her, to warn her about how the Creepers were exploiting her and afflicting her life, but I was afraid.

After our meal, as we dove into a fresh batch of sopapillas, she became very serious. "Are you doing okay, Owen?"

"Sure." She could tell my answer was dishonest.

"You've made some outlandish statements lately, and you seem really on edge all of the time. I've also noticed Lance and your other friends haven't been coming around. What's going on? I know Jared and Conner's deaths were difficult for you, but is there something I should know? I'm worried about you."

There was something she desperately *needed* to know, but I was reluctant to say it. How miserable. I could try and assure her I was fine and she had nothing to worry about, in which case she would likely know I was full of crap, or I could tell her the brutal truth and endure harsh criticism and compound her concerns.

I tried a backdoor approach. "You know how you and I have never been the type of people who believe in spiritual things? Well, I've had some experiences recently that are making me question things—everything really."

She appeared to be taking me seriously, so I plunged deeper. "I've always needed to see something in order to believe it, but that's just it, Mom. I've been seeing spiritual things—spiritual *beings*."

She leaned away from me and took a deep breath. I didn't know how to take that. I waited for a response. She motioned for the waiter. "I'll have a margarita to go, please."

That was my mom. When in doubt, get the alcohol out.

"What exactly are you seeing?" Her tone was accusatory.

"Well . . ." I hesitated. "I see evil things attaching themselves to people. They hate people—all of us, for some reason."

"Yeah, you mentioned that before." She was referring to the night she came downstairs with a Creeper, and I confronted them both. She didn't believe me then; I don't know why I thought she would believe me now, but I gave it my all.

"I know it sounds ludicrous, but why would I lie about this?"

She wasn't buying it.

"Mom, there are these disgusting Creepers that—"

"Disgusting what?"

"I call them Creepers. It's just something I made up, but I think they may actually be demons."

That was it. She went ballistic. "You sound just like my parents! They blamed everything on demons! I couldn't do anything without them warning me about demons!"

"Really? Did they ever say anything about seeing them?" My zeal offended her.

She dropped her chin and glared at me. "Of course not. They were cruel and irrational, but they weren't crazy."

Umm . . . no offense taken, Mom.

I drove us home and hoped we wouldn't get pulled over and busted for having alcohol in the car. My mom didn't concern herself with such things.

We listened to the radio, and she quizzed me to see if I knew the meaning of Latin root words such as "acidus," which was her way of avoiding more talk about paranormal apparitions. She was one of the few females on the planet who could care less about bringing closure to a situation. We would no doubt go on living our dysfunctional lives under the same Creeper-ridden roof without discussing the outlandish claims I just presented to her, for the second time.

We arrived at our house, and I was surprised to see Mrs. Greiner's car. What was Ray Anne's mom doing on our doorstep? I didn't know why she was there, but I was glad. Her presence helped keep the spiritual atmosphere clean, if even momentarily.

My mother handed me her margarita cup and greeted Mrs. Greiner with superficial enthusiasm, then invited her inside. Mrs. Greiner respectfully declined to come in and explained, "I'm hosting a prayer meeting at my house at ten o'clock tomorrow morning. Some moms are getting together to pray for the Lincoln Forest students and our community. I realize your work load may conflict, but I wanted you to know you're invited."

The expression on my mother's face was priceless. She tried to look grateful, but wasn't able to mask her uneasiness. "I'll be there if I can."

Not likely.

They stood in our driveway and chit-chatted for a while, mainly about prom. Mrs. Greiner made sure my mom knew to be at her house at five o'clock on Saturday evening to take photos. She eventually left, and my mother and I went inside our graffiti-stained house. She turned on the TV right away, hoping to drown out the awkwardness looming between us. I had something to say, though.

"Mom, I'm sure you aren't considering going to that prayer meeting tomorrow, but I just wanna assure you, it would be a serious waste of your time. I know for a fact that prayer doesn't change a thing."

That's when my dog started barking. My heart skipped a beat, and I discovered I had yet another enemy in pursuit of my soul. A Creeper named "Faithless" came charging through the living room wall right at me. I ran out the front door and sprinted all the way to Ray Anne's. I didn't look back. If the vile thing was behind me, I didn't want to know.

Ray Anne came outside, and I tried telling her about the Creeper while straining to catch my breath. It was no surprise that she had some questions for me.

"What were you doing when the Creeper showed up?"

"I was talking to my mom."

"What did you say right before it appeared?"

I had to think about it a second. "I told my mom I know for a fact that prayer doesn't change anything."

"Way to go, Owen."

"What?"

"Don't you get it?" she said, placing her hands on her appealing hips.

"You think that somehow summoned the thing?" I asked.

"Yes, I do. Your faithless comment led it right to you."

That was hard for me to believe.

Speaking of unbelievable . . .

16. Desirable Date

Ray Anne was nice enough to come with me to my house to help run off that "Faithless" Creeper, but it was nowhere to be found. I drove her home anguishing over the inevitable—it would reappear soon.

Experiences like that made me all the more desperate to figure out why certain people glowed. I'd give anything to have the power to drive Creepers away.

I hardly slept. I was on edge all night.

When I got to school on Tuesday morning, there was talk about another suicide, but it turned out to be a false alarm. There was a girl who was deathly ill, but rumor somehow had it that she hung herself. How the facts can become that warped and exaggerated is beyond me.

I passed Lance and Meagan on my way to second period, and that "Suicide" Creeper was back. It was actually in the process of attaching itself to Meagan. I hated feeling so helpless, so unable to intervene. It was moments like that when I really despised the Watchmen's neglect.

The Creepers were writing on everything like crazed sociopaths. There were wicked words plastered on tables, lockers, desks, walls, even on the floor.

I was headed to fourth period when a refreshing, familiar scent overpowered the hallways. There had to be a Watchman nearby. I turned in every direction but didn't see one. As I ran upstairs to the second floor, I sent Ray Anne a text: **There's a Watchman here somewhere. I smell him.**

The instant I reached the second story, a blinding light hit the left side of my face. There were five breathtaking Watchmen at the other end of the hallway. This time they weren't staring up into the ceiling. They peered out directly at all of us. There was not a single Creeper in sight. They knew to run for cover.

The Watchmen looked like they were about to charge or something. I didn't dare approach them. I found refuge beside a section of lockers, shielding myself from the eye-piercing light between sporadic glances.

As the few remaining students rushed to class, I came out from my hiding spot and stood in the middle of the hallway opposite the Watchmen. That's when they began striding in sync, charging in my direction. I watched with amazement as they blew on the lockers, walls, and everything in their path, creating this unbelievable wind tunnel. The rotten graffiti disintegrated and disappeared.

As if that wasn't astonishing enough, they reached through the walls and pulled Creepers out by their necks, lanky arms—whatever they could grab. I hightailed it back to my cowardly post beside the lockers. They passed right by me, all of them holding at least three Creepers in each humongous hand, dragging them forcibly along.

The Creepers thrashed and hissed like they feared for their immortal lives and appeared to beg for mercy.

The Watchmen made a sharp turn and stormed down the stairs, clearing an entire flight of steps in one stride. My knees were weak, but I managed to follow. I watched from behind as they traveled the downstairs hallway, again blasting the graffiti into oblivion and snatching even more Creepers. They got to the end of the hall, then hurled the life-sucking fiends right through the locked doors and out of our ransacked school.

"Owen Edmonds." I jumped when Principal Maxwell called my name. "Do you have a hall pass?"

I didn't answer. The Watchmen took their graffiti-cleaning, Creeper-butt-kicking awesomeness into the cafeteria. I desperately wanted to follow, but the "school police" wouldn't allow it.

"Get to class." She wasn't about to make an exception. It occurred to me to ignore her and chase after the Watchmen, but I didn't want to end up locked away in some back office for the remainder of the day with no chance of seeing them again. I had lunch in twenty five minutes. Hopefully they would still be performing an exorcism on my school at that time, and I could continue spying in awe.

I sat down at my desk and read a text from Ray Anne. **I'm not surprised a Watchman is here. Look what time it is.**

10:47 a.m. *So what?* A minute later it dawned on me. Ray Anne believed the Watchmen showed up because her mom and the other ladies were praying during that time. I was hesitant to believe that, but what else is new?

Unfortunately I didn't see any more Watchmen that day, or that week.

Saturday afternoon eventually rolled around, and it was time to shower and get dressed for prom. The only thing keeping me from conjuring up some elaborate last-minute excuse to get out of going was knowing that I was about to see Ray Anne in that form-fitting red dress. I could hardly wait.

My mom said I looked like a million bucks in my tuxedo. I had to agree.

We took separate cars to Ray Anne's, and by the time we arrived, lots of people were already there. For a fleeting moment, I felt like a normal eighteen-year-old. Yeah, my shackled mother's chains scraped against the pavement as she ran up the driveway to hand me Ray's corsage. But still, I was about to participate in a time-honored American tradition. I would knock on the door and check out my prom date. There's nothing paranormal about that.

I must say, the sight of Ray Anne in that little red dress did not disappoint. I actually diverted my eyes away from her multiple times for fear her on-looking father would see right through me. I was in full blown desire mode. Man, she looked amazing. And her perfume was working its voodoo magic on me.

There were six other couples there, including Justin and his date. All of the parents took a million pictures. My mom got teary-eyed at one point. It was a little awkward, but I saw a few of the other moms get just as emotional, including Mrs. Greiner.

Ray and I chose not to do the limo thing. I didn't want to be confined to such a tight space with a handful of people who just might be escorting Creepers for the evening.

Before I left my house, I had placed a long-stem red rose on the passenger seat of my car. When I opened the car door for Ray Anne, she blushed and thanked me repeatedly. We drove to the restaurant, and I stared at her as often as I could without wrecking my car. She couldn't take her eyes off of me either.

We had a very nice dinner with the other couples, and with the exception of two Creepers at the other end of the restaurant and several explicit graffiti words, the atmosphere was elegant and relaxing.

By the time we paid the ticket and left, the sun was beginning to set, and the sky was a breathtaking collage of bright orange and pink. I don't normally notice such things, but I've heard the mundane becomes exquisite when you're falling in love.

As we drove to the prom, I wanted so badly to skip out on the high school crowd and spend the evening alone with Ray Anne, just the two of us. I thought for sure she would hate that idea, but I went ahead and tested the waters, so to speak.

"So, you're really looking forward to prom, right?"

"Um, yeah. I guess so."

Her response lacked enthusiasm, so I probed some more.

"You want to go, don't you?"

"Of course! I mean, you want to, right?"

"Well, we don't have to—I mean if you don't want to." I was starting to think things just might go my way.

"Honestly, I've never cared much about going to prom," she said. "Most of my friends have dreamed about it since they were little girls, but not me. I agreed to go because my mom—our moms—seemed so bent on seeing us go."

I went for it. "What if we ditch the plan, Ray? What if we do something else entirely tonight?"

"Like what?" She could hardly contain her excitement.

"I have an idea. I just have to stop off at the store for a second. Is that okay?"

"Sure, but what do you have in mind?"

"It's a surprise. Are you alright with that?"

Of course she was perfectly fine with that. Ray Anne was that kind of person. She didn't have to be in charge all of the time. And I knew she wouldn't nag me all the way there or badger me in an annoying attempt to make me tell her where we were going.

I parked the car. "Okay, I know it's totally weird to go into Walmart dressed like this. Do you wanna stay in the car?"

"No way! I'm coming too!"

We walked into the Creeper-filled store and noticed someone taking a picture of us pushing a grocery cart in our formalwear. It was really funny.

She forgot her lipstick at home, so while she went to the makeup isle, I quickly filled our basket with a huge blanket, a carton of strawberries, multiple bags of chocolate candy, and cold bottled-waters. As expected, lots of people gawked at us as we went through the self-checkout line, but Ray made the best of it. She put a plastic grocery sack over

222

her shoulder and walked around like it was her purse. She cracked me up.

We talked non-stop during the drive, and it was nine o'clock at night by the time we got to Galveston Island, nine-fifteen when we arrived at our destination. I parked in front of a colorful vintage-looking carnival that sat facing the ocean. It was old but cool looking. A handful of people were there enjoying the nightlife and ocean view.

Ray's face lit up like a child. "This is beautiful. How did you know about this place?"

"My mother used to bring me here when I was young. I have a lot of great memories of being here."

I bought tickets, and we got on the mermaid-adorned merry-go-round. Ray Anne sat with both feet on one side of a giant seahorse, and I stood beside her, conveniently holding on to her waist in case she started to fall. The night air blew off the ocean, making it windy yet refreshing outside.

I was far more leery of getting on the rusty Ferris wheel than Ray Anne was, but I sucked it up and rode. I didn't want to ruin the special moment by pointing out how freaky it was to look down from way up there and see Creepers scattered among the people, so I kept that to myself. I also didn't mention that the toothless man operating the ride had a Creeper named "Insanity" linked to him.

It really was spectacular to see the ocean from up there at night.

We survived the ride, and after walking around and taking in the scene for a while longer, we wandered back to the car. I drove us to the only part of the beach where people were still allowed to park vehicles on the sand. I positioned my new blanket near the shoreline, and Ray Anne took off her high heels, then came and sat down. It was amazing how brightly the moonlight shined. We could see each other just fine. Of course, I had a little extra help. Ray Anne's phenomenal glow illuminated the ground around us.

At first, we munched on our strawberries and chocolate and laughed about all kinds of things, but after a while, our conversation became more personal. She asked me questions about my childhood, and I shared the ugly truth—how my mom had been an alcoholic for as long as I could remember and how I had no relatives to speak of. She was really surprised to hear that about my mother.

Things got a little intense for me when she asked about my father, and I tried to explain the pathetic situation. I'd hardly talked about it to anyone, but the few times I had, I felt ashamed admitting that I had never met him. It was humiliating.

"I bet he'd be so proud of you if he could see what an amazing person you've become."

In her attempt to say something kind, she unknowingly hit on a major nerve.

"He doesn't want to see me," I said. "He's never wanted anything to do with me."

It took Ray Anne a second to figure out how to respond, but as usual, her words were uplifting. "I'm so sorry, Owen. I'm more sorry for him, though. He messed up the biggest blessing in his life. He's really missing out."

I wanted to thank her, but there was a lump in my throat. I needed a change of pace. I took out my phone and picked out a music playlist. Yes, I had a playlist of slow music; I can admit that.

"Would you like to dance with me?" I stood and reached out to her.

She put her soft hand in mine. As I pulled her body close, my cold stomach did a flip-flop, and I felt myself beginning to breathe faster. She put her head on my chest near my shoulder, and I inhaled the tantalizing vanilla scent of her hair.

"Did you purposely play this song?" She smiled at me.

"No, I really didn't." A 1980s classic, *Lady In Red,* popped up first on my playlist.

As we swayed back and forth together, I marveled at how, when I was getting ready just a few short hours ago, I never would have guessed I'd be dancing with Ray Anne in the moonlight next to rolling waves. And when I knocked on her door a month ago, I had no idea that I would completely and totally fall for her.

"Ray, I want you to know something." I waited for the next wave to crash, then continued. "I really care about you. A lot."

My affectionate words made her shy, revealing a side of her I'd never seen. "Thank you. That's very sweet."

She started to say something, then stopped, then started to say something else, then stopped again.

I chuckled. "You, of all people, at a loss for words?"

"I'm sorry. I guess I *am* at a loss for words."

"Why?" I leaned back and gazed straight down into her captivating face.

She struggled to speak her mind. "I just didn't expect . . . I mean . . . I knew we were . . . but . . ."

The crashing waves hushed again for a few brief seconds, and I whispered into her ear. "It's okay, Ray. You can tell me. You can tell me anything."

We were barely moving anymore, and my arms were now wrapped around her, holding her tight.

"I guess I didn't realize when we blew off prom that we would end up alone in such a . . . well, a place that's this romantic."

"Is that a problem?" I asked, staring intently at her glossed lips.

"I just want to be careful," she said. "I love that we've become such good friends, but I guess I'm afraid of taking things any further."

I heard what she said, and I really did care, but I couldn't resist. I leaned in to kiss her.

She turned her face and quickly went back to resting her head on my chest. Needless to say, the rejection was crushing.

I cleared the air. "I'm sorry Ray. I didn't mean to—"

"No, it's not your fault. You didn't know."

"Didn't know what?"

She bit her lip. "I don't want you to make fun of me if I tell you."

"Why would I make fun of you?" I couldn't imagine saying anything cruel to her.

"Well, that's what they've all done."

"Who?"

"Other people I've told."

"What? Just tell me."

She hesitated a moment, then blurted it out. "I'm saving my first kiss for my wedding day, okay? I've never kissed anyone." She buried her face in my chest. "Go ahead. Start teasing me."

I laughed. "I'm not gonna tease you."

"But you think it's stupid, right? Well, I don't care. It's not stupid to me."

"Hey, I didn't say it was stupid."

She sat down on our now sand-filled blanket and motioned for me to do the same.

"So what do you think?" she asked.

Honestly, not kissing until marriage did seem over the top, but at the same time, I couldn't help but respect her for it. "You really wanna know?"

"Yeah, I do."

I sighed. "I think it's awful."

"What?" She was instantly offended.

"Wait." I smiled. "Let me finish. I think it's awful for *every* guy, except for the incredibly lucky one who gets to have that kiss."

Her pout instantly became a grin. "Thank you. Seriously, it means a lot."

I nearly leaned in and tried to kiss her again but remembered that was a no-no.

"Owen?"

I sensed she was about to break my heart.

"I want us to stay good friends, and I'm worried that if I open up my heart to something more, it will lead us down the wrong path."

I was perplexed. "Well, since we can't even kiss, isn't 'friends' the only choice we have?"

"That's what I'm talking about. You don't even know how to be more than friends without fooling around. I want something more meaningful than that. And I want someone who loves the Lord like I do."

She might as well have clobbered me in the face with a fistful of sand. "Are you saying I'm not good enough for you?" I sounded hurt because . . . well . . . I was.

"No," she said. "I'm saying *I'm* not good enough—not strong enough—to date you. I think it would pull me away from my commitment to save sex for marriage and make it difficult for me to serve God with all of my heart."

I suppose that was her attempt at putting a humble spin on things, but it still seemed to me like she was saying I flat didn't measure up.

I felt a dire need to prove myself.

"Look, we both know I'm not a church boy and faith does not come naturally to me, but I really am trying to be open and learn—more so now than ever before. And if you're asking me to keep my hands off you because you've set your heart on saving yourself for marriage, I'll do it. I'll respect your wishes because . . ."

I almost took the coward's way out and said something about how much I admired her, but I somehow found the guts to speak the uncensored truth.

"I'll respect your wishes because I love you, Ray."

And I meant it.

With all of my heart.

17. Living Dead

I had just enough time on Monday morning to get ready, eat breakfast, and leave something in the microwave for my mom. For the first time since my world imploded, I slept like a rock and pressed snooze on my alarm, like, five times.

I slid into my car and made a mental note, *Only six weeks left of high school, and then graduation.* I didn't want to think about the next phase of my life. I only knew *who* I hoped would be with me.

I was just about to back out of my driveway when Jess called.

"Oh my God, Owen, did you hear?"

"Hear what?"

"Lance's girlfriend Meagan shot herself. She's in the hospital. She didn't die."

I instantly felt sick. "Where is she? What hospital?"

"I don't know for sure. I'll let you know. Let me call you back."

I drove around in a daze. I couldn't believe it. She gave in. She let that Creeper talk her into ending it all. The more I thought about it, the more enraged I became.

If only Lance had taken my warning about Meagan seriously. He refused to even consider what I had to say. And I begged that Watchman for help, and he blatantly ignored me, too. He could have destroyed that brainwashing Creeper with next to no effort and saved her life, but he just stood there, useless.

I knew this would happen. For the first time ever, I loathed being right.

I pulled over onto the side of the road and voiced my outrage to the supposed god of humanity. On the slim chance that he actually did exist, someone needed to stand up to him. I was more than willing.

"What's the matter with you? How can you sit back and let this keep happening? If those Watchmen work for you, you suck at commanding your army!"

I didn't care if he had the power to annihilate me. I wasn't done talking. I had one more thing to get off my chest. I gripped the steering wheel so hard my fingers turned white, then spoke the truth.

"I hate you."

I instantly saw them out of the corner of my eye. "Murderer" and "Faithless" were closing in, careening toward me from the left side.

"Is this your way of punishing me? Do the Creepers report to you for duty, too?"

I threw my car in reverse and sped off with no place to go. I only knew I needed to get as far away as possible, and fast.

I was nearly to the freeway when Jess called and told me Meagan was at Cypress North Hospital. I wanted to be there for Lance during all of this, but that could go either way. He might be glad to see me or want to strangle me. It was a risk I was willing to take.

The press was already there. I ignored the reporters and squeezed into the crowded waiting room with what looked like nearly our entire senior class. I was glad to see Ray Anne. She explained the horrific situation. Meagan shot herself in the head with her father's pistol and was on life support in intensive care. Oddly enough, Lance wasn't there. I imagined he was devastated. I texted him: **I'm at the hospital. Where r u?**

I had just sent the message when he walked in with his parents. He looked awful, like *he* needed to be on life support. I stood. Lance surveyed the room with puffy, bloodshot eyes, then walked straight over to me. I understood why he couldn't speak. He was trying to keep it together, to stuff his emotions.

I didn't want to cause him to crack, so I didn't speak either. All I knew to do was give him a pat on the back, and I think he appreciated it. Soon everyone bombarded him with sobs, hugs, and questions.

All of us sat crammed in that tiny waiting room all morning, anticipating an update. Several teachers and counselors arrived on the scene. The cops showed up, too, and kept an eye on the sign people. The weirdos were there in full force, chanting outside the emergency room entrance.

One minute my thoughts were dominated with concern for Meagan, and the next minute—I'm ashamed to admit—I was consumed with my own issues. This was the first time I'd been in a hospital since I morphed into a visual telepathic—I still wasn't sure what to call my state of existence. I put my hand over my icy stomach and contemplated making up a story in the hope that a doctor would order an X-ray of my midsection. Maybe if I told them I ate glass or something they would take a look at my insides.

I so wanted to know why my stomach was freezing all of the time. I wasn't willing to risk a psychological evaluation, though. If they ordered that I take one, I'd be in over my head, for sure.

I sat there feeling claustrophobic, not just because I was shoved in the corner of a tight space and weighted down by the heavy sadness in the room, but because several students, one teacher, and even a nurse were all linked up to Creepers.

Around lunchtime, Lance and his parents got to go back and see Meagan and her family. Meanwhile, a doctor explained to the rest of us that Meagan's situation was bleak and that the family requested that we please carry on with our day. They would post updates online about Meagan's progress as often as they could.

Ray Anne gave me a sorrowful goodbye, then got in the car with her friend Joanna to head to school. I didn't feel like sitting in class, so I drove home and agonized over the reality that Meagan was on death's door.

Other than a brief call from my mom to check on how I was doing after the morning's events, I spoke to no one that afternoon. I powered up my laptop and added to my depressing timeline of events, then turned on the TV and tried to escape my nightmare of a life for a while. My dog was sprawled out by the couch, snoozing at my feet, and the fact that she wasn't growling was hugely comforting.

I was just about to go pick up some fast food for dinner when Lance texted me. I was surprised to hear from him.

Can u come to the hospital?

I didn't bother stopping to grab something to eat. I figured things had taken a turn for the worse with Meagan, and I needed to get to Lance as soon as I could.

When I arrived, he was already in the waiting room looking for me. I could see the fear all over his face.

"Hey. Is she . . ." I didn't know how to ask if she was about to die.

"It doesn't look good. They've had to restart her heart twice. I'm holding out hope, but the doctors say—"

I'd never seen Lance cry before, and I had no idea what to do. He wiped his face and tried to tell me again.

"The doctors say that we should consider letting her—"

He still couldn't say it, but I knew. He struggled to gain his composure then explained, "I know you don't know her family very well, but they said you could come back there, you know, to be with me during all of this."

I really was glad he reached out to me, but honestly, I was scared out of my mind to be anywhere near a dying person. What would I see? I didn't want to face it, but I had to, for Lance.

The Intensive Care Unit was quieter than I imagined it would be. We had to pass several hospital rooms before we came to Meagan's, and it made me super uncomfortable to see glimpses of people lying there, fighting for their lives. Some were done fighting, I'm sure. My uneasy reaction to that environment was more confirmation that, even if my future plans weren't in jeopardy, I would have made a lousy doctor.

I wanted to be strong for Lance, but when I saw Meagan's limp body in that hospital bed surrounded by all kinds of monitors and life-sustaining machines, I nearly lost it. Her entire head, including her face, was wrapped with gauze, but I was actually grateful for that. Seeing her face would have made it even harder.

Her shackle was still intact, along with three bulky chains.

I stood in the back corner, out of the way. Meagan's parents and grandparents were there. As expected, they were totally distraught.

Some time later, Meagan's older brother arrived. He flew home from college to be there, and the scene became so emotional and intense when he entered the room that I stepped out into the hall.

I stood there witnessing Lance and Meagan's relatives fall to pieces, and I felt brokenhearted for all of them.

I needed a breather. I walked down the hall and took a sip out of a water fountain. On my way back, I noticed a room with the door wide open and an elderly lady propped up in her bed. She looked to be a century old, but what caught my attention was the glow at the foot of her bed. She had no shackle around her neck, no cords or chains, and she was luminous, like Ray Anne.

I took steps in her direction and noticed there were no guests in her room. I inched my way just inside the doorframe and stared at the comatose great-grandmother.

I nearly screamed when she lifted her head and looked at me. "Is that you, John?"

I looked over my shoulder. "Um, no ma'am. My name is Owen."

"Come here, son." Her tone was kind, and although her eyes were closed again, she was smiling. I walked toward her but stopped a good four feet from her bed. She reached out her wobbly hand and called for me to come closer.

She gripped my hand the best she could with the little strength she had. Her knuckles were enormous.

"You remind me of my son John." She grinned again. "He died in 1964."

I had no clue what to say to that. I just smiled and secretly marveled at how deeply set her eyes were. It was also really strange to see her shackle-free neck. I rarely saw anyone's neck anymore.

She seemed to fall asleep instantly, so I took that opportunity to check out the foot of her bed. She was a frail woman, but was giving off an amazing concentration of golden light. It penetrated through the bed sheet and clear down to the floor.

She returned to consciousness. "It's so nice of you to come see me."

"Sure." I didn't know what else to say. I did have a question for her, though.

"Ma'am?"

She turned her face and attempted to look at me with her cloudy eyes. I figured I could speak frankly given the circumstances. "You have this wonderful glow around your feet. Do you know why?"

Her exhausted body managed to let out a laugh. "I'm going home soon," she said just before drifting off again.

Clearly she was in no state of mind to answer my question.

235

As I stood there a few final seconds, beholding her wrinkled face, I thought of Meagan and how she was far too young to die.

I needed to get back to Lance. I draped the nice old lady's arm over her chest and let go of her hand. I had just stepped into the hallway when an announcement blared through the intercom. I don't claim to know much about hospital protocols, but I knew the term "code blue" was not good.

A team of medical personnel went racing by. To my horror, they charged into Meagan's room. I followed a few steps behind. What I saw next will never, ever leave me.

A female doctor was positioned over Meagan, straddling her on the bed, clutching an electric paddle in each hand. The only thing louder than the monotone sound of Meagan's cardiac flat line was the high-pitched squeal of the defibrillator charging.

"All clear!"

The doctor was just about to plunge the paddles against Meagan's chest when Meagan's dad shouted above the chaos, "No! Stop!" He collapsed at her bedside and wailed. "Let her go. We have to let her go."

Lance fell into a chair, put his hands over his face and sobbed. I stood paralyzed, not knowing whether to approach Lance or leave him alone.

I remained in the hallway, reeling with uncertainty and grief. That's when the supernatural world trespassed onto the scene. I watched as two Creepers paraded through Meagan's hospital room like victors claiming a much-anticipated prize. One named "Death" pounced on her chest and began pulling Meagan's chains loose and removing her cords right through the gauze, callously winding them around her neck and encircling her locked shackle. Its movements were swift and jerky, and it appeared to want to choke her even though she already had no pulse.

The other Creeper, "Damnation," stood by, taking in the heartache and despair in the room like some sort of intoxicating incense, visibly delighting in people's pain. Once its putrid partner completed its task, "Damnation" moved in. It charged right through the foot of Meagan's bed and stood on her—inside of her—just below her midsection. It glared down at her, then plunged its filthy hands into her stomach, ripping a shadowy-looking figure right out of Meagan, leaving a huge, dusty, gaping hole.

My knees buckled, and I hit the cold floor.

I watched in utter shock as the two spiteful monsters dragged what appeared to be Meagan's soul out of the room—out of this earthly realm altogether!

I couldn't comprehend it. *Did I really just see that?*

A nurse felt my forehead and handed me a cup of water, but I dropped it. She tried to help me up, but my legs were too weak.

The next few minutes are a blur, but I know at some point a nurse helped walk me to a nearby chair, and I sat there while the commotion around me continued. Medical personnel scurried in every direction while Meagan's family wept loudly around her lifeless body. The ICU was no longer quiet or calm.

My hands were trembling ferociously, and it took me forever to text Ray: **Meagan is gone. U wont believe what happened.**

I called my mom, and told her the grim news. She was sad, of course, and she offered to come get me, but I assured her I could drive.

I found Lance standing at Meagan's bedside, holding her hand for a few final moments. He knew any second they would come and take her body away, out of his life forever. I could only imagine how he was feeling.

I stood back and waited. Finally he turned around and approached me. I wrapped my arm around his shoulders, feeling totally inept to try and console him. But I was committed to being there for him—as best I could given the atrocity I'd just witnessed.

That's when he snapped.

"You knew this would happen. What did you do to her? Did you talk her into this?"

"What?" His accusations were absurd and no doubt driven by overwhelming stress and grief. I tried to calm him. "Look, you need time to process this and I—"

"Why is it that when people get around you, they end up dying?" He raised his voice, drawing attention from everyone around, including Meagan's family. "You're psychotic! I don't want you anywhere near me!"

I didn't understand his drastic change in attitude toward me, but then again, I didn't understand much of anything that took place that evening. I decided it was best to leave. I was too emotionally drained for his words to hurt me at that point, but I knew better than to stick around and try and talk it out.

I was nearly to the exit door of the ICU when a nurse called out to me.

"Excuse me, sir?"

I looked back.

"Excuse me. Are you a friend or relative of Mrs. Ida Knowles?"

Who? My mind was jumbled enough. I didn't need this.

"I saw you talking to Ms. Ida earlier this evening, but then I couldn't find you. Did you hear?"

It dawned on me that she was talking about the nice old lady. "Did I hear what?"

"Ms. Ida passed away a few minutes ago."

More death. More queasiness.

"Would you like to go pay your final respects?" she asked.

That seemed a bit much. I didn't know her at all. "Isn't her family here?"

"No, she doesn't have any family that we're aware of."

The last thing I wanted to do was look at another dead person, but it seemed pitiful that no one was there to acknowledge her passing.

I reluctantly walked to her room, not knowing what to expect, but seeing her actually struck me as breathtaking. She looked peaceful, even beautiful in a way. Her glow was gone, but there was no scary dusty wound in her abdomen like I'd just seen on Meagan and also on Jared.

What's more, I could tell Watchmen had just been there. Their one-of-a-kind scent lingered in the room.

"Goodbye Ms. Ida," I whispered.

As I left the hospital, I kept reliving Meagan's deathbed assault in my tormented mind, despite how hard I tried to suppress it. I was sure I'd just witnessed the single most terrifying scene the underworld has to offer.

As usual, I was wrong.

18. Oppressive King

In all of my efforts to find answers and somehow make sense of my deranged world, I was not just at ground zero; I was six feet under. Every traumatic thing I'd recently seen had left a permanent wound on my sanity, but witnessing what looked to be Meagan's soul being snatched right out of her dead body was, without question, the most traumatizing of all my inexplicable experiences.

Over the next few days, I quit eating, quit going to school, quit living, really. The only exception was I did stay in touch with Ray Anne. My mom made a few attempts to get me out of bed, but her concern and nagging were no match for my determination to isolate myself, at least for a while, until Meagan's demise stopped replaying in my mind.

The funeral was scheduled for later in the week, Friday morning, but I had already decided I wasn't going. I didn't care what people said about me for not being there. I was done—done with Lance and done with burying the dead.

Besides, I was sure Meagan was not resting in peace—far from it—so why go listen to people go on and on about how she was in a better place?

I didn't know where those thieves took her, but I was sure it was dreadful.

I left the house Thursday afternoon, not because I had a desire to change out of my pajama pants and get some fresh air but because my dog was growling at my closed closet door, and I couldn't deal with whatever was behind it. I was fed up with being on edge and on the run from Creepers all the time, but they were so freaking scary that I couldn't help myself.

My destination-less drives were getting old. I eventually returned home but wished I hadn't when I arrived. A patrol car was in my driveway, and Officer Smith was at the door. I figured slamming a U-turn and flooring it would raise some suspicions so I parked. I approached the officer while sipping on my bottled-water, trying to look like I didn't have a care in the world.

"Hello Owen." He was one of those guys who nearly fractures bones when he shakes your hand. "I need you to come down to the station with me, right now. We've got some more questions to ask you."

It sounded like he was telling me to go, not inviting me. That dreaded heart-racing sensation hit me in the freezing gut. I agreed to meet him there and drug my feet back to my car.

I texted my mom and also Ray Anne, but I told my mom the truth about where I was headed and told Ray Anne a fib. I was trying to make a good impression on Ray. Certainly a police investigation was a giant step in the wrong direction.

Once at the station, I was escorted to an official interrogation room where a shackled detective named Benny pulled up a chair across the table from me. His protruding gut made it difficult for him to lean over and write on his old-school yellow notepad.

"Can I get you something to drink, Owen?"

I was way more concerned with why they had me there than I was with thirst or hunger. "No thank you. I'd just like to get started, if you don't mind."

He glanced to the side, and I counted four cords spewing from the back of his head.

"Sure," he said. "Please recount the chain of events that took place the day before Jared and Conner's deaths. Start with what you did that morning and early afternoon, then explain, in as much detail as possible, what happened once you met up with the two boys. Leave nothing out, please."

I knew the police had increased suspicions, or maybe even new evidence that somehow pointed to me. That weighed heavily on me. I'd watched enough episodes of *Dateline*, however, to know that it's absolutely key to stick to the same story, to keep every single aspect of my account exactly the same as the first day I told it.

Even if I wanted to come clean and disclose the truth about the freakish water and all, it was way too late for that. The fact that I deliberately hid it from them was incriminating. My plan was to stay with my original story, no matter what.

And that's what I did. I spoke for about fifteen minutes. Detective Benny got quiet and scribbled some notes that I unfortunately could not decipher. He was concentrating, no doubt looking for holes and inconsistencies in my testimony. My pulse was pounding so hard I could have sworn he felt it reverberating off the table.

I tried to act normal, even though normal was a thing of the past for me and I was petrified of adding a prison sentence to my already messed up life.

I didn't kill them on purpose.

I said it over and over in my head as if reassuring myself I wasn't a real murderer and certainly didn't deserve to be locked up with convicted killers. The problem was I didn't believe that. I had committed a selfish act that resulted in the loss of two lives, and I felt sure justice demanded some sort of penance on my part. Nonetheless, call it human nature, but I was not willing to admit guilt and succumb to punishment. I was determined to stay free—well, as free as one can be when malicious spirits are after you.

"Owen, some of your classmates have expressed concerns about you, about your mental and emotional stability."

"Really? Who?" I knew Lance was bothered by my recent behavior, but I never would have guessed he would expose me to the cops. I was sure he was among those who betrayed me, though. I couldn't imagine who else would have squealed.

"Well for starters, your girlfriend Jess says you've been acting delusional and even claiming to see scary creatures. She said you recently jumped on top of her and nearly smothered her, supposedly because you believed you were protecting her from some unseen being that was out to get her?"

If there was still oxygen in the room, my lungs didn't know it. It was all I could do not to punch the table.

"She's my ex-girlfriend, and with all due respect, sir, what does that ridiculous accusation have to do with Conner and Jared's deaths?"

"Following their autopsies, the cause of death appears to be the result of having ingested a hazardous substance of some kind. The problem is these two young men don't fit the profile of kids who wanted to kill themselves, and we have to do our due diligence to investigate all other possibilities, including homicide."

I was in the middle of trying to come to grips with the seriousness of what he just asserted when I suddenly realized Ray Anne was exactly right; Creepers can be summoned by certain behaviors or words. I now knew that for certain because two seconds after that detective said "homicide," that "Murderer" Creeper sliced right through the wall and stood towering over me. You have no idea how difficult it is to try and act normal with one of those things staring you down.

"But I've already told you everything I know." I was hoping he'd let me hightail it out of there at that point.

"But I haven't told you everything *I* know, young man."

"Okay?" I held my breath and waited for him to present some form of physical evidence that I couldn't possibly explain away.

"Conner's mother said her son came home that evening complaining that you made him drink something that left him feeling very sick. Are you starting to connect the dots, Owen? He died of poisoning and said *you* were the one who coerced him into drinking the 'weird water,' as he called it. And your classmates are saying you're not in your right mind. That doesn't look so good, does it?"

He had me cornered. I had no choice but to pull the ripcord. "I'd like to speak with my lawyer."

I didn't actually have a lawyer, but I figured it was time to get one—fast.

Although Detective Benny released me to go home, I was sure my insistence on involving legal counsel sealed the deal in his mind, and he knew I was 100% guilty.

I left the interrogation room in a hurry, and, for whatever reason, the "Murderer" took off in a different direction. I imagined I wasn't its only prey. Perhaps it went to harass someone else for a while.

I was nearly to my car when I spotted my mother across the parking lot, walking swiftly in my direction.

"Owen!" She looked scared. "What did they want?"

She already suspected I was out of my mind and guilty of deception. She really wasn't going to like what I was about to say.

"There's been a huge misunderstanding. Some of my friends made ridiculous accusations about me to the police, Mom. They think I had something to do with Conner and Jared's deaths."

Just as I predicted, her face turned white as a bleached sheet.

"I hate to say it, but I need a lawyer."

During a crisis like this, most parents would want to talk through the situation and ask thousands of questions. Not my mom. She instructed me to go home, then we didn't say two words to each other. I figured I'd wait until the next day to ask if she was going to help me find—and pay for—a good lawyer.

I called Ray Anne and told her I just got back from running some errands with my mom and held out hope that she wouldn't somehow find out where I actually had been. She asked me to come over and help her with some math homework, and I jumped at the chance to see her.

I showed up around 8:30 p.m., but as it turned out, I wasn't much help with her schoolwork. We were alone in her living room, sitting side-by-side on the couch, and all I could think about was how badly I wanted to pull her on top of me and feel her curvy body against mine. Every time she looked at me with those mega-blue eyes of hers, I seriously regretted promising I would refrain from kissing her. I actually felt a tinge of resentment that she would even ask that of me.

I guess she sensed I was straining under the pressure of temptation because she scooted over and put some space between us. I sat there miserably conflicted. I wanted to respect her commitment to "purity," as she called it, but at the same time, I wanted so badly to persuade her to give in to me. My desire for her was so strong that I practically ached.

"You want something to drink?" she asked.

I was in the middle of thinking, *no, I want you*, when a massive Creeper poked its ugly head through the wall. Its name was "Lust."

"Is everything okay?" she asked.

I was taken aback. I never intended to lust after Ray Anne. I didn't want to be a Dan Mitchell in her life. I guess I had allowed my thoughts and selfish desires to digress lately. I was so stressed and mentally and physically fatigued that I felt helpless to tame my sensual desires.

"I'm fine. I'd love something to drink," I said, all the while suffering the intense frustration of having my carnal appetite unquenched.

I knew that "Lust" monster wouldn't dare set its mucky foot in Ray's house, not with her glowing family around. Sure enough, it backed away and disappeared.

We sipped on some blue Kool-Aid for a while, then I headed home.

I crawled into bed and couldn't resist texting Jess: **I can't believe you tried to get me arrested.**

Less than a minute later, my phone rang. It was her. She spoke without taking a breath.

"Listen to me. I know you're probably furious, but the police came to my house and questioned me, and at first I didn't say much, but the more they asked me about you, the more I found myself being honest with them and telling them all kinds of stuff. After they left, I felt really bad, like I had betrayed you or something, and I thought about telling you, but I just didn't know how. I don't think you did anything bad whatsoever to Jared and Conner, Owen. I'm so, so sorry."

I was prepared to really sock it to her, but I lost all momentum after she groveled for my forgiveness. Honestly, I kind of understood where she was coming from. I knew from personal experience that it's incredibly distressing to lie to the police. What continued to aggravate me, though, was that she still didn't believe me about the Creepers.

"Jess, that day when I told you something was trying to attack you, and I threw myself over you, and that night when I met you in the park and warned you about spiritual influences, did you believe me at all? Are you even slightly willing to consider that I'm telling the truth?"

After a long moment of silence, she proceeded with a predictable response.

"Owen, what do you expect? I can't possibly believe what you're saying. No one could. Besides, your claims are really terrifying."

I was well aware how terrifying my claims were. That was all the more reason to take them seriously. Oh well. There was no sense in trying to convince a shackled person to believe me.

By the time we hung up, I was exhausted and desperate to get some sleep, even though I knew I would likely have another dreadful nightmare about Meagan's deathbed assault. Sure enough, I tossed and turned for hours and had a miserable night.

I thought my mom was going to tear into me on Friday morning when I announced I wasn't going to Meagan's funeral, but surprisingly, she seemed understanding. She offered me a truce. She wouldn't give me any grief over missing the funeral if I went to school. I agreed to her terms.

I think she had had her fill of attending funerals, too. She stayed home and graded papers, and once again, neither of us brought up the investigation or my need to find a lawyer.

It felt weird sitting in class after being out the whole week. My teachers were so beat down and frazzled that not one of them said anything to me about my consecutive absences or making up my work. Half the school was out, anyway, attending the funeral.

The hateful Creeper graffiti was steadily beginning to litter the place again, and so were the Creepers. By now, I could look at a certain student or teacher and recall which Creeper tended to torment that person. I would see someone, like my friend Sammy, for example, and have absurd thoughts like, *Hey Sam. Where's "Aggression" today?*

I was navigating my way through everyone's lagging chains to get to fifth period when out of nowhere, the Creepers all began frantically charging in the same direction. I hoped the Watchmen were back to clean house, and I wasn't about to miss it. I followed behind, delighting in seeing the look of terror on their wretched faces.

One by one, they threw themselves onto the floor, lying prostrate in single-file lines that stretched clear across the commons area. I dashed up the stairwell overlooking the cafeteria to get a better view. People bumped into me as I parked myself on the landing halfway between the first and second floors, and one guy even shoved me, but I refused to budge.

That's when I noticed the Creepers were lying in a pattern. Every other Creeper faced the same direction opposite its neighbor so that their heads were beside each others' feet. They grabbed one another's ankles, creating these tight Xs with their bodies that formed a uniform blanket over the entire floor and sent chills rippling up my spine.

The bell rang and the hallways cleared, but I stood there enthralled.

Like the pounding of ten thousand bass drums, I felt it in my chest when, all at once, they began chanting in unison. It was loud, much louder than I'd ever heard them communicate before.

At first I couldn't understand them, but then I heard them clearly proclaim, "Hail the King!" They shouted a few more phrases I couldn't make out, then echoed, "Grandinem rex!" all rolling their Rs in one accord with their toxic tongues.

I knew exactly what that meant. It's Latin for "Hail the King!"

I gripped the handrail with my freezing but sweaty palms and voiced my conclusion aloud. "They're shouting 'Hail the King' in one human language after another."

For a brief moment, I was elated to have solved the mystery of their ritualistic mantra, but an inevitable realization seized my mind. *If they're shouting for their king then he must be—*

I was only halfway through my realization when my body was overcome with a feeling of intoxication. My hands slid down the metal banisters as I sank to the ground, too dizzy and heavy to remain standing. I kept my gaze fixed on the freak show unfolding in my school cafeteria even though my gut was full of adrenaline, nausea, and euphoria, all at once. I'd never experienced such a manic high or depressing low before, and I struggled to comprehend what was happening. I felt sweat drop from my forehead to the floor.

At that precise moment, I saw two Creepers crawling on their hands and knees, trampling on top of their prostate coconspirators while straining under the weight of what had to be their one-and-only king. They escorted him on their boney backs. He was the same intimidating height as the rest of them and had an equally emaciated build, but he was adorned in opulent purple and gold attire, nothing like his disheveled army.

His porcelain doll face looked far more feminine than masculine, and he was exceptionally beautiful, like an attractive young woman. Unlike the others, there was nothing branded on his flawless forehead.

Is that God? I wasn't sure.

He dominated his two slave escorts with reigns that attached to dreadful face harnesses. Every slight twist of his wrist inflicted intense pain as evidenced by their shrill shrieks, which only seemed to excite him.

He seemed to bask in the Creepers' lavish praise as if it infused life into his soul-less existence. Once he trod over his submissive subjects, they rose to their hands and knees and crawled behind him in a massive entourage without ever lifting their brainwashed heads, continuing to shout unwavering devotion to their corrupt king.

I physically could not turn away. His presence had a seduction power that mesmerized—more like hypnotized—my entire being, and it took every ounce of willpower not to bow down and worship alongside his enslaved fanatics.

He didn't repulse me like the Creepers did. Instead, I was riveted by his presence.

I shoved my face between two banisters to steady my wobbly, swollen head and watched as their spellbinding king finally came to a halt in the front and center of our commons area. The Creepers were now huddled together on their knees at his feet with their hands lifted high in the air, praising and pledging their unwavering allegiance to their dictator, although visibly troubled and tormented by his presence. They didn't dare look him in the face.

The king gracefully lifted one delicate hand as if to silence them, and all activity instantly ceased. He then paused, reveling in the manipulative power he held over them, then abruptly shoved his other hand straight out, signaling for the Creepers to move back. They did so at once.

I remained perched on the stairwell bewitched by the most foreign feelings of both ecstasy and despair when I saw the ground literally open. The floor tiles disintegrated, revealing what can only be described as a place of untold, unimaginable anguish.

The walls looked like human body tissue and stretched down so far that I saw no ground floor, though it appeared as if fire simmered below, lighting the insidious pit. Out of the tissue hung the dusty remains of countless arms, legs, and heads—all kinds of human appendages reaching, flailing, cursing, and begging. I also saw Creepers there, crawling up and all over the pulsating walls while jabbing any shadowy soul that dared to try and claw out of the grotesque, flesh-like entrapment.

It was a smoldering hot, hate-filled place of torment that somehow exacerbated the chill in my stomach. All I could think about was how badly I didn't want to go there and how no human being belonged there. The Creepers shuddered and clearly dreaded the place as well.

Their pretentious cult leader lifted his index finger, positioning his long fingernail in the direction of a certain Creeper, then motioned for it to come forward. "Traitor" came and stood impishly by his side, then spoke into his ear. The king grinned with satisfaction, revealing a charming, appealing smile. There was nothing ugly about him. Even his eyes were striking and rich.

The king called more Creepers forward, only they didn't stand by his side. They knelt before him with their battered heads hung in shame. It appeared the "Traitor" was exposing the Creepers—perhaps naming those who had somehow failed in their assignments—and I was sure they were about to be disciplined in some savage manner.

Sixteen disgraced Creepers were brought before the mob and awaited judgment. I held my breath as the king glared down on them with hatred, then kicked each one of them in the chest, hurling them violently backwards into the sweltering hole behind them. They immediately went to work inside the pit, patrolling and punishing what I presumed to be imprisoned souls of the dead.

The king gave a subtle nod to the "Traitor," releasing it to rejoin the others.

I knew by then that their king couldn't possibly be God. If the Creator of the universe existed, surely he didn't need an informant to tell him *anything*. To be God is to know everything already. Even in my disoriented stupor, I was confident of that.

The king resumed his exalted position up front, parading himself again on the crooked backs of the same two conquered Creepers. Like the ocean tide rushing up the shore, the ground closed over the deplorable pit, concealing the living dead. To my amazement, the dirty cafeteria floor returned.

That's when the king's demeanor changed. He narrowed his eyes and spoke as if he was outraged and overcome with desperation, even fear. The intensity and hostility with which he gestured toward his soiled soldiers was frightening and sickening, and it reminded me of the old footage I'd seen of Adolph Hitler addressing his Nazi army. I was both fascinated and repulsed.

I couldn't understand the Creeper king's words, but I could read his body language. He was mobilizing his blood-thirsty troops around a deadly mission, rallying them to attack. He pointed outward and also to the ground as if referring to my fellow classmates and my school. He motioned toward certain groups of Creepers, giving them specific instructions.

In the midst of his tyrannical rant, what looked to be drops of thick blood began leaking down his pale face, only it was black, like motor oil. That's when the word "Destroyer" appeared on his forehead, as if just freshly sliced into his skin with an unseen blade. I covered my mouth, attempting to suppress my gag reflex.

I had already suspected that something disastrous would go down soon. Now I was certain. The energy in the room changed. The Creepers were no longer cowering but were now poised for action, frothing at the mouth to carry out their depraved king's commands.

Just as quickly as the twisted chain of events began, they concluded. The Creepers' merciless, yet revered king quite literally faded before my eyes. His reenergized subjects dispersed, fleeing in every direction.

I sat there feeling lifeless on the stairwell, wondering if everyone I'd ever known who had died was trapped in that unthinkable place of suffering.

"Owen?"

It was Ray Anne, thank God. She helped me to my feet, and I hugged her with all the little strength I had.

"You're trembling. Are you okay?"

I wanted to tell her what I just witnessed, but I didn't know where to start.

"No, Ray. I'm not okay! None of us are! Something terrible is happening!"

She looked at me with compassion and assured me, "It's gonna be fine. Just calm down. Why don't you come to my house after school, and we'll talk?"

I went straight to my car and planned to sit there until school got out and it was time to go to Ray Anne's. The only thing keeping me from hyperventilating was the assurance that she was there for me. She had become a lifeline in the midst of my deplorable circumstances.

Unfortunately, as much as I needed and clung to her friendship, I was unknowingly about to seriously sabotage it.

19. Vexed Soul

I sat nervously in my car, counting down the minutes until it was time to drive to Ray Anne's. My phone alerted me of a text message, and I nearly jumped through the roof of my car. It was from Jess: **Are you going to Jason Townsend's party tonight?**

I didn't respond.

Finally, school let out. I couldn't get to Ray Anne's house fast enough. She welcomed me inside, and we sat in her dad's cramped office.

"So what happened to you today? I couldn't believe it when I saw you slumped over on the stairwell."

I had to warn her. "Ray, I know every day or two, I have some ridiculous story to tell you about things you can't see or hear or anything, and you always seem to believe me, which is so awesome. But I have to warn you. This is gonna be the most unbelievable thing I've ever told you—ever."

As usual, she took a moment to mull over what I just said, then told me to proceed while supplying her undivided attention.

I started at the beginning and anxiously explained how I saw the Creepers all scurrying toward the cafeteria and throwing themselves on the floor. I then described the unbelievable sensation that came over me and disclosed every detail I could recall about the king's opulent appearance and oppressive behavior. I feared that as I spoke about the ground opening up, she would finally scoff in utter disbelief, but instead, she grabbed a nearby throw blanket and listened all the more intently.

When I recounted seeing what looked to me like human souls suffering torment, she didn't hold back. Tears streamed over her pretty cheeks. She had attended Meagan's funeral that morning—and many others in the months past—so this all weighed heavily on her empathetic heart.

Once I finished telling her everything, I figured she'd have some questions for me, but I was not expecting this one.

She wiped her face then whispered her request as if she knew it was scandalous. "Owen, I want to see what you see. Will you take me to the water in the woods so I can drink, too? I've been thinking—"

"No!" I stood and shouted so loud that Mrs. Greiner came running around the corner asking if everything was okay. Ray and I assured her all was well, then I sat back down and tried to calm myself.

"Ray, that is never, ever an option. Do you understand?"

"But why? I could be so much more helpful if I could see the—"

"Because it's not safe! It will make you sick—really, really sick."

I knew full well that water actually had the potential to be fatal, but I wasn't about to share that. If she knew the role I played in Jared and Conner's deaths, I was sure she'd despise me for the self-centered monster I was and want nothing to do with me. There were also the legal implications of confessing my crime, but that actually scared me less than the risk of losing Ray's respect.

She finally reverted back to discussing the morning's events. "What do you think you witnessed today, Owen? The arrival of an alien leader? Some sort of reincarnated king?"

After all of the intense research and scrutinizing I'd been doing lately, I was beginning to lean toward a certain theory about the Creepers, but I was reluctant to admit it. At the risk of sounding childish, I wanted her to go first. "What do you think I saw?" I asked, knowing full well what she would say.

She spoke with absolute conviction. "I believe you've been seeing the satanic world all along, and today you peered right into the depths of hell."

Although it felt strange to admit, I was inclined to agree. I officially believed in the demon world. I still couldn't reconcile my doubts about God, though. It made sense to me that the Watchmen reported to a higher authority, but their refusal to annihilate the Creepers made me question the existence of an all-powerful deity. At the very least, I questioned the nature and character of one such being.

Still, Ray Anne was relieved that I was finally starting to see some things her way for a change. Unfortunately that made me second-guess myself. I worried if my feelings for her were clouding the issue and causing me to lose objectivity.

She leaned in and, in a hushed tone, begged me one more time. "So what harm would it do if I could see all the spiritual stuff, too, like you?"

I pled my case again, trying to keep my voice down. "Ray Anne, you can never drink that water. Promise me you won't ever go looking for it. Please, don't make me sorry I told you about it in the first place."

She agreed and then knelt next to the couch where I was sitting. We lingered in the heavy silence a while, then she asked if she could pray for me. I said she could, but it was simply out of consideration for her. Prayer was her thing, not mine.

Her words were kind. My thoughts vacillated between the possibility of God's existence and the life-altering scene I just witnessed at school. She said "amen," then sat by me a while. Her presence was enough to bring immense comfort.

I took that opportunity to affirm how I felt about her.

"I understand you have your reasons for wanting to remain just friends, Ray Anne, but I want you to know that I'm fully committed to you. I don't want to go out with anyone but you. So maybe in your heart I'm not your boyfriend, but in my heart, I'm all in."

She smiled and offered up another one of her guarded roadblock statements. "Thanks. I'm just trying to use wisdom and be careful. 'Friends' isn't a bad thing, you know? You wanna watch TV?" She clearly hoped to lighten the moment.

I hung out there for another hour, then left so they could have dinner. They invited me to stay, but I was too drained to carry on an intelligent conversation with her parents.

Ray Anne walked me to my car. "I guess you heard about the big party everyone is going to at Jason Townsend's house tonight," she said. "His parents are out of town, and it's gonna be crazy. I don't want to go anywhere near that place. I know of several people who are bringing weapons—like, guns and knives. I guess people are paranoid now that Conner and Jared were supposedly murdered. They think there's some psycho student among us who's out to get us. Pretty scary, huh?"

Wow. I had no idea everyone now assumed Jared and Conner were murdered, much less by a student.

"Yeah. I don't wanna go to that party either," I said. We exchanged our goodbyes, and I left.

The last place I wanted to be in my cursed condition was a party, but as I drove home, I found myself worrying about Jess. I sent her a text and tried to discourage her from going tonight, but not surprisingly, her mind was made up.

My mom called to tell me she picked up dinner for the two of us. As we sat at the breakfast table eating our burgers and fries, I could tell she had something she wanted to say. Finally, she opened up.

"Owen, you know I'll stand by you through thick and thin, no matter what, and of course I'll get you the legal help you need, but there's something I need from you."

"Okay?"

"I need the truth. I'm not accusing you of harming those boys, but if you did, I need you to tell me, right now."

It wasn't like her to want to get to the bottom of anything. She always preferred avoidance and an "ignorance is bliss" life philosophy, so her insistence on knowing the truth caught me off guard. I didn't feel comfortable confessing to her, but I also didn't want to lie to her, not straight to her face.

For one moment, I considered coming clean. Certainly my conscience would benefit from the relief of telling at least one person the honest truth about what really happened in the woods that evening. But she refused to be honest with me. My whole life, I knew she was hiding something, but when I dared to question her, she closed up and gave me shallow answers we both knew didn't add up.

"Mom, all we did was go play basketball at the park, then jog and goof around in the woods for a while. That's it. They're just focusing so hard on me because I happened to be the last one to hang around Jared and Conner and they're desperate for leads, but I've done nothing wrong. I promise."

She looked at me the same way I'd always looked at her after she fed me a story I wanted to believe but couldn't. We threw away our trash and went our separate ways.

I tried to find something to watch on TV, but I was too preoccupied to settle on anything. In between trying to suppress mental images of the horrendous scene I witnessed at school, I couldn't shake the sinking feeling that Jess was in some sort of trouble. I told myself I'd never do another kind thing for that girl after she ratted me out to the police, but I decided to stop by the party, just long enough to check on her and put my concerns to rest.

Jason only lived a few blocks away from Ray Anne, so I was careful to park around the corner, as far away as I could from Ray's street. The odds of her driving by the party were slim, but I didn't want to take any chances. It wouldn't be the end of the world if she found out I was there, I guess. I just didn't want to have to explain why I went. If she suspected I still had feelings for Jess, it could really mess things up.

I knocked on the door and hoped they would let me in. My reputation wasn't what it used to be, to say the least. I was now considered psychotic by most of my former friends.

Some girl I recognized but didn't know opened the door, and the smell of beer, weed, and Creepers accosted my nose. It was a typical high school party scene, only for me, chains, cords, and the presence of evil beings were now part of the mix.

The music was loud, but that didn't bother me. What did concern me was that Dan was standing in a dim corner, clearly hitting on some blonde freshman girl. I looked around for Jess, but didn't see her, so I texted her. She said she was on her way.

Although it was difficult to talk over the music, a guy from my third period class initiated a conversation, and we went back and forth for a while about college plans. I was jealous of how promising a future he had. Mine was clear as mucus. I maintained I was going premed at UCLA, but that was just for appearance sake.

The evening got interesting when I spotted a group gathered around a table where two girls were playing with a ouija board. Oddly enough, my mom warned me on numerous occasions to stay away from those things and never ever touch them. I could see now that she was right to caution me.

The two girls touching the pointer giggled and gasped as it slid across the board, spelling out answers to their personal questions while onlookers debated whether the movement was motivated by ghosts or the girls. I cringed observing how Creepers were, in fact, manipulating the pointer, no doubt lying and deceiving with each response. They didn't care about the girls' insignificant inquiries. This was a prized opportunity to make new connections with fresh ignorant prey.

My classmates thought they were summoning the gentle spirits of people who had died long ago, gaining insight from loving souls who now existed in an eternal, more enlightened realm. In reality, they were begging reprobate forces of evil to oppress them.

I walked over and wasted my breath. "You guys shouldn't be doing that. Seriously. It's not good." They proceeded without hesitation.

I headed toward the snack table and had just scooped up a handful of peanut M&Ms when I spotted Jess making her way toward me through the crowd, trying not to spill her beer. Dan walked up behind her and put his arm around her neck, then decided to take a pot shot at me.

"What's this madman doing here, looking for his next victim?" Clearly, rumors were going around about me behind my back. Jess stared at the floor, hurt that he would say such a thing.

I laughed. "You know us psychopaths. We're always up to something."

He tried to smile, but I could tell my comment made him uneasy, just as I intended. I turned around, thinking our exchange was finished, but he opened his big mouth again.

"Everyone, I'd stay alert if I were you. We've got a murderer among us."

"Dan, stop!" Jess tried to shut him up, but that was an utter waste of energy. He didn't care one bit about her feelings, and he despised that she would dare take up for me.

"I'd watch what I say if I were you," I said, knowing few people could actually hear our conversation. "I'd hate for you to become the next victim, wouldn't you?"

I realized that sounded as if I just threatened his life, and that probably was not the wisest move given the current police investigation I was caught up in, but seeing the look of fear on his face made it entirely worth it. And as a bonus, it shut him up.

He and Jess disappeared into the crowd. I waited a few minutes, then went looking for her. I was passing through the hallway when she grabbed me by my sleeve.

"Owen, I'm so sorry. I didn't . . . he can be really mean sometimes."

She had obviously had too much to drink and strained to form coherent statements.

"Don't worry about it. Look, why don't you let me drive you home?"

"No, I have to stay with Dan."

I was willing to walk away at that point, knowing I'd at least offered to help her, but I saw something strange— brilliant, actually—that captured my attention. Near the bottom of Jess's midsection was a super tiny, laser-bright light. I stared for a while, not knowing what to make of it.

"What?" She could tell I was perplexed.

I pulled her toward me and took a closer look, then gasped. I suddenly felt sure I knew what it was.

"Jess, you've got to come with me right now. And put down that drink."

"Why? What's going on?"

It was not only difficult for her to hear me above the noise, but her mind was in an alcohol-induced fog.

I opened a nearby bedroom door then carefully pulled Jess inside, closing the door behind us.

"I said we have to go. Let me take you home."

"Why?" She took another big swig of beer before I grabbed the bottle and set it on top of a bookshelf, too high for her to reach.

"Hey, give me that. You never let me drink *anything*."

"This isn't about protecting you from toxic water or evil beings. It's nothing like that. Don't you know?"

"Know what?"

I couldn't believe it. She didn't have a clue. I took a deep breath and blurted it out. "Jess, you're pregnant."

She looked stunned for a moment, then laughed. "What are you talking about? I'm not having a baby." She stumbled and landed on the edge of a neatly-made bed. "You've really lost it now, Owen." She fell backwards onto the mattress and grinned, dismissing the seriousness of what I just said like she always did.

I sat down beside her, hoisting her up to a sitting position, then said it again, only with more compassion this time. "Jess, you're pregnant. You really are."

"How would you know that?"

There was no sense in going down the path of explaining what I could see emanating from her body, more like her womb, I guess. "Please, this once, just trust me. It's the truth."

"But I . . . I don't . . . understand."

She started crying. I wasn't sure if it was because she actually believed me or it was just a meaningless display of emotion in response to having too much to drink.

"I've done so many things lately that you would be unhappy about," she said. "Why are you even talking to me after what I did to you, you know, with the police and all?" She looked up at me with an adoring expression.

"We can talk about that later. Why don't you let me take you home now?" I was just about to help her up when she leaned over and wrapped her arms around my neck, burying her head in my chest.

"Thank you for always being there when I call you and need you." She stared into my eyes, and I got the impression she wanted to kiss me. I held my breath, repulsed by the smell of alcohol on her's.

That's when the bedroom door flung open. I fully expected to see Dan standing there, ready to go to fists having caught me sitting on a bed holding his girlfriend. The last person I expected to see was Ray Anne.

I couldn't believe my eyes.

Neither could she.

20. Evil Ambush

"Ray Anne!" I called out after her, but she had shoved her way through the crowd and was nearly out the door. "Wait!" I rushed to catch up.

Once outside, she bolted on foot in the direction of her house. I sprinted behind until I was close enough to reach out and touch her.

"Ray Anne, stop!"

She finally quit running, and we both hunched over in the dark street, gasping for air.

"I know you were surprised to see me like that with Jess, but it's not what you think."

"Let me guess. You were saving her from a spiritual attack, right?" I'd never seen Ray Anne so furious.

"No, it was something else. I'll tell you if you'll just calm down."

"No, Owen! I won't calm down! You promised never to lie to me." Her voice cracked and she began to cry, causing my heart to explode in my chest.

"I didn't lie to you. Please just let me explain."

"When I saw your car parked outside," she said, "I figured you had a good reason for being there, and I came to offer my help if you needed it. Do you know how foolish I feel right now?"

She stormed off, wanting nothing to do with me or my excuses. I walked right behind her and delved into an explanation without her consent, but she was way too angry to listen. We were halfway to her house when she turned around and let me have it.

"Has this all been a big joke to you? You've made up these absurd stories about shackles and Creepers and seeing into hell, and like an absolute fool, I've allowed myself to believe you! You aren't *committed* to me," she said with disgust. "You don't even know how to be a loyal *friend*. I can't believe I actually took you seriously!"

She turned to keep walking, but I grabbed her arm to stop her. She jerked away. "Leave me alone. I'm not sure exactly what I believe anymore, but I know I don't believe you!"

She looked up and shouted at the night sky. "God, are you even there? Why did you let someone deceive me again? How could you do this to me?"

That kind of contempt toward God was completely out of character for her. I realized I needed to give her some space and time to collect herself.

I was just about to ask if I could please simply walk her home—it was pitch dark outside—but in that instant, three Creepers came charging up the street, heading straight for me.

"Ray, I know you don't want to hear this right now, but—"

"Oh, shut up," she said, continuing taking angry steps toward her house.

I wondered how close the corrupted trio would dare to come near me with Ray Anne's glowing presence only a few feet away. I kept close to her and waited to see what calculated move they would make next.

Within seconds, I recognized one of the Creepers. It was "Faithless," the bully that had been stalking me lately. The others, "Betrayal" and "Distrust," fanned out in front of Ray Anne, all three glaring directly at her and overlooking me entirely. While keeping up with her brisk pace, "Distrust" plunged its hand underneath the neckline of its grimy garment and pulled out what looked like a black burlap sack. It rummaged through the contents without taking its hateful eyes off Ray Anne, then quickly pulled two bulky chains from the bag.

The Creepers were closing in on her, yet careful not to trespass into the aura beaming around her feet.

"Ray Anne, you have to listen to me. Something is happening."

"Whatever. I'm so done listening to your wild stories."

"Distrust" tossed a chain to each of the Creepers lurking on either side of Ray Anne. I watched in bewilderment as the one named "Betrayal" locked its wrist inside the singed metal cuff, then took pride hoisting the chain high into the air and whipping it toward Ray Anne in an attempt to loop it around her neck. It fell just short and slammed to the pavement.

"Ray Anne!"

"I told you to leave me alone!"

"But they're after you!"

"I don't believe you. Besides, you said Creepers are supposedly scared of me, remember?"

"Faithless" and "Betrayal" kept hurling chains at Ray Anne's neck until finally, they both managed to encircle her throat. Meanwhile "Distrust" pulled cords out of the bag, only they were much longer than the ones that hung from people's heads, at least fifteen feet long.

Ray Anne wept and despaired aloud. "I can't trust anyone. That's the way it's always been. Everyone lies to me!"

"I didn't lie to you. I only went there to make sure that Jess was okay and that—"

"Oh, she looked just fine to me, sitting there in bed with you!"

"No, it's not like that."

By now, "Betrayal" had discarded the black bag, throwing it near my feet. It then began the sickening process of burrowing the cords into its hands, two in each palm. That's when I noticed the letters R—I—G on the bag, but I didn't have time to process that.

"Ray Anne, please!"

She stopped and faced me, turning her back on the Creepers while tears flooded down her face. "How many times do I have to tell you to leave me alone? I'm almost home. Just go away!"

With the cords now nestled deep into its decaying flesh, "Betrayal" swung its arms into the air, sending the grisly cords flying up behind Ray Anne, then falling and pounding her directly in the back of the head where they somehow stuck.

I grabbed one icy chain and also yanked at a skin-piercing cord, but the torture tools didn't budge.

"Stop it, Owen! I mean it!" I must have looked like a lunatic to her, tugging at what appeared to be absolutely nothing.

"There are three Creepers attacking you! You've got two chains looped around your neck and four cords plastered to your head! This is serious!"

Physically exhausted and emotionally spent, Ray Anne collapsed and sat back on the curb, covering her face with her hands as she continued to cry. "I'm so confused. Why won't you just admit that you want to be with Jess? Why sneak around?"

I didn't answer. I was totally absorbed observing the Creepers' next wicked maneuver. I'd heard their monotone whispering many times before, but now, with Ray Anne in their clutches, they were all three moaning in a low pitch, eerie chorus. As if music to their ears, mobs of Creepers began pouring out of the shadows, moving in from every direction and lifting their voices as one.

They formed a circle around us both, but clearly feasted their predatory eyes on Ray Anne.

She suddenly became less weepy and far angrier. "That's it. I'm through—through with you, through with your crazy lies, through with trusting people. From now on, I refuse to trust anyone but myself!"

The Creepers groaned louder as if energized by her suffering and self-reliance.

"I know you're upset, but you have to stop this, Ray. Please, don't say anything else. Let's get you home." I thought perhaps the presence of her glowing family might help drive away the army now encamped around us. I reached down to help her up, but she slapped my nervous hand away.

"I'm not going anywhere with you. Just leave me alone. I want to sit here by myself. Go away!"

"But if I leave, you won't be by yourself." I fought back a flood of emotions as I exhausted myself trying to explain. "You're in the center of, like, a hundred Creepers right now, and they've come together to do something to you, to hurt you somehow. Please Ray, I need you to believe me!"

The sight of her bound in chains and cords, being victimized by a gang of Creepers, was more than I could take. Her glow was still there, but it was only keeping them slightly at bay. They were several human arm lengths away, but attacking her, nonetheless.

"Sorry, I can't believe you. Not anymore, Owen. I just can't."

I was desperate to convince her I was telling the truth. I mustered the confidence to approach the familiar Creeper named "Faithless," one of the two cuffed to a chain clinging to Ray Anne's neck. It was so tall that my head was right in line with its wrist, allowing me to get a decent look at the cuff. I used my cell phone for light. The giant didn't seem to notice.

"Who's Tori Deanne Lansing?" I asked.

"What?" She looked surprised.

"Tori Lansing! Do you know that person?" I was frantic, desperate to get through to her.

"Yes, I know her. She and I despised each other in elementary school. We made each other's lives miserable. But how did you—"

"Is your mom's middle name Ruth?" I had already run to check out the inscription on the other Creeper's cuff. I couldn't imagine why Ray Anne's mom's name was on there, but I thought perhaps the fact that I was able to state her middle name would serve as proof for Ray Anne that I truly was seeing supernatural manifestations.

"Yeah. How did you know that?"

I ran to her and slammed to my knees, then squeezed her shoulders. "Those are the names written on the cuffs of the two Creepers that have you bound in chains. I swear. You have two huge chains around your neck, these awful cords stuck to your head, and a gang of Creepers working together to harm you."

"I . . . I don't know." She wouldn't allow herself to believe me. It was beyond frustrating. I stood, thinking perhaps I should run and get her brother or parents. That's when hope came alive in me again. I saw seven immense Watchmen running in our direction.

"Ray Anne, they're here. They're here to help!"

"Who?"

"The Watchmen! They've come to free you!"

I anticipated that at any second, the horde of Creepers would begin squealing and fleeing every which way.

They didn't. Instead they formed an even tighter circle. The ones on the outside turned and faced the Watchmen and began hissing like poisonous snakes while the others kept up the sickening groaning melody. I stood there in stunned devastation as the Watchmen slowed their pace, then came to a stop just short of the circular wall of Creepers.

"What's going on? Do something!" I shouted at the shining Watchmen.

They looked agitated, like they wanted to move in and crush the Creepers but didn't have permission or something. I didn't understand.

"Ray Anne, they're just standing there!"

"What are you talking about?"

"The Watchmen!"

I began waving my arms and calling out to them, trying to get their attention while pleading for help.

They didn't move a massive muscle.

I looked back at Ray Anne. She was shivering.

"Are you alright?"

"I feel awful," she said. "I'm so confused and scared."

"Ray Anne, listen to me. You're playing right into their hands. You've got to stop this. Everything is gonna be okay. I just need you to come back to your senses. Remember who you are, what you believe, and what you stand for. Can you do that, for me?"

She cried for a moment longer, then took a deep breath and nodded her head, assuring me she would try to get a hold of her runaway thoughts and emotions. She grabbed my hands and closed her eyes. After a short time of silence, she quietly uttered, "Heavenly Father, please forgive me for saying I can only trust myself. I know I can trust you."

In that instant, the chaotic noise around us escalated so severely that I covered my ears. The Creepers howled in terror as the Watchmen moved in, grabbing handfuls of them at a time and hurling them some one hundred yards away. "Distrust" snatched the chains and cords off Ray Anne, chunking them back into the sloppy bag, then narrowly escaping the Watchmen's wrath, disappeared into the night.

In less than a minute, there wasn't a single Creeper in sight, but the Watchmen remained poised to fight, looking all around for stragglers. Their attention then shifted to Ray Anne. She remained balled up on the curb, releasing tears that streamed from a fractured but faith-filled heart.

I nearly ceased to breathe as one of the Watchmen lowered to the ground, positioning himself right in front of her. For what seemed like the millionth time in recent weeks, I couldn't believe my eyes. The exquisite Watchmen looked into Ray Anne's face with the purest of compassion, then took his humongous hand and wiped a tear from her check with the tip of his finger.

I threw myself to the ground beside him and looked straight up at him. "Thank you! Thank you so much!" He didn't even glance in my direction.

He and his splendid companions peered into the sky, then ran off, disappearing in the opposite direction from which they came.

"They're gone now—all of the Creepers and the Watchmen, too," I said. We sat in the soothing silence for a while, relishing the new calm that finally engulfed us.

I couldn't deny that I'd just seen Ray Anne's prayer cause a drastic change in the unseen realm, but I wasn't sure if it was her prayer or just her personal resolve to resist their manipulation that actually made the difference.

I eventually described the spectacle that just unfolded, including how a Watchman responded to her with great affection. I also took the time to explain what really happened earlier that night and how there was absolutely nothing going on between Jess and me. Ray Anne was shocked and deeply concerned when I told her that Jess was pregnant.

"I'm sorry I freaked out on you," she said. "I have a huge fear of being lied to, and I sometimes overreact."

I took responsibility for not trusting her enough to simply have told her that I was worried about Jess and planning to go to the party to check on her. Then I asked her why she was so afraid of others' deception. She became very tense, and I could tell it pained her to answer.

"When my little brother was dying, my mom didn't want to burden with me with the tragic news, so my parents kept it from me. They felt like Justin could handle it far better than me, so they told him the truth, but kept assuring me Brent was just sick and not to worry.

"The day he died came as a total shock to me. I later learned that my dad wanted to tell me, but it was my mom who insisted they keep it from me. It hurt so badly because, even though I was young, there was so much I would have said and done had I known I only had a short time left with my brother.

"I've forgiven my mom for that, but it still bothers me at times."

I realized in that moment that I was guilty of thinking Ray Anne had never suffered any real family trauma, certainly nothing on par with me. But I was wrong. She'd been through a lot, actually.

We spent some more time talking about Brent. She shared a few of her dearest memories of him, then explained how horrible it was watching him become increasingly sick. She also described how his death forever changed her parents, especially her mother.

"Speaking of my mother," Ray Anne said, wiping her eyes and clearing her throat. "You said her name, and also Tori's name, was written on cuffs? I don't understand that." As always, she was quick to jump to a new subject, but I was relieved that she was acting more like herself now and back to taking my stories seriously.

To me, it was obvious. "I think you must have worn those chains and cords at one point, but you somehow got free. The Creepers were trying to use your past against you, so to speak."

"What makes you so sure?" she asked.

"The bag with the chains and cords displayed three letters. I didn't make the connection right away, but it's clear now. Your initials were on there, R-I-G. Ray Anne Isabel Greiner. I'm guessing those chains and cords once belonged to you, and they've kept them to torment and exploit you with them when the opportunity arises."

"Owen!" She jumped to her feet, scaring me half to death. "Think about it. Most of the Creeper notes have numbers with three letters. I bet they're writing down initials."

That made sense but seemed far too primitive. Surely the Creeper code was harder to crack than that.

I had to concede. "Perhaps that's correct," I said, "but how could we ever track down who the initials belong to?"

I took out my phone and pulled up the images of the notes, specifically a shot of one with the most frequently seen code, 0602SGM.

"Who do we know with the initials S-G-M?" Ray Anne pulled out her phone and panned through her social media contacts. There were two seniors at our school who qualified: Spencer Monroe and Stella Murphy. That was a start.

"I'm friends with both of them," Ray Anne said with great enthusiasm. "I'll text them right now and ask their middle names."

It was nearly midnight, but they both responded immediately. Spencer's middle name was Michael. Stella's was Grace.

"Oh my gosh! They're planning to do something to Stella," Ray Anne said. "Unless there's someone else at our school with those very same initials—and what are the odds of that—she's their target."

That's when a new wave of clarity washed over me.

"Maybe their plan isn't to just hurt Stella, but to use her to bring destruction to *lots more* people."

"What makes you say that?" she asked.

Stella had been talking nonstop for months about her upcoming surfside party. On the night of graduation, all the seniors, juniors, and a handful of the in-crowd sophomores would flock to her parent's beach house on Galveston Island for a riotous party.

The date of graduation, by the way, was June 2, or should I say 0602?

21. Shocking Betrayal

Over the next two weeks, no students committed suicide, which was a welcome surprise. Still, I feared the Creepers were revving up to deal the most devastating deathblow yet, a grand finale of sorts to conclude the worst school year in history. Ray and I were confident that, based on the surprisingly simplistic Creeper code, it would take place at Stella's party the night of graduation.

One Saturday afternoon, Ray Anne brought her little pink Bible with her to my house and proceeded to flip through it while sharing what she called "the plan of salvation." On multiple occasions, she had insisted the reason her family glowed is because they'd each confessed their sins to God and asked Jesus to be their Savior, to which I always responded, "It can't be that easy. If it was, everyone would glow." Besides, I'd observed Christians flocking in and out of church, and there was always a good mix of glowing and shackled people.

There was another impossible variable in that equation, but it was nothing I would ever disclose to Ray Anne. Her family asking forgiveness for *their* sins was one thing. My asking was something else entirely. Think about it. I'd not only spent the bulk of my life arguing against the existence of God and taking pot shots at Bible-toting people, but I was guilty of what had to be an unpardonable sin—committing and covering up not one, but two murders. And as a shiny cherry on top, I had literally shouted to God that I hated him.

Ray Anne's persistence paid off, though. While seated beside her on my couch one Saturday afternoon, I agreed to give the Christian thing a try. She spoke a prayer, and I repeated after her. We said "amen," and I lingered there in the off chance that some glorious feeling or energy would soon wash over me.

Just as I predicted, nothing happened. I didn't start to glow, Creepers continued taunting me without hesitation in the days following, and my conscience still accused me night and day of my unforgivable guilt and incurable skepticism.

The issue was settled for me: religion was not the answer to my crisis.

The following Monday, my mom had arranged for me to meet with a lawyer. He asked lots of questions, and I stuck with my original story basically word-for-word. I didn't mention anything about the water and instead suggested that, after dropping me off that night, Conner and Jared must have ingested something they knew they shouldn't. "Conner accused me to his mother as a cover-up," I said, "using me as a scapegoat since he knew his parents would be furious with him. He wasn't about to rat out Jared, so he blamed the whole foolish stunt on me."

My new lawyer wholeheartedly believed me and agreed to represent me. It was his belief that, since graduation was just one month away, the authorities were intentionally going easy on me but would pounce on me right away after I graduated. If they pressed me before then, it could create an unnecessary surge of negative publicity, and seeing as our senior class was already limping into graduation, they didn't want that for our morale-depleted community.

Throughout the next few weeks, every second Ray Anne would allow me to spend with her, I did. We brainstormed all kinds of Creeper plots that we imagined could possibly go down on the second of June and anticipated how we would counterattack given each particular scenario. Ray Anne frequently dropped hints about how much more helpful she could be if only she could see into the spirit world, too, and I cautioned her over and over about what a grave mistake that would be.

The last Friday in May, Mr. and Mrs. Greiner went out of town for a few days, leaving Justin and Ray home alone. I fantasized about Ray Anne inviting me over and us taking advantage of her parents being gone, if you know what I mean, but quickly reminded myself that would never, ever happen. Ray Anne was firm in her conviction not to fool around before marriage, something I truly admired but frequently had a hard time respecting. I knew to pressure her was to lose her though, so I didn't dare. I also didn't want to draw that "Lust" monster to me again, so I tried to behave.

Ray made plans to have a friend over, and I sat at home watching TV and feeling sorry for myself because I didn't have a single friend, except for her, of course. I was sick of being alone.

It was no relief when my mom's boyfriend dropped her off at one o'clock in the morning. She came stumbling through the door tethered to a Creeper named "Regret." My dog went berserk until I brought her into my bedroom and stuffed a towel under my door. Valentine finally laid down, but wouldn't allow herself to fall asleep for several hours. I had an impossible time sleeping, too.

By Saturday afternoon, my mom was rid of the Creeper and had a long list of errands for me to run. I always did my most in-depth thinking in the car, and that day, my thoughts turned to graduation. It was just one week away, and, with the exception of my mother, I had absolutely no one to invite. She was a complete loner, and I was too now. It was a depressing realization.

I questioned whether I should even show up for graduation. I was much more focused on what would go down that night than during the official ceremony that morning, anyway.

I was on my way home at about four-thirty in the afternoon when I received a text from Lance: **Hey. We need to talk. Meet me at the fields.**

There were several acres of grassy fields with trails not far from Lance's house where he and I used to go to ride our bikes when we were younger. I didn't want to admit it, but I had really been missing hanging with him lately. I'd also been worried about him and wondering how he was coping in the aftermath of Meagan's death.

It took me about twenty minutes to get there, and I was slightly confused when I arrived. His truck was there, but several of our friends' vehicles were there, too. I didn't see anyone, though. I parked, then got out and looked around. My stomach was chilled, but within seconds, I was melting in the Texas heat.

My heart skipped a beat when, all at once, ten or so guys emerged from behind their parked vehicles, all glaring at me with stern faces. I couldn't believe it. Lance had lured me into an ambush.

"Hey guys. What's going on?" I tried to stay collected even though I knew I was in big trouble.

Lance spoke up. "I don't know if the cops are on to you or not, but we are, and we're ready to enforce justice on behalf of Jared and Conner."

"And this is your way of getting justice? Tricking me into coming here so you could all gang up on me?"

I didn't deny the fact that I deserved to be punished. I only confronted the deceptive, brutal way he was going about it. I knew there was no sense in trying to reason with him, though. He was joined to a Creeper named "Rage."

Lance took steps toward me, then cursed in my face, making all kinds of violent threats. That's when the Creeper made its move, performing a vile maneuver that I suspected was possible after reading up on demonic manifestations, but hoped I would never, ever have to witness.

"Rage" entered Lance. It literally pried its way in through Lance's back and took residence inside of him. It somehow shifted its shape so that its huge frame was concealed within a much smaller human host.

As if that wasn't gruesome enough, Lance's appearance instantly mutated. His skin turned gray like a Creeper's and his face became distorted, reflecting nearly identical facial features as "Rage" and staring me down with the same dead eyes.

I stumbled backwards, revolted by the Creeper's bodily invasion. As Lance continued spewing hateful words at me, I observed that it was the Creeper doing all of the talking, moving Lance's mouth at will. And his voice was lower. That startled me. Lance was officially a slave to his iniquitous intruder's dominating spell.

I wondered if the other guys could see or hear Lance's morbid metamorphosis, but they paid no attention to him. All eyes were on me.

One by one, they pressed in around me, festering with nothing but vicious intent. My adrenaline was in full force, and although I was scared, my plan was to give them hell and go down swinging. I knew they would put a serious beat down on me. I just hoped they didn't pound me to death.

Before I could get in a single jab, I felt a sudden sharp pain as one of them bashed me in the back of the head with what I assumed was a good-sized rock. I caved to my knees and covered my head, bracing myself for their merciless group attack. They kicked me in my ribs, punched me in the head, and even pulled me by my hair. I tried to block my face, but they twisted my neck, then struck me right in the mouth with repeated blows.

I heard them shouting at me, calling me a murderer and a liar. I was sure I saw several Creepers wailing on me right along with them as well.

As the distinct taste of blood flooded my tongue and I felt my sense of consciousness quickly fading, I truly believed I was about to die.

At first, I feared Creepers would swoop in and abduct me right out of my flesh, leaving that horrific dusty hole in my abdomen and plunging my soul into that fiery place of nonstop suffering. But my final thoughts turned to Ray Anne. Believe it or not, I lamented the idea of another man winning her heart in my absence and stealing her long-awaited affection right out from under me.

I wanted to live, but I was no match for the pack of wolves devouring me without restraint. I finally yielded to the inevitable and accepted that this was how I was going to die.

I honestly believe they would have beat the very last breath out of me had it not been for an elderly man who happened to drive by. He laid on his horn and threatened to use his rifle on them if they didn't cease that second and retreat to their vehicles. They reluctantly complied and sped away, leaving my wounded body in the street in a swarm of dirt.

"Son, are you okay?"

"Yeah." It really hurt to say that.

"Let me call you an ambulance."

"No." I didn't want the police to get involved. I was hoping to stay off their radar. "Please, I can get up. I just need a second."

He stayed there smoldering in the heat with me, all the while pleading for me to let him call for help, but as I finally stood upright some twenty minutes later, he relented and helped walk me to my car.

"I'm gonna drive straight home. My mom will look after me," I said, hoping to assure him he could leave me at that point. I thanked him the best I could having just been bludgeoned and all. To this day, I credit that man with having saved my life.

I was covered from head to toe with blood and bleeding profusely from my bottom lip. I'm sure I could have used some stitches in multiple places, but I wanted to steer clear of hospitals. After seeing Meagan's soul seized from her body, hospitals would always be portals to the dreaded underworld of the dead in my mind. Besides, I was in no condition to go anywhere but home. Seeing Lance possessed by a Creeper was distressing, to say the least.

Once inside my house, my mom took one look at my blood-soaked appearance and went nuts. I felt grateful that she was both home and sober. She pleaded with me to go to the emergency room, but I refused. She pulled out a huge First Aid kit I never knew we had, demanding to know who hurt me.

I didn't dare tell her Lance was the ringleader. She knew where he lived, and my mom was one of *those* moms. She wouldn't have hesitated to go pound on his door and bash him upside the head with a sharp object if she knew he had just hurt her boy. I didn't want her anywhere near him. I told her I got in a fight with some guys from another school and tried to downplay the whole horrendous thing.

After I was bandaged, had sipped on some chicken noodle soup, and had a chance to recoup in bed for a few hours, the reality of what just happened began sinking in. I was grief-stricken by Lance's ferocious plot against me, but sickened by his fate. Out of the two of us, he was in far more danger in that grassy field than I was.

As the sun set on what was shaping up to be the one of the worst days of my life, I called and texted Ray Anne repeatedly but she didn't answer. At first I didn't think much of it, but when I hadn't heard from her two hours later, at eleven-thirty at night, I started to wonder if everything was okay.

Just before midnight, her brother Justin called me. He asked if I had seen Ray Anne, and I told him I hadn't heard from her since that morning. I could hear in his voice that he was deeply concerned.

"When did you last talk to her, and what did she say?" I asked him.

"It was right after we ate dinner. She grabbed a garden shovel out of the garage, then told me she needed to use the car, but she wouldn't be gone long. She was going to look for something in the woods. That didn't make any sense to me, but I blew it off. Now I wish I had asked more questions."

I dropped the phone and covered my gaping mouth with both hands.

"She wouldn't! She didn't!"

I picked my phone up and told Justin that I would look for her and call him back.

I'm sure it was painful to get dressed, but I didn't notice at the time. My mom was asleep on the couch. I didn't bother wasting time waking her and trying to come up with some explanation as to why I was hobbling out the door that time of night. I drove like a madman to the woods and nearly went into cardiac arrest when I saw Ray Anne's car parked there.

I pulled a flashlight out of my glove box then ran into the woods as fast as I could, straining to breathe with what felt like numerous broken ribs. I'd never shown Ray Anne where the water was. Maybe she was just lost and actually hadn't found or ingested any of the lethal substance. I held out hope.

I called her name many times as I made my way to the infamous wooded spot, but there was no response. In a matter of minutes, I could hear the familiar, odd sound of the rushing water.

I shined my light in every direction and yelled for Ray Anne, but didn't see her. My thoughts were erratic and anxious, and I felt like I was dreaming, like I couldn't wake from a nightmare. That's when I saw the pile of dirt, a shovel, and the hole. I ran to take a closer look.

"Oh no. Oh God, please no."

Clearly she had found the water, but I refused to entertain thoughts about what happened next. It was too excruciating to consider that she might have swallowed the stuff hours ago and now be lying lifeless in the woods, God knows where. I pressed on, frantically calling her name and shining my light all around, clinging to the expectation that she was still alive.

That's when my world flat lined. I saw her body off in the distance. She was lying on her side in some shrubbery, not moving. I flew over there and crashed onto my knees beside her, crying out her name.

"How did you find me?" she whispered, still not moving.

I let out the single biggest sigh of relief of my life and collapsed in the dirt beside her.

"Ray, tell me you didn't drink that stuff!"

"I did drink it, and I don't regret it. I just wasn't prepared for my stomach and head to hurt this bad. It's so painful that I haven't been able to move. I don't feel like I can get up."

"Ray Anne, we have to get you out of here right now." I began the process of scooping her into my arms.

"Are you mad at me?" she asked, maintaining a kind tone despite her extreme discomfort.

I didn't have time to explain things. I had to get her into my car and to the hospital right away.

"Come on. We have to get you out of here right this instant!"

"Please just give me more time. I don't think I can stand. Does this throbbing start to ease up after a while?"

"You have to come with me now. I know it hurts, but you've got to get up. I'll help you."

I didn't wait for her permission. I lifted her off the ground then took quick strides in the direction of my car, ignoring the countless aches penetrating my body.

She wanted to walk and winced in pain as I lowered her to her feet. She grabbed her gut just like I'd seen Conner and Jared do and also had done myself.

"I don't feel good, Owen."

"I know. I'm taking you to the hospital."

"What? Why? Don't I just need to go home and sleep it off like you did?"

I eased her into the passenger seat of my car, then got behind the wheel and sped in the direction of the ER.

"Ray, you're gonna hate me once and for all for this, but there's something I haven't told you. I haven't told a single soul. But I have to tell you now. It's a matter of life and death."

"I think I'm gonna vomit," she said while looking for something to barf into. I handed her an empty fast food sack. "It's weird. I need to throw up but can't."

"Yeah, I know that feeling. It's terrible."

I realized now was less than an ideal time to confess to being a murderer, but I owed it to her to be honest for once and tell her that she was most likely about to die. I endured the lump in my throat and smothered an avalanche of emotion as I made a second attempt at coming clean.

"I need you to listen to me. This is really hard to say, but you deserve to know the truth. Ray Anne, there's a very strong chance that you may not survive this."

"What do you mean?"

I finally had her attention. That's when I made my heinous admission.

"It's my fault, Ray. It's my fault that Jared and Conner are dead. They were mocking and challenging me about my visions, so I took them to the water and served it right to them. And it killed them. It literally poisoned them to death, and it's likely gonna do the same thing to you!"

Even after hearing my devastating news and seeing me come unglued, Ray Anne stayed calm. She didn't utter a word for the rest of the car ride, and I knew better than to

292

press her. I couldn't tell if she hated my guts or not. The important thing to me was that we successfully arrived at the emergency room.

When two medical personnel greeted us, I told them she drank something lethal and needed to be admitted right away. They asked me what exactly she ingested, and I said it was toxic waste from the ground. I didn't know how else to describe it.

I was instructed to sit in the lobby and wait. That's when I called Justin and told him I found his sister in the woods, and she was so sick that I brought her to the emergency room. He was shocked. I didn't tell him she was most likely dying. He'd already lost one sibling. The possibility of losing his twin sister would definitely destroy him.

I wandered aimlessly up and down the hallway, preferring to grieve and agonize without being gawked at by a waiting room full of nosy onlookers. I realized that, at that very second, Justin was probably informing his parents that their only daughter was hospitalized, and they were scrambling to make arrangements to come home from their trip.

Even though I was far less to blame in this situation than when Jared and Conner drank the fatal water, I felt just as guilty. No, I hadn't led her to the stuff and urged her to drink it, but I did drag her into this insane world with me through my constant stories. Her desire to help me and others was likely now her undoing. It was totally unfair.

I stood leaning against a wall, desperate to receive an update on Ray Anne's condition, when I saw Officer Smith and Detective Benny walk through the double doors and begin looking all around, no doubt searching for me.

I felt sure this was it. I was in no state of mind to defend myself or cover my tracks with clever lies. This whole ordeal had gone too far. I had no choice. I had to tell the police about the deadly water, even if it cost me my freedom.

I walked straight over to the two men and was surprised when Benny reached over and hugged me. I guess my sullen expression and battered face compelled him to extend some tenderness my way.

"You need to come with us." Officer Smith directed me to get in the car with Benny and him. I saw Justin and his friend in the parking lot, but they didn't see me in getting into the back of the squad car. I was grateful for that.

We all three sat in the parked car, and Benny turned and glared at me from the passenger seat. "Why don't you cut the crap and tell us what's going on so we can help you, son?"

He was right. I had to quit clinging to the same insufficient story. It was time to retell what happened the night of Conner and Jared's deaths and also explain what just went down with Ray Anne. I didn't care that my lawyer wasn't present.

"I've been living a lie, and I'm sick of it."

Detective Benny pulled out his digital recorder and motioned for me to keep talking.

"On March nineteenth, I was in the woods with Jess Thompson, and we stumbled on this odd underground water. She threatened to drink it, and I begged her not to, then I did something really stupid and drank it myself. I was just trying to protect her.

"In a matter of minutes, I got this really bad stomach ache and migraine, so I drove Jess home as fast as I could, and by the time I got to my house, I honestly believed I was dying. I was shocked when I woke up the next day and was completely fine. Believe it or not, that bothered me. I was expecting to die and have everyone grieving over my death, but instead, I woke up to another ordinary, depressing day.

"That's when I started making things up."

"What kind of things?" Benny asked.

"I pretended to see people wearing shackles and chains and having these gross cords draping from the back of their heads like they were enslaved by aliens or demons or something, and I was the only one who could see it. At first it was cool, like, just a fun thing in my head. But then I got carried away and started telling people and even said I could see these huge evil beings attacking certain people.

"It's not like I'm crazy. I just really liked the attention. I liked the feeling of being in control for a change, I guess."

"Did you tell Jared and Conner these stories?" Officer Smith asked.

"Not exactly. They heard about it from someone else. That day we went to play basketball, they brought it up and started giving me a really hard time about it. They ridiculed me to the point that I wanted to make them pay, but not with their lives. I thought if I took them to the woods and gave them some of the water, they would get sick, like I did. I never meant for anything worse than that to happen. I swear!"

Benny looked angry. "Why didn't you tell us about this right away?"

"I got scared. Even though I never dreamed that the water could be deadly, I feared that if it somehow turned out to be, it would look like I killed them. I was also pretty ashamed and embarrassed, I guess, about how out of control my fantasies and storytelling had become, and I dreaded having to come clean about it."

Benny wanted to know why Ray Anne drank the water, and I explained that she just wanted to see the supernatural stuff like me, even though I warned her over and over not to do it. "More than anyone else, she has believed my lies," I said. "She believed it so much that she sought out the water and was eager to drink it."

They asked me to show them where the water was, so I did. They drove to the woods, and I led them right to the tragic spot. Benny had arranged for some forensics people to meet us there and get water samples. My future hinged on the results. If it was clean like Mrs. Barnett claimed it was, it looked as though I just might escape imprisonment after all, even though nothing could convince me that was ordinary water. If it was toxic, I'd have to defend against accusations that I intended to kill my friends.

If Ray Anne didn't survive, it didn't matter to me if I got locked up or not. I'd be shattered no matter where I laid my head at night.

It was almost four o'clock in the morning when they dropped me off at the hospital. I held my breath as I approached the nurse's desk and asked for an update on Ray Anne. I was relieved to hear that she was recovering in a regular hospital room. That's all that the nurses could disclose to me.

Visiting hours weren't for another four hours, so I planned to go home and change out my bandages and get cleaned up. My busted bottom lip was really aching.

I texted Justin and told him I would be back at the hospital at eight o'clock in the morning, and he said that was great because he would be at the airport picking up his parents at that time. He was glad to hear that Ray Anne wouldn't be alone.

I showered and ate some toast, then laid down for two hours before returning to my least favorite place on earth—the hospital. I entered Ray Anne's room and hated the sight of her lying in a hospital bed. I took a seat in a chair by her bedside and stared at her beautiful face while she slept, lifting my eyes continuously to make sure her pulse was still registering on the machine.

It had been a long time since I felt joy, but it surged over me in waves now that I knew she survived the night and would likely be okay.

I couldn't wait for her to wake up and look at me with those big blue eyes of hers. I must have dozed off though because, the next thing I knew, Ray Anne was up and cowering in the corner of the room, staring at me.

"I'm so glad you're okay. What are you doing?" I asked, perplexed by her odd behavior.

She didn't answer. I took two steps in her direction but stopped when she raised her voice.

"Don't! Stay away!"

"What's the matter?" I thought perhaps she was afraid of me now that she knew I was responsible for Jared and Conner's deaths, or maybe it was the sight of my busted up face. "I'm not gonna hurt you, Ray. I promise."

She continued to stare at me like I was the devil. "What's wrong?" I asked again.

"I see it."

"See what? Do you see people's shackles?" I was both shocked and comforted at the thought.

Nothing could have prepared me for her response.

"I see yours. You have a shackle around your neck, Owen."

22. Yearning Heart

I raced out of the hospital like I was on fire. In a way, I was. Once I learned that I was shackled and enslaved like nearly every other doomed human being, my last few shreds of hope went up in flames.

What a sick joke. There I was on a mission to discover how to free others, and all along, my soul was pinned in the same unrelenting trap.

Once home, I rushed upstairs and beheld my undesirable reflection in the bathroom mirror. I was bruised from yesterday's beating, but other than that, everything looked normal. I marveled at the irony. I could see others' brokenness and bondage with such clarity, but my own eluded me.

"Perhaps Ray Anne was lying to me," I thought. "She wants to get back at me for concealing the deadly nature of the water, so she told me I'm shackled, knowing it would drive me insane." The problem with that theory was that Ray Anne was not one to lie about anything. Also, I saw the terror in her face as she beheld my appearance, and I didn't think she could fake that.

Helpless feelings of defeat seized my body, and as I stumbled into my bedroom, I felt inexplicably heavy, like gravity had a heightened hold on me. To add to my misery, the one person I would normally run to at a time like this now considered me a monster. I was sure Ray Anne would want to stay as far away from me as she could. She'd probably seek out other glowing people and pity the rest of us from afar.

I entertained the idea of ending my life, but I didn't consider it for long. I wasn't about to give those Creepers reason to celebrate. Besides, the last thing I wanted to do was die. In my condition, death was to be avoided at all costs.

I curled up in a ball under the sheets and wrapped my arms around my frostbitten gut while contemplating another form of escape. I had to leave, leave Cypress behind and go somewhere—anywhere but here. I'd start a new life, only this time I'd tell no one about all the heinous things I could see. I'd also be careful not to develop any ties or feelings for anyone. It was too painful.

I fully realized that in a matter of time, my new plan would likely land me under a highway overpass swatting at Creepers alongside some homeless companions, but if that was my fate, so be it. What I wasn't willing to do was stick around and keep exhausting myself trying to rescue people.

Who was I kidding? If the Creepers were planning to rain down hell at Stella's party next weekend and carry out some vicious plot against my schoolmates, there wasn't anything I could do about it. Maybe if I glowed, I could help in some way, but the harsh reality was, I didn't. I was a shackled freak. I needed to accept that. And if faith and prayer somehow comprised the formula for getting free, I was destined to remain bound in chains.

I got out of bed and started throwing clothes into the biggest duffle bag I owned. I decided I'd drive west on Highway 10 and see where it took me. Maybe I'd leave the country at some point and settle down in a different hemisphere.

I had access to the funds my mom stashed away for my college education. I figured I could pulse out some cash and live off that for a while until I got a job doing God knows what.

I knew better than to think that I could outrun the Creepers or my sadistic sightings, but at least I could remove myself from the constant drudgery of seeing people I cared about be abused by unseen perpetrators. And I could stay away from the people who hated my guts and, quite honestly, wanted never to see me again anyway.

There was just one thing I had to do before I left. I needed to know how many chains and cords I had and what was written on them. I was sure that not knowing would drive me mad. That meant I had to see Ray Anne one last time.

Around one o'clock, I texted her brother: **You guys home with Ray yet?**

He responded and said his family was home. I drove over there unannounced and rang the doorbell. I wasn't expecting Ray Anne to answer. She grabbed my hand and pulled me onto the grass, then gave me a long hug. I wasn't expecting that either.

"Owen, I'm so sorry about the way I reacted to you this morning, but don't worry. We'll get you out of that shackle. You'll see. And oh my gosh, the Creepers are terrifying! You told me they were dreadful, but in my wildest imagination, I never dreamed they would be this scary. But you're right. They do avoid me and my family, thank God!

"And I can see the glow, Owen! It's all around my feet!" She lifted one foot, then the other, marveling at the sight. She was clearly on a high of sorts, reveling in her new superhuman senses.

She didn't seem to be holding any grudges against me. Still, for numerous reasons, I felt ashamed standing there in her presence. I wanted her to tell me what I needed to know so I could leave. The longer I looked into her face, the harder it would be to walk away.

"I need you to do one last thing for me."

"What do you mean, 'last thing'?" she asked. I didn't offer an explanation.

"Please tell me the names written on the cuffs of my chains and the words etched onto my cords. I've got to know."

I could tell she was nervous, but willing.

"You have three chains."

The mere thought made me ill. "Look at the writing on each of the cuffs. What do they say?"

"The first one says 'Susan Lynne Edmonds.'"

My mother. "Okay, and the next one?"

"It's Lance, Lance Gregory Wilson."

That was no surprise. I had no way to prove it, but I felt sure that chain was less than twenty-four hours old. I officially hated him now.

"And the last one?"

"Stephen James Grayson."

That name meant absolutely nothing to me, except the middle name was the same as mine. I had no idea who it was.

"What happened to your face? Why are you so beat up?"

I dodged the question and asked her to tell me what was written near the bottom of each of my cords. She stood behind me and looked closely without touching any of the skin-piercing strands, then proceeded to name my character flaws, calling out one insulting accusation after another.

"Deceptive."

"Unrepentant."

"Cynical."

"Lustful."

"Selfish."

I thought she was never going to shut up. *Five* cords? Everything in me wanted to defend myself, to launch into lengthy justifications about how those labels were wrong and how I was seriously misunderstood and misjudged. But I recognized that for what it was. If there was one thing I'd learned from living with my mother it was that human nature despises admissions of guilt.

If the "forces that be" pronounced those as my transgressions, there was nothing to do but accept it.

As I turned to leave, Ray Anne called out after me.

"Wait. Where are you going?"

I slammed my car door and began backing out of the driveway. She plastered her hands on my window and shouted through the glass. "Stop! We need to talk. I need your help with all of this!"

I really wasn't out to abandon her in her time of need; I just needed to get home and grab my stuff, then be on my way like I'd planned. I resisted looking into the review mirror.

Look at you, acting so selfish. My own thoughts turned against me, allying with the dark side—those condemning cords. "Shut up!" As I argued back and forth with myself, I realized I had plummeted to an all-time low, into hostile mental territory where psychopaths and schizophrenics live. The way I saw it, though, that was all the more reason to leave town and live an isolated existence.

I charged into my house and walked straight over to my mother. She was working on her computer with her back turned toward me. I ignored her greeting and dropped to the floor, taking a careful look at each of her numerous cuffs among the chains scattered all around.

"What are you doing?"

Sure enough, as I examined the eighth cuff, I found what I was looking for.

"Who is Stephen James Grayson?" I asked in an authoritative tone. I had to know why his name was on one of my cuffs and also hers.

My question appeared to strike terror into her heart.

"Who is Stephen James Grayson? Tell me, Mom!"

She started to cry, but still looked more scared than sad.

"Where did you—"

"It doesn't matter, Mom. Just tell me who he is and what role he played in our lives."

"Well, it's complicated."

"Try me."

She cried uncontrollably, then leaned over and caved into my arms.

"I'm so ashamed. I have so much regret. If I could go back, I swear to you, I would do things differently, son—I swear!"

That's when I knew.

"That man is my father, isn't he?"

I took her lack of response as an affirmation that I was correct.

"Why have you lied to me about his name all of these years? I don't understand!" I released her from my arms, outraged by her deception.

"Because I promised his parents, your grandparents."

"What are you talking about?" I said. My hands trembled and lips quivered.

She asked me to give her a moment, then went to grab some tissues. I walked in circles and then sank into the sofa. She lowered onto the floor by my feet, nervously clutching my hand and looking down as she spoke.

"I loved your father very much," she said, overcome once again by emotion. "We were young and in love and anxious to get married. Neither of us cared about having some big elaborate wedding, so we eloped, just the two of us.

"I never intended to get pregnant right away, but I did. I wondered how he would take the news since he had just started his college education, and we barely had two pennies to rub together. He had high hopes of becoming a successful doctor someday like his father.

"I knew his mother wasn't very fond of me, but I decided to confide in her about the pregnancy, thinking perhaps his parents would be supportive and offer to help us through what was sure to be a challenging time. But instead, she was cruel to me. She told me I was not an acceptable match for her son and even accused me of getting pregnant just to trap Stephen into staying with me. Oh, that infuriated me!

"I spent the next few days agonizing, thinking perhaps they were right—he deserved someone more refined and intelligent than me, someone from a wealthier family. And I convinced myself he would resent me for the timing of the pregnancy. I was too terrified to tell him.

"One morning when Stephen was at school, his parents came by our apartment. They said they had the perfect solution and made me an offer that would benefit everyone.

"What kind of offer?" I asked.

She covered her face. "They agreed to pay me a large sum of money every year for the next eighteen years, ensuring you had a good childhood and received a quality education. It was enough for me to get my education, too."

"Under what condition, Mom?"

She looked in every direction except at me. "Providing I left town and agreed not to contest an annulment. And never said another word to their son—ever."

"So . . . you're saying my dad didn't . . ." I couldn't believe what I was hearing.

"He never knew about you, Owen. I'm so sorry. Your dad never knew he had a son." She shook with each violent sob while I sat there astonished, piecing together a few of the many loose ends that had troubled me over the years.

I stood and vented my frustration, releasing nearly two decades of pent-up anger and confusion.

"Now I understand why you cried for three days when I told you I wanted to become a doctor. I was following in the footsteps of my father and grandfather and didn't even know it!

"And now I get how we've had such a nice standard of living on your unimpressive salary!

"And I know why there aren't any pictures of my dad. You didn't want me to know what he looks like. You didn't want to run the risk that I might seek him out and tell him what you've done!"

"Please forgive me." Her voice quaked as she begged. "I did what I thought was best at the time. I know now that his parents were wrong, and I should have just told the truth and trusted Stephen to love me and accept me—to accept us. I just couldn't at the time, and then it was too late to go back. He eventually got remarried."

She wiped her soaked face, then made a pathetic confession. "And we've needed the money, Owen."

"How dare you! What I've needed is a father!"

She wailed, then pled with me again. "I told myself that when you grew up, I would help you find him, and you could get to know each other. I had no idea he wouldn't make it."

"What did you say? What happened to my father?" I'd been to hell and back in recent days, but I'd never hurt like I did in that instant.

She wiped her face and explained through involuntary gasps, "It's hard to say. About a year ago, he traveled to a remote part of the world and was never heard from again. He's presumed . . . well, they think he's likely . . ."

"Dead?" She was too weak of a person to say it, so I did.

"I'm so, so sorry, honey." She reached out to hug me, but I jerked away. "Can you please forgive me?"

Just hours ago, it was me pleading for Ray Anne's forgiveness, but my dishonesty spanned a matter of weeks. My mom had been lying to me my entire life.

"Sorry, Mom. I can't let this go."

I grabbed the last few things I wanted to take with me and threw them in the back seat of my car. She chased after me.

"Where are you going?"

"I'll be gone a few days." I only said that so she wouldn't report me missing right away. By the time she realized I was gone for good, there would be no finding me. At least that was my hope.

I hardly noticed my surroundings as I drove for hours along the flat stretch of highway, lamenting the truth about my father.

By late afternoon, I reached San Antonio and took a random exit and drove west. My mom called me nonstop until I turned my phone off. Ray Anne called multiple times, too.

I rehearsed the conversation over and over in my mind, obsessively recounting my mother's words leading up to where I learned that my father was presumed dead. All these years, she poisoned my mind with the idea that he wanted nothing to do with me when in reality, he never even knew I existed. Evil takes on many forms, but to me, that was wickedness personified.

I arrived at a small Texas town and saw a sign that said, "Welcome to Hondo—This is God's country, please don't drive through it like hell." Certain streets looked like the set of an old western movie, and I marveled that towns like this still existed.

There wasn't much to see. It was hardly dusk, and already everything was closed. If it weren't for the few cars on the road, I would have written the place off as abandoned.

I made my way to a dilapidated motel. My room was supposed to be non-smoking, but the instant I opened the door, I knew whoever stayed there last ignored that rule. I sat down on the corner of the king sized bed and took in the moment. I was truly alone. That realization brought both comfort and fear.

It occurred to me to get out my laptop and search online for information about my dad, but I wasn't ready for that yet.

I ate snacks out of a vending machine for dinner, then secluded myself in my room watching the sports channel on a television set that belonged in an antique shop. All of a sudden, someone pounded on my door. I was on my feet in two seconds flat, preparing to defend myself.

"You in there?" I heard a male voice with a strong southern accent. He didn't sound menacing, so I opened the door a few inches. There stood a little old man with a thousand wrinkles, only a few teeth, and a broom in his hand—and a glow.

"Say, that your fancy sports car ov'r 'dare?" He pointed his shaky finger at my Camaro.

309

"Yes, it is."

"I saw you got a flat tire. You need help changin' it, you let me know. Name's Earl. I'm the maintenance man 'round here."

I walked out to my car, and sure enough, the front passenger side tire was flat. I could see that I had parked right on top of a broken bottle.

It's embarrassing to admit, but I'd never changed a tire, and I didn't know how. That's the sort of thing you miss out on when you're fatherless.

"If you don't mind, Earl, I could use your help."

He was the brains behind the operation, and I was the brawn. He admitted his eyesight made it nearly impossible for him to see at night, and I concealed the fact that the glow emanating around him was what helped me to see.

I shook his hand and thanked him for his help.

"Say, you gonna be 'round tomorra'? You're a strapping young man, and I could use your help fixin' some things 'round here. I can pay ya' thirty bucks for your time. What you think 'bout that?"

I could tell he anticipated I would jump at the chance to earn thirty whole dollars. I went ahead and agreed to assist him for the sole purpose of observing and studying him. Maybe I would learn something new that would help me in my quest to rid myself of the shackle of shame groping my neck.

I had no idea that the advice I needed most would come from an even more unlikely source.

23. Open Eyes

Earl banged on my door at exactly seven in the morning, and even though I was expecting him around then, it still made me jump. He greeted me with a cup of coffee and a pastry. I didn't normally drink coffee, but I made an exception.

We got started immediately. I helped him clear all the furniture out of three motel rooms that needed the carpets cleaned, then tightened a loose ring around a plumbing pipe and hauled a massive amount of tree limbs to his truck.

Earl talked a lot, and I was careful to pay attention, searching for clues as to how he managed to break free from a shackled existence. He asked questions about me now and then, too, but I gave only vague answers.

By the conclusion of my time with him, I picked up on something that seemed significant. Just like Ray Anne and her family, Earl was a very kind-hearted person. He was patient, a hard worker, and oddly content with his less than lavish life. I noticed that, even though his job consisted of little more than grunt work, he took pride in it and did everything with a willing, even grateful attitude.

I retreated back to my musty motel room with a new goal in mind. "Perhaps if I just make more of an effort to be a good person and resist those five ugly attitudes branded onto my cords, my shackle will fall off. Maybe this whole thing is far less complicated than I've been making it."

It occurred to me that, in order to free myself from my chains, I might also need to let go of my grudge against my mother, but that seemed impossible. While it was easy to forgive my dad—he never abandoned me after all—I didn't have it in me to forgive my mom, or Lance for that matter. I decided to worry about that later and focus on proving I had what it took to overcome the indictments on my cords.

On Tuesday morning, I was itching to get back on the road. I went to tell Earl goodbye, and when he tried to hand me thirty dollars cash, I insisted he keep it—my first attempt at proving I was not a selfish person. I left and went straight to buy a new tire. When the mechanic asked where I was headed, I rattled off something about going to visit my grandmother in the hill country.

As I drove away, I realized I had just been deceptive. I didn't mean to blow it so quickly.

I saw a sign saying the City of Medina was the apple capital of Texas, and since I like apples, I figured I might as well go there. Clearly, I had no master plan for my new life.

As I drove mile after mile, I noticed there were just as many shackled people in that part of the state as there were back home. There weren't quite as many Creepers hunting these territories, but I still spied them around. They were not confined to one geographic area, unfortunately.

On Tuesday afternoon, I gave a ten dollar bill to a homeless woman begging at a stoplight but then mouthed off at an old guy who was driving so slow he caused traffic to back up for nearly a mile. I figured my temperamental outburst negated my act of generosity, and I bemoaned the fact that I was no closer to earning my way out of my shackle, despite my sincere effort.

One thing was certain: being good all the time was way harder than I thought it would be.

I checked in to a Holiday Inn in Medina and powered up my phone for the first time since Sunday. I had eighteen voice messages: thirteen from my mom, four from Ray Anne, and one from Detective Benny.

I was relieved to hear that the results of the water test came back clean, clearing me of any potential charges and dismissing me as a suspect. It was good news, for sure, but it didn't change the fact that I would always believe I was guilty. I had no idea how the lethal nature of that water escaped modern testing methods, but I was sure it was venomous. It also remained a mystery to me why Ray Anne and I survived drinking it while it cost my two friends the ultimate price.

The rest of my nomadic week was basically uneventful, except for the maddening ongoing battle to behave myself. The more I tried to think and do only pure-hearted things, the more I became aware of what a pathetic failure I was. In a matter of days, I had acted on all of the attitudes I vowed to suppress, and not just once or twice, but over and over again.

I arrived at the most disheartening conclusion: I wasn't enslaved by the shackle. It was my moral deficiencies that truly held me captive, infringing on my thoughts and actions no matter how hard I tried to subdue them. I decided Earl, Ray Anne, and everyone else who glowed were just really exceptional people, not at all like me.

It sure is excruciating living with the knowledge that I, along with most of the world's population, was rotting on a sort of spiritual death row, awaiting inevitable execution by Creeper without any hope of redemption.

I woke up Saturday morning on a stiff bed in Fredericksburg, a small Texas town that's apparently very proud of its German heritage. I'd had a cup of coffee every morning since Monday, and I was craving one again now. I drove to a quaint cafe in the middle of nowhere. It was difficult to fathom that I was missing my own high school graduation that morning.

I'd texted my mom and Ray Anne just to tell them I was okay. I was sure my mom knew by now that I had run away and was beside herself with worry, but I still had no intention of ever returning.

I sipped on my drink and powered up my laptop, fighting back anxiety. I'd had enough time to mull over the little bit of information my mom gave me about my father. I was now hoping to learn as much as I could about him.

I searched his name online, and all kinds of information came up. I spent the next hour not reading much, but instead fixating on pictures of him.

If at any time I was going to second-guess whether he really was my father, all doubt vanished when I saw how much he looked like me—or I looked like him, I suppose. We had the same dark brown, wavy hair, green eyes, facial features, and stature. I resembled him far more than I did my mother.

As I scanned the web, I learned that he was a cardiologist with a thriving private practice, and he frequently traveled to third world countries to perform surgeries for impoverished people. I saw that he was married, but nearly choked on what was left of my coffee when I discovered that he had an elementary-age son and teenage daughter.

I'm not an only child. That was nearly impossible to comprehend.

What I read matched what my mother told me. He and five other doctors went to Africa in March of last year, and none of them was ever seen again.

His wife was a pretty lady, a blonde with a nice smile. I'm sure his disappearance was devastating for her, not to mention their children.

I read one article after another, clinging to everything I could that revealed anything about his past, his accomplishments, and what kind of man he was. The most informative article was written by a reporter from Tulsa, Oklahoma, his hometown. She interviewed my dad just days before he vanished.

He acknowledged that he was going into dangerous territory, and when asked why he would risk his life to provide medical help for a small tribal group, his answer was not at all what I expected:

"I'm going to serve and meet their medical needs the best I can, but my primary focus is to share the Gospel. There's not a person on earth who doesn't need and deserve to hear about the Savior's death and resurrection on his or her behalf."

My dad was a devout Christian? That blew me away. In that sense, we were nothing alike, but I definitely admired his desire to help people and willingness to go out on a limb for others.

As I continued reading quotes, reciting the very words he once said, I longed so badly to meet him, to look him in the face and tell him I exist. I would have given anything for the chance to spend even one minute with him.

I marveled at his bravery and selflessness and felt sure that, although the pictures didn't allow me to see it, he had to be glowing.

If he was still alive and I could simply call him on the phone, perhaps this would all feel too good to be true. But the fact that I had come this far only to still be worlds away from him was the most severe of let downs.

There wasn't a single statement he made in that article that didn't move me somehow, but it was the final quote I read that changed the course of my life. When asked why he was willing to make such extreme sacrifices and risk his life for others, this is what he said:

"I interpret the fact that I see and empathize with their suffering to mean I'm the one who's called to intervene and help. I refuse to run and hide behind the comforts of my prosperous life and leave it up to someone else to try and save them."

How could it be that his words, spoken over a year ago, could serve as such sobering advice for my situation at the time? Even having never met one another, my father just reprimanded and motivated me to action. How astounding.

I instantly became aware of what a coward I was for running off and leaving Ray Anne and my classmates, knowing full well an invisible army would soon launch a large scale attack on their lives.

I knew what I had to do.

I rushed back to my motel room and threw my things together, then started the six-hour drive back to Cypress. I called and told my mom I was on my way home, and she thanked me profusely for coming to my senses. I knew Ray Anne was likely still at graduation so I sent her a text: **Sorry I left you. I'm coming back. We have our work cut out for us tonight.**

It occurred to me that no Creepers had bothered me while I was out of town. I wondered if it was because I was right where they wanted me—far away from home, despondent, and totally isolated from the people who cared about me.

It was after six o'clock by the time I turned onto my street. I was surprised but elated to see Ray Anne sitting in my driveway. We hurried toward one another, running faster as we drew closer. Finally, we were locked in an intense hug, clinging to each other like we were the only two people on Earth about to take on hell's army. And in a very real sense, we were.

I wondered how she could wrap her arms around me now that she saw my disgusting chains and cords. I'd never felt so hideous.

"Thank God you're okay," she said. I wasn't expecting such a warm welcome from her, not after how I treated her the last time I saw her.

"I'm so sorry I left you all alone when you needed me the most. That was so wrong. *I* was wrong."

Her simple response was like a splash of cool water across my parched soul: "All is forgiven, Owen."

Thank you hardly seemed an adequate response, but it was all I could say as I stood there, blown away by her merciful reply, relieved to be reunited with my favorite person in the whole world. "How was graduation?"

"It was good. I can't believe you missed it!" She socked me in the arm with a playful punch. "What happened to your face, anyway?"

The swelling in my lip had gone down, but the cuts were still healing, and my left eye still had purple around it.

"I got in a fight."

"Are you serious? With who?"

"Lance set me up. He jumped me with a bunch of other guys. I nearly died, and probably would have if this old guy hadn't pulled up and threatened to shoot them all. And Ray, a Creeper entered Lance and took control of his body. It was disgusting."

"That's terrible. Why did they want to hurt you?"

"Lance thinks I set out to murder Jared and Conner." It was an awkward topic to bring up with her. "You know that's not true, right?"

"Of course. I know you didn't mean for that to happen."

Ray Anne had questions about how the Creeper possessed Lance, but I deliberately changed the subject. I wanted to focus on how she was doing. "So, what's it been like?" I knew from personal experience that it's terrifying to suddenly behold a ghastly invisible realm.

"I can't believe what I'm seeing. Every day I witness something that freaks me out even more than the day before. It's so much scarier than I thought it would be."

"How's your stomach?" I asked. She explained that the awful chill in her belly had faded away, along with the headache, by the time she left the hospital. That was good news.

"Have you seen any Watchmen?" I asked.

"No, but hopefully we will tonight!"

I heard the front door fly open, and my mom came running out of the house and hugged me, then snapped at me. "Get inside, now!" The situation struck Ray Anne and I both as being funny for some reason, but we tried not to laugh in my mother's face. We went inside, just as we were told.

Ray and I needed to leave for Galveston right away if we were going to get to Stella's beach house by eight o'clock. Also, I felt really uncomfortable being around my mom after her big confession. That made me even more anxious to get going.

I tried to quickly smooth things over by telling my mother I just needed a change of scenery for a while, but I felt much better now and wanted to go hang out with Ray Anne and my friends for the night. She was hesitant to let me go again so soon, but what was she going to do—ground me? We both knew those days were over.

"I can't believe you missed your high school graduation," my mom said. I assured her it wasn't that big of a deal.

Seconds later, Ray Anne and I were blazing down the freeway, trying to mentally prepare ourselves for what was sure to be a wild night.

We were halfway there when she brought up Jared and Conner, causing me to squirm in my seat. "Have you thought about why you and I survived drinking that water, but they didn't?" she asked.

I told her I'd nearly driven myself mad thinking about it, but I just couldn't come up with a reasonable explanation.

"Do you have any ideas?" I asked.

"I think it all comes down to motive."

"What do you mean?" I had no clue what she meant by that.

"Think about it. Why did you drink the water in the first place?"

I knew it would be awkward, but I said it anyway. "I drank it to protect Jess."

"And why did Jared and Conner drink it?" she asked next.

I thought about it for a moment. "They were trying to show me up and prove how brave they were, I guess. What about you? Why did you drink it?"

She looked me in the eyes. "Because I wanted to help you, because I care about you."

I felt my cheeks blush and my cold stomach drop as if I'd just thrown myself out of an airplane.

"Do you get it?" she asked.

"Get what?" Her words of affection completely derailed my concentration.

"You and I drank the water for selfless reasons, but Jared and Conner's motive was completely self-centered. I'm not

320

saying they deserved to die because of that—not at all—but it's the motive that makes all the difference, nonetheless."

"But how could motive affect a person's bodily response to the water?"

"You still don't get it, do you? Whatever is in that water is not physical. It's spiritual. Its components supersede the material realm."

She acted like there was nothing preposterous about her conclusion, and I was dense for not realizing it as well.

"I understand what you're saying. I'm just not sure I completely agree with you," I said.

"That's okay. I know what I'm talking about." She asserted her opinion with complete confidence, which I found irresistibly attractive.

"By the way," she said, "I gathered with five glowing seniors at school this week, and I told them to be sure and come to the party and be prepared to give me some help if I ask for it."

"Didn't they want to know what you were talking about?"

"Yeah, and I told them I could see certain spiritual beings, and I might need their help warding them off."

"And they actually took you seriously?"

"Of course they did," she said. "Glowing people always believe. It's the shackled ones who are resistant to spiritual realities."

Her comment socked me in the gut, but I already knew it was true.

By the time we drove over the towering drawbridge and onto Galveston Island, the sun looked like it was sinking into the ocean. I was growing increasingly nervous and wondered if it was a huge mistake bringing Ray Anne along. I realized she was in a far better position to take on the Creepers than I was, but still, I worried for her safety.

As we neared Stella's house, Ray Anne began praying under her breath while I fought off the urge to do a U-turn.

I tried consoling myself. "Maybe we read too much into the Creeper notes, and nothing unusual is even gonna happen tonight."

Just one glance at Stella's beach house and I knew, without a doubt, something catastrophic was definitely about to happen.

24. Unimaginable Existence

I normally would have been impressed with such a posh vacation home, but that night, I hardly noticed it. All I could see were the eerie, impeccably straight rows of Creepers stretching from the back of the property, lurking underneath the elevated house, and spewing all the way across the front yard, stopping just short of the ocean. Hundreds of them stood within inches of each other, assembled in orderly fashion. They peered down each others' reeking necks.

Their filthy hands were crossed at the wrist and pressed against their concave chests. It reminded me of how dead people are positioned in their graves in horror movies. They poured in from every direction like rats, then filed into place as if they had rehearsed that formation many times before.

"I . . . I . . ." Ray Anne was so shocked she couldn't speak.

"This is it," I said with zero confidence and absolutely no desire to get out of the car.

"Call the police," Ray Anne said.

"And tell them what?"

"Just put them on alert or something!"

To appease her, I went ahead and called up my old friend Officer Smith and told him we were at a party in Galveston and heard some kids were going to bring weapons. I figured that would get his attention, and besides, it was true. He encouraged me to leave immediately and told me he'd give the island police a heads up.

I wanted to take his advice and get going, but my father's words echoed in my head. *I refuse to run and hide and leave it up to someone else to try and save them.*

We got out of the car and looked all around, desperately hoping to spot an army of Watchmen, but all we saw were more Creepers flocking to the scene like demented zombies.

Ray Anne clung to the belief that faith could affect the evening's outcome. "I should have told my parents to pray, but I was too scared that if I did, they'd get suspicious and not let me come."

Maybe that would have been best, I thought. Despite Ray Anne's glowing advantage, I worried I made a huge mistake bringing her along. There was no telling what the Creepers had planned.

"Hey there."

One of Ray Anne's friends walked up and started chatting with her like she didn't have a care in the world. Ray Anne did her best to act normal.

"Come on you guys. Let's go." She grabbed Ray Anne by the hand and pulled her toward Stella's house, gallivanting straight toward the army of Creepers.

"Um, give me just a minute, okay? I'll be right there." Ray Anne pulled her hand away and stayed put, right next to me. We watched as that girl, along with a steady stream of others, went bouncing right through the maze of Creepers, totally ignorant of their revolting presence.

"How long do you think they're just gonna stand there?" Ray Anne asked.

"Until each nasty one of them is accounted for, I suppose."

I heard laughter echoing from behind us and, without having to turn and look, knew exactly who was walking in our direction. It was Lance. He was Creeper-free, but once he noticed me, his whole demeanor changed.

"I thought you knew better than to show your face around here," he said.

I looked away and chose to focus instead on the real threat—the growing number of Creepers assimilating just ahead. Lance kept walking and put his arm around some red-headed girl.

It was nearly dark outside, and Ray and I were still clinging to my car like it was some sort of protective home base. If the truth be told, we both lacked the courage to walk past the hoard of Creepers and into the house.

A few glowing people approached Ray Anne, basically checking in and assuring her they were ready to help if needed. She thanked them, and left it at that. As they walked toward the house, we observed the Creepers lean away from their penetrating glow but not break rank or flee.

We stood there for over an hour, becoming more intimidated by the minute. The Creepers were scary enough in the sunlight; beholding hundreds of their shadowy figures under the faint grey moonlight was downright petrifying.

As their oversized garments whipped back and forth with continual strong gusts of wind, the Creepers remained so still they looked dead. We knew they would advance at some point, but we weren't expecting what happened next.

As if responding to some sort of sonar command, the Creepers dispersed all over the place, each rushing to form what appeared to be predetermined groups, as if manning their assigned posts.

"What do we do?" Ray Anne panicked, but I couldn't blame her. I was freaking out, too.

"Let's move." If we didn't approach the scene right then, I feared we'd chicken out completely.

We walked past hordes of Creepers and made it up two flights of stairs, then stopped on the outdoor deck that ran along the perimeter of the house.

"How about I go inside and look around for anything suspicious, and you keep an eye on things outside?" Ray Anne said. As much as I despised the idea of traipsing around in the dark with God knows how many Creepers, I figured it would be safer for Ray Anne to be inside.

"Okay," I said, "but keep your phone handy, and call me if you see anything suspicious." I promised to do the same, then watched my breathtaking best friend walk into the house and blend into the rambunctious crowd.

I looked out across the yard and saw countless Creepers clumped together, communicating and collaborating against us. I heard them rummaging across the rooftop above my head and watched them scamper up and down the exterior of the house, one after another. The place was overrun with them.

I walked the deck, circling the house multiple times and feeling grateful each time I survived a round. Being within arm's reach of that many Creepers and living to tell about it is truly cheating death.

I stood facing the ocean, wishing a tsunami would crash the shore and somehow drown only the Creepers, when I suddenly picked up on the distinct smell of gasoline. It was hard to tell where it was coming from, but on a hunch, I walked downstairs and into the front lawn.

The wind blew from my right, carrying the gas scent with it. I looked in that direction and saw at least fifty Creepers huddled in a tight bunch, moving slowly in unison underneath the house, which stood elevated some twelve feet off the ground. I also heard what sounded like water spilling.

I dreaded forcing my way between them, but I felt I had no choice. I held my breath then pushed my way through their soggy garments, trying not to barf as I stepped over their raunchy feet.

I finally made it through the gruesome group and panicked at what I saw. A man I recognized from among the sign people who often stood protesting outside my school—the crazed redhead—was pouring a huge can of gasoline all over the ground and onto the massive wooden beams supporting the house. A Creeper was linked to him, coaching him along with his persuasive powers.

"What are you doing?" I asked.

"Sending these wicked kids to hell where they belong," he said, continuing to dump massive amounts of gasoline all over the place. I grabbed my cell, but someone snatched it out of my hands and threw it.

"Hey!" I said, realizing the deranged man was not alone. The next thing I knew, I was lying face down on the cement, and my nose was throbbing. I felt pinned down, like someone was standing on me.

I twisted my neck and saw that there was, in fact, a man hovering over me with one foot lodged into my lower back.

"Get off of me!" I managed to roll out from under him. I scrambled to my feet only to endure a hard blow to the gut, knocking the wind right out of me. I fell backwards and landed on an empty gas can.

"Is everything okay?" A female's voice called down from the deck above.

"Call the police!"

"Owen, is that you?"

"Jess, it's me!"

The two men jumped on top of me, slapping a gasoline-drenched hand over my mouth to shut me up.

"Come on, Jess. Let's go inside," Dan said.

"Wait. I think Owen needs my help."

"Don't you dare go down there and cater to that psychopath," Dan said. "I swear if you do, I'll never speak to you again. Now get inside."

I heard the door slam shut. The two insane men kept me down in the dark and nearly smothered me to death while trying to keep me quiet as several more people approached the house and walked upstairs.

One of the guys finally let go of me and pulled something out of his pocket. It sparked a long flame, and both men laughed. That's when I went nuts. I contorted my body, kicked, and bit whoever's hand was over my mouth until I was free.

I jumped to my feet and tackled the guy holding the lighter, knocking him to the ground and wrestling the thing out of his hands. Once I had hold of it, I began sprinting through the yard then down the street. Both men came charging behind me, and so did a mass of Creepers. I ran as fast as my legs would carry me and, in an attempt to lure them away from the house, hoped they would keep after me.

Sure enough, they kept up the chase, tracking me for what felt like miles. Just as we neared a wood-framed house still under construction, one of the men grabbed and tripped me, slamming me onto the concrete slab. I held onto the lighter as if my life depended on it.

Once again, I found myself the outmatched victim of a brutal group attack. The two men pounded me, but there were numerous fists socking me and jagged fingernails tearing into my flesh. The Creepers had somehow joined the fight.

I crawled with one hand, clutching the lighter in the other, then finally fought my way back onto my unstable feet. That's when I made a straight dash for the ocean. The violent gang followed. I passed the shoreline, and when I got knee-deep, chunked the lighter as far out into the water as I could. That's when the two men clobbered me, shoving me under the tide.

I thrashed and clawed for my life, sneaking quick gasps of air before they would thrust my head under the water again. My strength was failing, and I felt the salt stinging the wounds all over body. I flailed my arms and fought like mad.

Then, for no apparent reason, they released me.

I immediately came up for air, sucking in oxygen while choking on sea water. In the midst of my gagging and coughing, I noticed the Creepers' drastic change in behavior. While the men rushed toward the shore, the Creepers turned and left me at a relaxed pace, without the slightest trace of aggression or urgency. It made no sense.

I strained to catch my breath, all the while watching in bewilderment as the Creepers disbanded, each meandering along its own path. The two men walked hurriedly along the beach, but in the opposite direction of Stella's beach house.

That's when I heard the sound of sirens.

I hobbled back toward the house as fast as I could, leaving a blood-soaked trail in the sand with each step. Once I could see the property, terror took over. There were not only police cars everywhere but ambulances, too.

I tried to move faster but was too weak. My mind was vexed by the possibility that, in my effort to save the day, I may have played right into the Creepers' deceiving hands, allowing them to lure me away while they executed their *real* plan of attack.

I was close enough to see my schoolmates scattered everywhere, trembling and crying, but still too far off to see if Ray Anne was among them.

I nearly collapsed, but kept pressing on, determined to get there. A guy approached me who I recognized from school but didn't know.

"Hey, are you okay?" he asked. Apparently I looked like a battered mess.

"I think so. What happened?"

"Dude, it was so freakin' terrible. Jess Thompson got in a fight with her boyfriend Dan—something about her wanting to go outside, but him forcing her to say inside. There was all this yelling and screaming back and forth, then Dan pulled out a pistol and, like, five or six other people pulled out weapons, too. The next thing I knew, people were shoving and pushing and turning on one another. And then shots were fired.

"Was anyone hit?"

"I don't know. I was one of the first people to get out, thank God."

I saw that my classmates were still pouring out of the house, some bleeding, most bawling.

"Was anyone shot? Please, tell me!" I demanded again.

"I'm sorry, I don't know."

I leaned against a car and tried not to hyperventilate. I felt like such a fool. What made me think I could outmatch spiritual forces? And why did I dare bring Ray Anne right to the battlefront?

I looked frantically for her. I stopped one person after another, asking if they'd seen her, but everyone was hysterical and concerned with their own wounds.

I saw Ray Anne's friend Joanna talking on her cell, sobbing into the phone. "Have you seen Ray Anne?" I asked in a panic.

"Hold on, Mom." She lowered her phone and looked at me with an anguished expression.

"Do you know where she is? Is she okay?" I asked.

"Owen, Ray Anne got shot."

My world quit spinning.

"No she didn't." I refused to believe her. I pushed past her, and asked someone else. "Have you seen Ray Anne Greiner?" The guy shook his head no, but the girl next to him pointed over my shoulder. I whirled around then exploded with emotion. The paramedics were carrying Ray Anne on a gurney.

"Oh God, oh God, no!" I ran over to her, but they warned me not touch her. "Is she alive?" I felt the sting of tears roll over my sliced cheeks.

"She's still breathing, but we need to get her to the hospital right away."

"Where are you taking her?" I asked, demanding to know why they were carrying her in the opposite direction of the ambulances.

"The Life Flight helicopter is coming for her," the female paramedic said, again urging me to back away. I followed close behind and noticed blood seeping through the white sheet draped over Ray Anne's stomach.

"Is she gonna be okay?" I felt a heavy hand on my shoulder. It was a police officer pulling me away, ordering me to leave Ray Anne and the paramedics alone while they waited for help to arrive. As he escorted me toward an ambulance, I heard the helicopter drawing near. I looked back over my shoulder, not knowing if I'd ever see Ray Anne alive again.

I knew what I had to do.

I turned and ran to her, exhausting the little energy I had for the chance to hold her again. All the voices and commotion around me faded into a distant silence as I raced to her and clung to her wounded body. I pressed my face to hers.

"Please Ray, don't leave me!" I begged from the depths of my soul.

I felt people tugging on me, trying to lift me off her. I stared into the sweetest face I'd ever known, then leaned in, attempting to get that kiss that I had hoped would be mine someday from the instant I heard she was reserving it for *the one*. I feared the worst, that she might not live to see that special day, and I didn't want her to leave this world without that—without a first and final kiss from me. But they were too strong. The police and paramedics pulled us apart despite how hard I fought to stay by her side.

I knew in my heart if we somehow both survived, we'd be together, just the two of us, for life.

Three men physically carried me to an ambulance. "I'm not going to the emergency room," I said while the paramedics laid me down under the bright lights. I wanted to find out where they were taking Ray Anne, but no one would tell me anything. They looked me over and urged me repeatedly to let them take me in, but I refused. I eventually staggered out of there, nearly fainting as I stood.

It was utter pandemonium. The press was swarming. All kinds of people were gawking. Students wandered aimlessly, trembling and sobbing. Others were in ambulances.

I happened to turn my head and spot Jess. She appeared to be okay. The tiny little light nestled inside of her remained dazzling. Dan was in the backseat of a Sherriff's vehicle, right where he belonged.

There were a few Creepers scouting the area, but most of them had moved on. Their masterful work was done here.

333

I couldn't believe how the night unfolded, and how quickly. I removed myself from the hectic crowd and blinding lights and took one laborious step after another down a pitch dark narrow road not far from the shore. I allowed myself the freedom to cry, to give in to the bitter pain.

It occurred to me that I had been played all along. Those Creepers tracking me—"Murderer," "Faithless," "Lust"—they weren't really after *me*. All this time, they were using me to get to Ray Anne, to try to weaken and destroy her.

I was sure she was their target all along, the predetermined victim of the Creepers' merciless, calculated attack this evening. They saw the power and purity in her, and they hated her for it. And like a blind fool, I fell right into their trap. I was so obsessed with my own plight and pain that I couldn't see the obvious.

I continued along that black desolate road and cried so hard I shook. I felt myself breaking, becoming vulnerable in a way that I never thought possible.

I traveled until I couldn't bear to take another step, then stopped under a dim, rusty street lamp, the first and only one I'd seen along that road. I fell to my knees and collapsed onto the palms of my blood-stained hands.

And that's when, for the first time in my life, I truly let go . . .

"God, I know you're there. I think I've always known, but I've been mad at you, maybe even afraid of you at times. But tonight I want to tell you something. I want to say I'm sorry—sorry for pushing you away and trying to control everything myself.

"I know I've failed miserably at being a good person and at trying to rescue people. I can admit that now. I'm the one in need of saving.

"I'm asking you, God, if you care about me at all, and if you really did send your Son to die for my sins—if all of that is true—I'm asking you to save me, to help me. If you'll have me, I want to belong to you. I mean it now, Jesus.

"And please, save Ray Anne. Save her life."

I opened my eyes and saw that a pool of blood had seeped from my forehead out onto the warm pavement. I lowered to the ground and laid there, having lost all ability and energy to sit upright.

I could still hear sirens in the distance, but all was calm and still around me. I found myself lost in the rhythmic crashing of the ocean's tide. It took me back, all the way back in my mind to that oceanfront carnival. I had an unforgettable time there with Ray Anne, but while lying there all alone, slipping in and out of consciousness, I dreamt of the evenings I spent at that carnival with my mother.

I recalled the sound of her laughter and the feel of her hands carefully lifting me onto the rides when I was too small to climb up on my own. I would beg her to stay a little while longer over and over again, and she would, over and over again.

How was it that all these years, I'd spent every day despising her for her shortcomings, continually rehearsing her failures, while overlooking all the ways she'd cared and sacrificed for me? There was no denying that she'd made some serious, costly mistakes. But so had I.

I vowed that if I lived, I would extend the same gracious words to my mother that Ray Anne recently afforded me—*all is forgiven.*

I didn't know what to make of it when I began hearing a loud racket, the noise of blaring music. I was disoriented but aware that it was getting closer.

A surge of intense light penetrated through my eyelids, blinding me as I strained to look. I saw a vehicle, a large pickup truck careening down the road, heading right for me.

I pushed up onto my arms, but they collapsed out from under me. I tried once more, but again, my strength failed.

I let my eyes drift closed and anticipated a massive jolt, knowing the tires would slam into me any second.

That's when I felt someone pick me up. I was lifted high off the ground, causing my stomach to drop and giving me a strong sensation of dizziness. I swayed with each step. Although I strained to see what or who had hold of me, my head was facing down, and I only caught glimpses of the moonlit sand and grass below.

I tried to stay awake but couldn't and reluctantly surrendered to the darkness.

I was too weak to open my eyes, but I felt warmth on my face and sensed I was lying beneath the sunrise. I could feel the grit of sand beneath my finger tips and under my elbows. I became desperate to see my surroundings, to determine if I was dead or alive.

At last, little by little, I beheld the shoreline. I blinked and balled my hands into fists, fighting to regain my physical stamina. It was working. I could feel energy surging through my veins, waking up my body. I drew in a deep breath and inhaled the most invigorating scent. I knew it well.

I managed to lean over onto my side. There, sitting beside me in the sand, was an enormous Watchman, peering down directly at me.

He spoke, and it felt like the rumbling of a massive waterfall reverberating against my chest. "Don't worry, she's going to live. You both are." He was smiling at me. Literally smiling!

He stood, and I marveled at his commanding presence.

"Wait!" I called out after him. "Where were you last night? Why did you let those vicious beings win?"

He graced me with an answer. "They didn't win, Owen. They fell into a carefully planned trap. You will see, in time."

I didn't want him to leave, but he was not subject to my orders.

I believed him. Ray Anne and I were going to survive, and we would be together. And somehow, some way, last night's tragedies would result in good. I felt confident of that.

I sat straight up, attempting to glance out across the waves.

That's when it hit me.

The sun wasn't up yet. The light I was seeing was emanating from *me*. It was glowing all around me. And that dreadful chill in my stomach, it was completely gone.

I felt warm and wonderful all over. More than that, I felt free—free to live and love and light the way for others by telling my unbelievable story. And this is just the beginning.

You do believe me, don't you?

For God so loved the world that he gave his one and only Son, that whoever believes in him shall not perish but have eternal life. For God did not send his Son into the world to condemn the world, but to save the world through him. Whoever believes in him is not condemned, but whoever does not believe stands condemned already because he has not believed in the name of God's one and only Son. This is the verdict: Light has come into the world, but men loved darkness instead of light because their deeds were evil. Everyone who does evil hates the light, and will not come into the light for fear that his deeds will be exposed. But whoever lives by the truth comes into the light, so that it may be seen plainly that what he has done has been done through God.

John 3:16-21

Efforts are underway to bring *The Delusion* to the big screen! Catch the vision and join the mission at **thedelusionbook.com.**

Want to be emailed when the sequel is released? Want to receive free *Delusion* bookmarks to use and hand out to others? Use the contact form at **thedelusionbook.com** to submit your email and mailing address!

Join *The Delusion* community at facebook.com/TheDelusionBook.

See the message concealed in the Table of Contents?

CPSIA information can be obtained at www.ICGtesting.com
Printed in the USA
LVOW130514020713

340954LV00005B/9/P